This Would Make a Good Story Someday

This Would Make a Good Story Someday

DANA ALISON LEVY

DELACORTE PRESS

To my parents, who taught me, from a very young age,
that the journey is always worth it

Text copyright © 2017 by Dana Alison Levy
Jacket art copyright © 2017 by Rebecca Ashdown

All rights reserved. Published in the United States by Delacorte Press, an imprint of Random House Children's Books, a division of Penguin Random House LLC, New York.

Delacorte Press is a registered trademark and the colophon is a trademark of Penguin Random House LLC.

randomhousekids.com

Educators and librarians, for a variety of teaching tools, visit us at RHTeachersLibrarians.com

Library of Congress Cataloging-in-Publication Data is available upon request.
ISBN 978-1-101-93817-1 (hc) — ISBN 978-1-101-93818-8 (lib. bdg.)
ISBN 978-1-101-93819-5 (ebook)

The text of this book is set in 12.2-point Sabon MT.
Interior design by Heather Kelly

Printed in the United States of America
10 9 8 7 6 5 4 3 2 1
First Edition

Chapter 1

Dear Mr. Levitt,

First of all, I'm really sorry I wrote over two hundred pages for my summer journal. It probably sounds crazy to apologize for doing more work than the teacher asked for, but I doubt any seventh-grade English teacher, even a seriously dedicated one (and I'm sure you are . . . otherwise you wouldn't be reading all these journals), asked for this. I never meant to write a book-length summer report, I promise. I mean, I do eventually want to write a book, and was actually planning to start a novel this summer (about mermaids or selkies . . . I haven't really figured out the story yet). But I barely wrote one chapter. Instead I kept writing this.

I thought I'd need to use a giant font and make stuff up just to fill the five-page journal requirement. After all, my ideal summer would have been to hang out with my best friends, Em and Vi (or Saanvi, if you want to be official), perfecting and finalizing our Reinvention Project before middle school (more on that later). We would have pretty much lived on the beach, Em and me learning to surf (Vi is totally petrified of sharks and refuses to consider getting on a surfboard; I blame that documentary on the Discovery Channel where they showed videos taken underwater of surfers and said that, to hungry sharks, the surfers look like sea turtles or seals). Then we would have practiced the new languages we were going to learn (I chose Latin, because I thought it was cool to speak something no one could understand, Em chose Mandarin so she can figure out what her dad's business actually does, and Vi chose Italian because she wants to move to Milan). And that was just the beginning . . . our plans were amazing.

So again, I am seriously sorry. The whole summer got completely out of hand, and our pre-middle-school Reinvention Project—well, let's just say it didn't go exactly as I had hoped.

Instead of spending the summer with my friends, I wound up on a cross-country train trip for a month and wrote around a zillion pages in my journal, mostly in self-defense. I needed some way to escape the endless family togetherness. Because really, gorgeous views don't exactly make my family less weird and annoying.

Did that just make me sound like Veruca Salt? You know, the horrible spoiled brat in "Charlie and the Chocolate Factory," the one who says "DADDY! I want an Oompa Loompa!" and ultimately gets attacked by squirrels? I swear I'm not a Veruca Salt kid. (And it would be particularly pointless to yell for my dad, since he lives in Alaska. More on this later too.)

I'm usually the one who gives my little sister the last marshmallow at the campfire, even if I haven't had one yet. And I always take the bad seat at the movies, and when we visit my great-grandma in the nursing home, I let her hold my hand for fifteen minutes even when she's clearly forgotten that she's holding it and I need to go pee.

In all honesty, the trip is impossible to describe, even in all these pages. It went from cool to frustrating to amazing to horrible and back again. But I was NOT thrilled about it at the beginning. It wasn't just that I would miss my friends. . . . It's a lot more complicated than that.

Ugh. I wrote this introduction so my journal would make sense, but I'm not sure it's working.

Let me start at the beginning.

My name is Sara Johnston-Fischer, though for a while I *was* trying to get people to call me "Rae," because it sounds more interesting than "Sara." (This was part of the Reinvention Project.) But I gave up, because no one really remembered.

Instead I get this:

From Mom and Mimi (also known as Carol and Miranda, also known as my parents. Yes, I have two moms. More on that later too): Sara, Sare-Bear, or Sara-Sweet. I can't even . . .

From Ladybug (my younger sister, real name Li, but she rarely answers to it): Say-Say or Woofy Dog. She wants everyone to play animal games, and once, ONCE, I made the mistake of joining her insanity and pretending to be a dog. No good deed goes unpunished, as she now calls me Woofy Dog. Loudly. In public.

From Laurel (my oldest sister): Say-Say or So-So (because I call her Lo-Lo), or Rae, occasionally. She at least tried. But since she's almost twenty and deeply committed to saving the planet, she has other things on her mind and usually forgets. Laurel's home for the summer, with Root (more on him in a minute too).

Earlier this summer everyone was away traveling, but my friends and I were all supposed to spend August right here in Shipton, Massachusetts, home of awesome beaches and some really boring historic houses. And this year, with the end of elementary school and the start of middle school, we decided to make August the "Reinvention Project" month. It's not like we wanted to be totally different people, just . . . new and improved.

In case you were wondering, we weren't losers back at Shipton Upper Elementary. We were . . . fine. Not too popular, not too shy, not too *anything*. Vi was the one who had the idea of reinventing ourselves. She decided she wanted to donate her hair (it was so long, she could sit on it) and try a kind of hippie-chic style (lots of layered T-shirts and embroidered jeans). I should mention that Vi is seriously into fashion, in an owns-a-sewing-machine-and-wants-to-be-a-designer-someday way. Anyway, she started the idea, but Em and I both said if we were going to do makeovers, it had to be *everything*, not just our clothes and hair. We needed new activities, new interests, and new skills. We couldn't just *look* different but be the same people, we needed to actually change.

They were such good plans. Our reinvention had to include our brains (new languages, researching social causes), our muscles (surfing and yoga for me, kickboxing for Vi, surfing for Em), and—of course—a "signature style." Because as Vi said, what was the point of changing in all these new and interesting ways if we looked exactly the same? And since three different elementary schools all feed into Shipton Middle School, we figured this was the perfect time to do it. Hundreds of new kids who had never met the *old* us would now meet the new and improved us!

So we brainstormed, made our lists, and were ready to stop talking about it and actually *do* it.

But within a week everything changed.

That's when—and I'm *trying* to get to the point (because you haven't even gotten to the actual journal yet!)—one of my moms, Mimi, who's a writer, won a fellowship sponsored by the National Rail Service to write while traveling across the United States by train. This was a huge opportunity, the kind of thing that could help her achieve her dream of publishing a book. (A dream, I might add, that we share. I *am* sympathetic to a fellow suffering artist. Obviously.) Tons of people applied for only two spots. Apparently, it's a big national competition for "serious writers to have time and space to create while immersing themselves in the magic of viewing the country by train." The winners could write anything at all that related to "the culture of rail travel," and in exchange, they were offered a free cross-country vacation with their families. Whatever all this "culture of rail travel" and "immersive experience" blah, blah meant, the fact was: this was a major win for her writing career, so obviously we were going.

The train trip also meant that our whole family could travel together out to California to bring Laurel back to college. She was home because . . . well, that's complicated too. I mentioned the environment, right? My older sister is reallyreallyreally committed. Like, goes to protests and rallies, chains herself to trees, gets arrested, and so on. And right before her school year ended, she and her "partner" Root (don't use the word "boyfriend," because it "perpetuates societal stereotypes, and he's not into that, dude"), well, they were part of a giant week-long protest. Tons of people were arrested, and it was in the papers and everything. And when it was over, Mom insisted that Laurel come home. At first Laurel said she wouldn't, that the cause was too important. Then someone fired a gun at a group protesting nearby, and Mom freaked out, and finally Laurel and Root agreed to come back "until things chilled out." Laurel's pretty amazing, actually. She's way braver than me about EVERYTHING.

Needless to say, Mom (who's a judge and quite big on law-and-order-type stuff) has *a lot* to say to Laurel about all this activism. Since Laurel's been home, she and Mom mostly stay out of each other's way, but Mom isn't exactly silent with her disapproval of Laurel's "reckless choices." Anyway, this train trip meant we could all travel back to Berkeley together. But in the meantime, Laurel's been home in her old bedroom, her hair cropped into almost a buzz cut, while Root pitched a tent in the yard because "he prefers his oxygen unsanitized by machines." Or something.

It's been . . . interesting, having Root here. Our neighbors, the Dunphys, kept hearing weird noises and would call across the yard, asking if things were okay. We would have to explain it was just Root "OMMMM"-ing after morning yoga. Even worse, their daughter Fiona, who's going into high school and is *totally* cool (she plays ice hockey and also won the library's read-a-thon four years in a row), brought back his *underwear* from their yard when they blew off the clothesline. Yes, Fiona Dunphy, possible future Olympian, handed me Root's boxer shorts. I hate my life.

Here's an example of life with Root:

SCENE: Our kitchen, which usually has at least four different kinds of gluten-free cereals or crackers lying around. Ladybug has a zillion allergies, and we're always trying to find food she actually likes. I'm sitting at the kitchen table with *A Homeschooling Guide to Introductory Latin,* practicing verbs.

MIMI:
You know, Li-Li love, I could try to get some gluten-free— AAAAAAAAAAAAAAAIIIIIEEEE!

(Mouse runs across the kitchen table and under a cloth napkin that's been left there.)

LADYBUG:
(reaching for the napkin) Mouse! MOUSE! Can we keep it? Let me hold it!

MIMI:

DON'T TOUCH IT! Do you know how many dis-
eases . . . UGH! Someone get me a broom!
Or a box! Or . . . GAAAHHHHH!

(Mouse, presumably freaked out by all the
noise, darts out from underneath the napkin and
attempts to hide in the open cereal box. Mimi
screams louder.)

ROOT:

(wandering in) Dudes, why all the intensity?
I could hear you through the windows. Totally killed the vibe on my tai chi.

MIMI:

There's a mouse! Grab that cereal box!
Crush it!

LADYBUG:

(standing on the kitchen table on the
verge of tears) NOOOOOO!

ROOT:

That's pretty violent. And it wastes a
whole box of cereal. Let's—

MIMI:

GIVE ME THAT THING! (Grabs the cereal box,
grabs *A Homeschooling Guide to Introductory*

Latin, slams book onto the box over and over. Throws box into the nearby garbage bag and flings the bag out the back door.)

SILENCE

ROOT:

Dude, that's some serious anger. Over a living creature. I'm a little freaked out, man.

LADYBUG:

(starting to cry) Is it dead? I wanted to make it a pet!

MIMI:

Look, people. I am not . . . Let's just . . . Hold on! We are talking about vermin! They spread disease! There's no—

LADYBUG:

What about Stuart Little?! Or Ralph, from *The Mouse and the Motorcycle*! Or—

ROOT:

She's right, my friend. Compassion begins at home, you know? Also, you should really recycle that box.

These types of situations happened frighteningly often. And that was *before* we even got on a cramped train together.

So yeah, it's been quite a summer, and this turned into quite a journal assignment. Mimi helped me type it up, so at least you don't have to read a bazillion pages of my bad handwriting (but she insisted on typing it *verbatim*— that's Latin for exactly how I wrote it. Oops, you probably already knew that). Anyway, you'll notice I added some extra things that I didn't write—notes, postcards I borrowed back from Ladybug's friend Frog Fletcher, and excerpts from Mimi's writing. (I have to give the postcards back when you're done grading. Apparently Frog was only willing to share them after Mom offered ice cream sundaes.) Consider it proof, so you know I'm not exaggerating. Trust me, that exaggeration would be *completely* redundant in this case.

But look on the bright side. . . . You only have to read it, and it probably makes a pretty good story. I had to live through the whole thing.

Chapter 2

TEAM JOHNSTON–FISCHER! (And you too, Root!)

I have BIG NEWS!!!! Please report to the dinner table at 6:00 SHARP for a family conference!

Here's a hint (try singing it!):

I've been working on the railroad/All the livelong day

I've been working on the railroad/Just to pass the time away.

Love and excited kisses,

Mimi

P.S. Root, we will be having a vegan dinner tonight, so you do not need to bring your own tofu.

P.P.S. Sara, so sorry, love, but I will not be able to take you and Em surfing tomorrow...for REASONS!

P.P.P.S. I know the cat barfed on the couch, and I haven't had time to clean it up! Sorry! I'll do it as soon as I can, but meanwhile...no one sit on the left side.

DEAR FROG GUESS WHAT WE ARE GOING ON A TRAIN RIDE!!!!!!!!! A REAL TRAIN AND WE WILL SLEEP ON IT AND GO ALL THE WAY TO CALIFORNIA ON IT!!!!! Okay Mom says I can't do more capital letters but I am very excited!!!!!!!!!!!!!!!!!!!!!!!!!!! Now she says she won't write any more exclamation points. But I am bringing Bruce the Roman and will take a thousand pictures and show them all to you when we come home. LOVE, LADYBUG!!!!!!!!

(Hi, Carol here. In case you're wondering if we're traveling with a strange Italian man, Bruce is a plastic Roman centurion soldier. Li's gotten VERY attached to him. We're not quite sure where he came from—Miranda thinks Li found him on the floor of the pediatrician's office. We should probably drop him into a bucket of bleach.)

It's possible we're crazy. Okay, it's likely we're crazy. After all, traveling with our three kids has never been what I'd call easy. Or even pleasant, necessarily. For those who wonder what exactly that means, take a look at my blog, They're Really Cute When They're Asleep, and find the post where I chronicled our fifteen-hour drive to Washington, DC. For new readers, I'll introduce the cast.

It was me, my wife (aka Superwoman), and our three daughters—known for purposes of their privacy and the avoidance of lawsuits as Animal Planet, the Scribe, and the Activist. Five people. That trip, known in our family as "The Time the Minivan Started Smelling Like Barf and Never Got Clean Again," took place when Animal Planet was only three, the Scribe was a constantly carsick nine-year-old, and the Activist was a sullen sixteen.

When we talk about that trip now, it is in the hushed tones of survivors. The Activist, who has since stopped being sullen and channels all her rage against those who despoil the earth, now says we should have pointed the Incredible Barfing Scribe (the carsick thing was really bad) at Congress as a protest.

I realize I am only dealing with three children. I know people have taken on greater challenges than this. My own sister Kate has volunteered at a foster home in Nepal and taken twenty-seven children on a public transit bus to Kathmandu. She never loses any of them. She also has, so far as I know, never had a zit, so whatever.

Me? I'm girding my loins for battle, or at least for an epic journey.

Together with the now six-year-old Animal Planet, twelve-year-old Scribe, and nearly twenty-year-old Activist, as well as the Activist's partner, who I'll call Tree, we are crisscrossing the country by train, diving into the small towns and big cities of America. The Scribe no longer gets carsick. Animal Planet, now that she knows how to read, can be silent for more than thirty seconds at a time. The Activist and Tree are thoughtful, compassionate, engaged young adults. What can possible go wrong?!

MIMI: Talk to family about the fact I will need their cooperation and input to make this work. Without their quotes and insights, I will have no book! Remind Ladybug that she can't only talk about poop. Remind Laurel that it can't be angry rants about the government. Remind Sara to say something. ANYTHING.

I'm in a state of shock. In the past twenty-four hours . . . no, wait, forty-eight hours . . . no, less than that . . . maybe thirty-six? WHATEVER. In the past few days, my entire summer plan blew up, exploded, shattered into tiny pieces that are beyond even the Gorilla Glue fix (thanks to Ladybug, I'm awesome at Gorilla Glue fixing). And to make matters worse, I can't even complain. There is *no* way that I would ever, in a million versions of my life, tell Mimi and Mom about the Reinvention Project. That idea is so horrible, I would rather stick a fork in my eye. Okay, not really, as that made me feel queasy and gross writing it down, but still. There are exactly two types of responses I would get from my moms:

1) "That is so WONDERFUL and TELL US EVERYTHING and HOW CAN WE CELEBRATE and MAYBE WE CAN BRAINSTORM TOGETHER!"

2) "There is NO WAY you are dying the ends of your hair blue, and WHAT'S WRONG with your *old* shirts, and DOES THAT SEEM IMPRACTICAL TO YOU? LET'S RETHINK THIS.

As I've said, the Reinvention Project is *not* just about how we look. I'm sure that would be Mom's first assumption, that "social media" and "today's celebrities" are turning us into fashion zombies. As if. No, we were totally clear: the project was mostly (okay, at least definitely partly) about *self-improvement*. The goal is to be more interesting and sophisticated in middle school, which *obviously* goes beyond looks. And yes, in theory we could do it in September when I'm home, but really? It's not going to happen. Once we walk into school that first day and start classes, we'll get sucked into the same old everything. If we were going to be different, it had to be at the start. Not that it matters anymore, but here was my list:

☆ Learn Latin

☆ Learn to surf, at least the basics

☆ Practice yoga every morning to develop Inner Peace and Mindfulness

☆ Change hair (*Note: this is Vi's idea. I've been growing mine for four years, and I'm definitely not cutting it, but dying the ends . . . that I can do.*)

☆ Start wearing dark gray or navy-blue nail polish (*and try not to pick it off in ten minutes*) (*Note: this is Vi's idea too. We'll see.*)

☆ Read at least five nonfiction books

☆ Pick a signature social cause to care about
(*Note: This one's Em's idea. I have lots of
causes I care about, but apparently we each
need a "signature cause."*)

☆ Eschew with a firm hand all old camp, soccer
team, and dumb club shirts and sweatshirts,
even if they are soft and cozy

☆ Consider jeggings

☆ Drink coffee

☆ Rebrand myself as Rae, not Sara

☆ Work on a novel, or at least figure out a good
story

Anyway, it's all irrelevant because now I'll be on this *ridiculous* train ride and won't get to do any of it. And like I said, there's literally no way I was going to explain to my moms that I needed to stay home because of the Reinvention Project. When I tried to say I would miss my friends too much and wanted to spend time with them, of course the answer was already out of my moms' mouths before I finished talking.

I'll see them in a few weeks.

We have the entire school year together.

I can write them and tell them all about it.

GAH.

Even Vi and Em were all "OH COOL! A CROSS-COUNTRY TRAIN TRIP! JEALOUS!"

But they have No. Idea.

Because now I need to explain what exactly Mimi writes. See, as a Fellow Author, I was totally curious how Mimi was going to incorporate "the culture of rail travel" into her writing. She's talked forever about writing a novel, so I couldn't wait to hear what she was going to come up with. But here's the thing: Mimi's kind of famous for her parenting blog. It's a big deal, with thousands and thousands of followers, and pieces in all kinds of crazy places like Oprah's magazine and the *New York Times*. She gets invited to speak at conferences and write for parenting magazines all the time. But the point—and the MAJOR problem here—is that the blog is all about our family. I mean *allllllllll* about our family. Here are some of her blog posts:

☆ How I said "cumbercukes" instead of "cucumbers" when I was little, and "capause" instead of "because," and how I used to sing the song from *The Wizard of Oz:* "Capause, capause, capause, capause, CAPAUSE! Capause of the wonderful things he does!"

☆ How when Ladybug was first toilet trained, she had to sing a goodbye song to her poop before she'd let anyone flush the toilet.

☆ How once when Laurel and I were fighting, I told her that I'd pull out her teeth while she was sleeping and put them under my pillow so I'd get money from the Tooth Fairy, and another time Laurel saved a snowball in the freezer until July so she could throw it at me.

☆ How once I found these white fluffy pads in the bathroom and made them into sleeping mats for my dolls.

I mean EVERYTHING.

When I was little, I didn't care, obviously, because . . . well, I was little. And of course Mimi doesn't use our real names. She used nicknames based on our personalities. "Animal Planet" for Ladybug, because she was always obsessed with animals, "the Scribe" for me because I've always kept a diary or journal, and "the Activist" for Laurel. The last one is kind of funny—she called Laurel that because Laurel was always . . . and I mean *always* . . . trying to prove that something wasn't fair. Of course now she really is an activist, forever fighting for environmental rights and stuff. And I'm still writing too, so I guess they were pretty good nicknames.

BUT THAT IS NOT THE POINT.

The point is, not only am I being pulled away from home right at the critical moment in our Reinvention Project when we stop planning and start actually crossing things off the list, but Mimi's writing project is a *continuation of her blog*! She's going to spend the whole time peering at us over her glasses, making notes on napkins and the backs of maps. And every time someone says something funny or stupid or interesting or *anything,* she'll be writing it down, and if the book actually gets published, the entire world will be able to read about every single embarrassing, ridiculous, *nonsensical* moment of my life. And yeah, it's not our names, but it's not like it's a secret. Let me tell you, I'm all for her dream of getting published, but I don't really want to have every comment, argument, family moment, and inside joke shared worldwide.

I tried to explain all this to Em and Vi, but I don't think they really get it. First of all, they were (understandably) totally bummed that I'm bailing on them right when we're getting to the good part of the Reinvention Project. I told them to go ahead without me, and that I'd try to do some of it on the train, but I don't know. Without us being all together, it seems pointless.

And they were kind of jealous, which, under the circumstances, is hilarious.

This is me trying to get them to understand:

SAANVI:

Wait! You're going to be gone for a month!
A WHOLE month? You're leaving us??

(Note: Vi can always be counted on for a dramatic reaction. But in this case she is not wrong.)

EM:

(interrupting before Vi's hysteria takes
over) You're going cross-country? That is
so cool! Will you see New Orleans? And
the Grand Canyon? LUCKY!

SARA:

Not lucky! It's not *just* that we get a
paid trip around the country. Mimi is
writing about the trip, and it might be
published as a book.

EM:

Oooh! That sounds cool. What kind of
book? Will it be a mystery? Like *Murder
on the Orient Express*? Or *New Orleans
Mourning*? Or—

SARA:

(cutting her off, because Em is obsessed
with mysteries) NO! Nothing like that.
It's nonfiction, about family travel.

                    SAANVI:
Like a guidebook?

                      EM:
Hmmm. I think it would be better if there
were a murder.

                     SARA:
YOU ARE MISSING THE POINT! It's going
to be like her blog. She'll be watching
everything we do, quoting us, capturing
the "moments when life gets real" and
basically making our whole trip public!
We're going to be like . . . like a reality TV show! Only in a book! She wants
us to have matching T-shirts!

                    SAANVI:
I could design you a team hat. That would
be fun.

I don't think they understand the scale of the problem.
Em was mostly bummed that I'm missing surf camp,
and now she'll be the only girl in the class. Saanvi was
upset that now we weren't going to be able to make over
my room, which was going to be an extension of our Reinvention Project. My room bothers her almost as much
as (okay, maybe more than) it bothers me. (Full disclosure:

it's still done in the unicorn theme I begged for when I was six. I have a unicorn mural on one wall, rainbow-unicorn framed "artwork" (though I use that word loosely) on the others, and rainbow shades on my window. Vi once said, unkindly but truthfully, that it looks like a rainbow fairy barfed in there. Anyway, now that project's ruined too.

I was trying to explain to them how horrifyingly embarrassing it was going to be, all trapped together on the train with Mimi poking at us like specimens, when Saanvi asked, "Is it because of the whole . . . L-word thing?"

It's not even the L-word thing. I mean, sure, it can be awkward introducing my moms, and sometimes people ask WAY too many questions. (I mean, seriously? Do I ask about how your parents had *you*??) But my family . . . well, I guess this journal will explain.

Sorry in advance, dear seventh-grade English teacher. Because I strongly suspect you will be getting the true and unfiltered version of the Johnston-Fischer Family Train Trip of a Lifetime . . . everything I WON'T be saying out loud.

Mimi can write her own story. . . . This one is mine.

Chapter 3

It's official. We are on board. Goodbye, Shipton, Em, Vi, surf lessons, and our adorable cats, Amos and Boris, who are being fed by Fiona Dunphy and will probably poop in our shoes to show how much they miss us. Goodbye, space to get away from Mom and Mimi, who have practically killed each other fighting about luggage and who needed (or didn't need) five pairs of shoes. Or space to get away from Ladybug, who has brought four stuffed animal cats and Bruce the Roman centurion. Or space of any kind, really.

And speaking of luggage, needless to say, Mom had one of her both-hands-up-in-the-air-are-you-crazy moments, and I had to put back around half of what I was planning to bring. My suitcase is tiny. Of course I insisted on my yoga mat, but I barely managed to fit my Latin book. At the last minute I decided to wrap the box of Vivid Life electric-blue hair dye in my new mandala T-shirt and hide it in the bottom. It was probably stupid to bring it, since it's not like I'm going to use it, but I felt too sad leaving it behind. After all, Vi, Em, and I all did a semi-blood vow (*like* a blood vow, but with red food coloring on our fingertips because Em's totally petrified of needles) that none of us would chicken out and we would all dye at least part of our hair. This was a tough one for me. . . . I actually *like* my hair, unlike most other parts of how I look, which are fairly boring. My hair's really long, and dark brown and shiny-silky. (At least when I've just brushed it. After a while it's kind of a snarled mess.) But a fake-blood vow's a fake-blood vow, so I'll do it. I chose blue for the bottom few inches, Em chose magenta for a skunk stripe, and Vi decided to bleach two white streaks in her new short bob. I pointed out that she may look a bit like that *101 Dalmatians* villain, but she didn't care.

Anyway, I tried to bring some new Reinvention Sara—I mean *Rae*—clothes, which mostly means avoiding all the ratty (but oh-so-comfortable!) old T-shirts and bringing three new ones I bought on Etsy with my allowance. But really, what's the point? Better to fill my whole suitcase with books. It's not like the Reinvention Project has much of a chance, even if I manage to practice a few Latin verbs.

Trains, it turns out, are all about tiny. Tiny sinks, tiny spots to store luggage, tiny closets that basically fit one shoe. It's cute, in a dollhouse-meets-Swiss-Army-knife way, though I'm not sure how we're actually going to fit. The beds are bunks that fold out from the seats, which we learned when the super-jolly train worker guy came through and demonstrated. He was so proud, you would have thought he'd invented them. Then Root started asking him about fuel efficiency and high-speed rail options, and they were BFFs before he finally left.

Here's the basic setup—me, the moms, and sometimes Ladybug are in one sleeper. Laurel, Root, and Ladybug the rest of the time are in another. Ladybug can't decide if she's willing to sleep away from the moms, but Laurel promised to tell her fairy stories every night, so Ladybug said she'd try. I hope she stays with them. Even three people in here is ridiculous. And Mimi snores, though she swears she doesn't. Every time we tell her, she immediately straightens up and pretends to look offended, saying "There must have been a bullfrog in the room last night! I never snore!"

Today's train ride is only as far as New York, so we won't even be using the cool beds. We'll spend the day in New York, then get back on the train tonight, which is when the real trip begins. The train leaving New York is called the Crescent Line. It travels to New Orleans. If we went straight through, it would take around thirty hours to get there. We'll be taking over a week, getting off the train at different spots to "explore the sights and sounds and smells of our country!"

That last part is a direct quote from Mimi. She is very excited about all this, and especially excited to "get the real, the honest, the hilarious, and the hideous moments of togetherness on a train." Personally, I think I could do without the smells of our country in the summer. The smells of our house are bad enough.

Anyway, first New York City. Then we go overnight to Greensboro, North Carolina, and will wake up there tomorrow, like magic. We'll see.

I'll be sharing what our National Rail guide calls FUN FACTS about the various places we're seeing. Though I have to be honest . . . some of these are seriously not that fun. I guess it's all a matter of opinion. I've also added my own not-so-fun facts about this trip. Don't think the National Rail Guide will be publishing them any time soon.

Fun Fact!

New York's Penn Station is the busiest rail station in the country.

Not-So-Fun Fact!

A homeless guy wearing a dress tried to bite Ladybug. In fairness she was saying "WOOF, DOGGY!" really loudly at the time, but of course she was talking to me, not him. Still, he couldn't have known that.

A concern: Penn Station was only a "quick" four-hour ride. I have serious misgivings about all this. The train was fun for around twenty minutes, and then we all got bored. Mimi was writing, Mom was deep in some legal reading, and Ladybug and I played cards for around an hour until I realized that (1) I think I hate cards, and (2) Ladybug cheats TERRIBLY. When I accused her of looking at the hidden cards on the edge (we were playing Concentration), she started laughing like it was the best joke in the world. In the end she won five games and I won one. Mostly because I cheated too. The only good part is that Mimi didn't bug us for our "thoughts and perspectives," as she was busy typing, then deleting, something for the whole time.

7:30 p.m.

I love this city! We visit cousins in New Jersey every year, and we'll come in to see Broadway shows and visit museums, but this time we walked all around. In no particular order, here are examples of the awesomeness:

The High Line: This is an elevated park that used to be an old rail track and is now full of gardens and art and literally a bazillion (okay, not literally, but TONS of) tourists taking selfies and wedding photos and everything in the world. I think I heard seven different languages.

Soup dumplings: These Chinese pork-and-crabmeat dumplings filled with broth are DELICIOUS. If you don't know that they're full of broth and casually take a bite, they *will* explode all over you. Cue hysterical laughter when Laurel proceeded to do exactly that. Also, Ladybug told every single person who worked there *or* ate there that she was Chinese like the dumplings. So that wasn't embarrassing at all.

Books of Wonder: This is a big bookstore filled floor-to-ceiling with children's books, including tons of autographed ones. While we were in there looking around, I spotted at least two ACTUAL authors talking to the staff and signing books. Not sure I'd ever want to write for kids—I think I'd rather write real grown-up books—but if I did, I would totally want to see my books in this store.

NYU, or New York University: It's right in the middle of everything and is definitely where I want to go to college. There were students everywhere, sketching, dancing, working on computers, hanging out. They were the coolest people I've ever seen.

One group of students was protesting offshore oil drilling, and Laurel and Root walked straight over and talked to them, and they all did this righteous fist-bumping thing and promised to follow each other on Instagram. It was all very hip and grown-up, and I admit I kind of wanted to jump in, but I was too embarrassed. Plus my sandals are leather and I was afraid if the protesters were vegan, they might get mad. Though I realized after we left that Laurel was wearing her "Piping Plover: Tastes Like Chicken" T-shirt, which means they couldn't have been too uptight, since the shirt basically suggests we eat these endangered birds that are super-protected. Root hates that shirt, by the way. He thinks it's cruel and exploitative to an endangered shorebird species. Laurel said she of course supports the birds, but the shirt is funny and, like Walt Whitman, she's allowed to contradict herself. Root got quiet after that.

Of course with this group there's always some drama. Root and Laurel tried to meet friends way up at the top of Central Park, but Root refused to take a taxi, even though we were far away and there was no easy subway connection. They tried to take a bus and got totally lost and wound up in Queens, which is, it turns out, across a bridge in a totally different part of the city. (It's called a borough, by the way, and New York has five of them: Queens, Brooklyn, the Bronx, Staten Island, and Manhattan, which is the part I always think of as New York.) By the time they got back to the restaurant near the train station, they were forty-five minutes late and Mom was spitting mad, saying that Laurel couldn't "maintain the basic premise of responsibility by showing up on time."

When they came in, Laurel was drenched in sweat and refusing to speak to Root, who had been mildly traumatized by an angry woman on the bus. Apparently she didn't appreciate his comments on recycling. Needless to say, hearing all this didn't improve Mom's mood.

She had her Judge Johnston voice going, which is never a good sign. "You realize we have a train to catch, right? This trip will not allow for the anarchist approach to time management that you seem to prefer!"

But Laurel, who—unlike me—is totally unfazed by the Judge Voice, waved her hands like she was brushing away a fly. "Mom. Please. The train isn't for two hours. Let's consider the worst-case scenario, shall we? Imagine this: you guys start eating dinner without us, and we—WAIT FOR IT!—have to get something else to eat! The horror!" She put her hands on either side of her face, pretending to be overcome with shock.

Mom is *not* a fan of sarcasm, so that was like waving a red flag in front of a bull, and she started in on a rampage about responsibility and consideration for others and immaturity, which lasted until the chicken satay arrived.

MOVING ON.

Dinner was Thai food, which has the advantage of being something everyone's willing to eat, and also awesome. Ladybug brought Bruce and posed him with the seriously fancy radish flowers next to the pad Thai. So far she's taken photos of Bruce:

☆ Standing on a soup dumpling

☆ Next to a mural on the High Line

☆ In front of a graffiti-covered parking garage

☆ On the shoulder of a very patient police officer

☆ Photo-bombing an Indian wedding (That one's my favorite.)

You know, maybe this trip won't be so bad. I mean, I miss my friends and all, but Mimi hasn't been bugging us too much about "opening up and sharing perspectives," at least so far. And it *is* pretty amazing to be out of Shipton and seeing the world. Somehow it's easier to imagine reinventing myself in a place like New York.

Maybe this will work out after all.

Chapter 4

I'm going to kill Mimi. No, really, I'm usually a nonviolent person, but this . . . this is ridiculous. Once we got on the train, she informed us that we should go to the dining car after we settled in, because she had a "delightful surprise." Given that this trip was her most recent "delightful surprise" (and the arrival of Ladybug was another one—and yes, that worked out pretty well, but I wasn't so thrilled at first, I can assure you), I was more than a little nervous. And with good reason. Her "surprise" turned out to be ANOTHER FAMILY OF NATIONAL RAIL FELLOWSHIP WINNERS.

Yes, that's right. There were two grand prizes, two fellowships for writers to travel together, "enjoying the camaraderie of a shared passion for writing," and offering a chance to "make lifelong friends." So now we're not only zigzagging around the country while Mimi writes about every moment of it, nagging us to "add our voices" whenever possible (and, oh yes, she's back to asking me to share my "insights"), we are doing so glued to *other people,* so that I will not only be annoyed with my family's unrelenting weirdness, but I'll share the embarrassment with

34

strangers who'll be stuck with us for the rest of the month. Same travel schedule, same hotels, same EVERYTHING.

Obviously, I don't really want to kill Mimi. But maybe I'll try to become an emancipated minor, which we learned about in English class last year. I swear at this point I feel like the courts would agree that I'd be better off on my own. I could go live with Laurel maybe. Or . . . hmm . . . she lives with around nine people in a pretty small house. Maybe I'd move in with Em. Honestly, what is the point of parents if they are going to be so mind-bogglingly thoughtless? The really incredible part is that Mimi seemed to think I'd be happy about this. Because there's a thirteen-year-old BOY in the other family.

"This is a friend for you!" she said, actually sounding baffled that I wouldn't be grateful. "I know how hard it is not to have people your own age here! Now you'll have someone on your level."

Because some boy from Texas is *on my level*.

There should be tests you have to pass to become a parent, I think. We had to fill out an eight-page application to adopt the cats, and yet . . . somehow parents can just happen? I CANNOT EVEN BELIEVE MY LIFE.

8:00 p.m.

I'm calmer now, thanks to my deep yoga breathing. (In through the nose, out through the mouth, smell the flower, blow out the candle. It really works!) Also, I asked Laurel about what it takes to become an emancipated minor, and I don't think that's an avenue I'm going to pursue. But I guarantee that I will not be joining the get-to-know-you chat that Mimi has in mind. In fact, I think this marks the beginning of my staying away from everyone. Let them hang out—I'll be hiding. Until California, if necessary.

To recap: I did not agree to be quoted extensively for publication. I did not agree to befriend some random Texas dude who probably has fifty opinions about my family and me after looking at us. And I definitely didn't agree to show up for some photo op for National Rail. So no. Nope. Nopenopenope. I'm staying right here.

9:00 p.m.

Just got back from the stupid photo op.

Mom is apparently not remotely interested in free will or individual rights. I can't believe she's a judge—she's the least fair person in the universe. Maybe I should file a complaint.

Sorry if this all sounds overdramatic, but . . . my family. GAH. Why??? Why do they have to be so . . . FRIENDLY?? Jeez. It's bad enough being all together all the freaking time. But now we're supposed to be besties with these total strangers? Please. After our oh-so-awkward introduction, I'm sure they're going to want to stay far away from us anyway.

It's hard to imagine getting off to a worse start.

I suppose I should back up.

Around half an hour ago Laurel, Root, Ladybug, and I headed out to go to the dining car, and while I was (obviously and naturally) totally annoyed that we had to do this, Ladybug was crazy excited about making new friends. She was flying Bruce on an X-wing fighter that someone gave her, swooping and zooming into the walls as the train swayed. And Root was right behind her, going, "It's pretty chill, actually, feeling the rhythm of the tracks below us, letting the motion of the train push and pull, push and pull. . . ."

Then we got to the door of the dining car, and Ladybug ran through, catching her toe on the edge and flying into the car. She was fine, but Bruce flew off the X-wing and sailed, pinwheeling—sword-over-feet-over-sword—through the air.

We all watched him go, too stunned to even yell a warning. Then he landed with a HUGE splash in a coffee cup.

I didn't think a cup could even hold that much coffee—it seemed like more liquid flew *out* than could have possibly fit *in* the mug. It was like some kind of horrible magic. Luckily, it wasn't scalding hot. Unluckily, it splashed a full-on tidal wave of brown liquid all over the tiny old woman whose cup it was. She didn't seem to speak much English, but, if I had to guess, she sure knows plenty of swear words in whatever language she was speaking. (Romanian? Latvian? Czech?? No idea . . . didn't sound like there were a lot of vowels.) Her husband, on the other hand, looked like he was trying not to laugh.

Of course Mom and Mimi ran over, and it was all "We're terribly sorry!" "We'll pay for the cleaning bill!" "Let us get you another coffee!" and so on, while the woman kept yelling at them in whatever no-vowel language she spoke and her husband silently rocked back and forth, laughing. Finally she flounced out of the dining car with a last, totally venomous-sounding yowl. (Armenian? Dutch? Hebrew?) Ladybug ran over and grabbed Bruce, shouting, "HE'S FINE! BRUCE IS FINE, DON'T WORRY!"

Silence.

After the Grand Flounce-Out, every single person in the dining car was staring at us. Their faces were somewhere on the spectrum between seriously annoyed and mildly amused. We were all trying to mop up coffee (which of course I got all over my shorts . . . I look like I rolled in poo), and Mimi was dithering and apologizing to the whole train car, and Ladybug was still bellowing in her ALL CAPS voice that BRUCE WAS FINE.

Through all this, I noticed a boy who was at least five inches shorter than me, wearing a totally normal outfit except for the *giant cowboy hat*. And he was laughing his head off. Like we were some kind of hilarious reality TV show. *Nugatory ac nebulo,* that was what he was. (I admit I haven't done much Latin yet, but the insults are pretty awesome.)

Finally the waiters took away all the wet coffee-smelling napkins, and Mimi calmed down and introduced us to our New Train Friends. . . . I could see the capital letters as she was talking. *I* call them the annoying people who will make this trip even more embarrassing than it was before. First Mimi introduced me to Travis, aka Cowboy Hat, as though I'm some exotic species, or perhaps a spokesperson for the Nation of Youth. Honestly, the whole meeting-at-the-dining-car was so hideously awkward, I tried practicing my yoga breathing to calm down, which only resulted in Cowboy Hat asking me if I had asthma and needed my inhaler.

For now the NTFs are Gavin, an engineer from Texas who writes thrillers under a pen name, and Travis (giant cowboy hat guy). I guess his grandmothers or some old lady relatives are meeting us in Atlanta, which only means it's going to get worse. Soon we'll also have crabby uptight old people with us, judging by Laurel's piercings and Root's poncho (though in fairness we *all* judge his poncho). But for now it's just the father-and-son team.

Travis stuck his hand out to shake mine, which, I have no idea, is maybe a Texas thing, or a fake-polite, let's-make-fun-of-the-weirdo thing . . . who knows? Of course, my hand was filthy from trying to wipe up coffee, but I didn't know what to do, so I put my hand out too, then pulled it back before he could really get hold of it.

I can see the headline now: Girl Too Confused by Life to Understand Handshaking

WHHHHHYYYYYY???

But before we could rework the whole teach-Sara-how-to-shake-hands thing, Ladybug asked if she could put Bruce on the brim of the cowboy hat. Travis knelt down so that Bruce could be stuck in the braided band, and that's when I shuffled into a seat and put my earbuds in. It's bad enough if he's going to laugh at me, but I better not see him making fun of my sister.

Mimi kept trying to catch my eye, but I stared down at my iPod and refused to look at her. This was NOT my idea.

Anyway, I went and sat in the dining car with this ridiculous other family that we're now apparently attached to, but I stared at my lap and ignored everyone. So all I really know is that the boy talks a LOT. And he's moderately amusing. But in a most annoying way.

Laurel, Root, I know you feel STRONGLY about stopping the drilling for oil in the Arctic, but it's important you understand that just because you CAN lecture someone for three hours straight in the café car doesn't mean you SHOULD. I'm sure those women would have been VERY INTERESTED, if only they had spoken English!

Love,

Mom

Finally back in our room. While we were in the dining car with the endlessly talking Texans, the train left New York through a two-and-a-half-mile tunnel under the Hudson River (thanks, Root, for another Fun Fact!) and into New Jersey. It was kind of cool—while everyone blathered on, I just watched a purply-pink sunset happening out the window. *Sunset over New Jersey* . . . Could be a good title for a book. Maybe about a girl who runs away from her family and lives happily ever after in a tree house with her friends.

Fun Fact!

Newark, New Jersey, is the third-largest insurance center in the US and home to the best Tibetan art collection in the world. (Really? Who compiles these facts? Seriously random stuff here. Does the insurance thing have anything to do with the art thing? The mind boggles.)

Not-So-Fun Fact!

We passed what I guess was once an apartment building that's all broken windows and really crazy graffiti, including some pretty mean things about the president.

It's kind of mesmerizing, watching the towns zoom by in the darkness. Sometimes we go along a row of houses and I can look right into their windows, which are wide open to catch the breeze. The train whistle blows again and again, every time we cross a road, and we can see the red lights flashing as the cars wait for us to pass. It's pretty noisy on the train, actually, rumbling and squeaking and chugga-chugga-chugging constantly, not to mention all that whistling. Plus it keeps swinging around turns and jiggling my hand. . . . My handwriting's not usually this bad, I swear!

Whew. I'm exhausted. Time for bed. Ish. Not sure I'd call them beds when they're so tiny you can't even roll over. Hope I sleep. I will say, it's pretty cool that while we're sleeping we keep flying along, traveling hundreds of miles. We'll be in states I've never been to before, only I won't even be awake! (Hopefully.) Tonight we go through Delaware, Maryland, and Virginia. Here's one more . . .

Fun Fact!
Elkton, Maryland, which is right on the Maryland–Delaware border, was once famous as a place for couples to elope—they'd run away and get married without having to fill out any paperwork or get permission. (I don't think I'll mention that to Laurel and Root. That's all we need.)

Mimi definitely snores. Or else there is a freaking HUGE bullfrog in our room.

You know what? I'm done wallowing in self-pity. Just because I'm on this trip with a bullfrog and a tiny Roman soldier and my whole family (plus *Root*), that doesn't mean I have to give up my dreams! No, every person who's ever done anything important has had setbacks and prevailed in spite of them! In fact, Mimi is forever babbling on about how kids today need "grit" and "tenacity" and "stick-to-itiveness," and guess what? Sara—whoops!— *RAE* Johnston-Fischer has that to spare!

I had pretty much figured there was no point in trying to do much on my list without Em and Vi, but starting right now, I'm recommitting to the Reinvention Project. Who cares if Travis the Texan thinks I'm weird? Or if I have to wait until we have Internet to email Em and Vi? I'll keep up, I'll learn Latin and practice yoga and read my nonfiction books, and try out my new casual-but-hip look (arty T-shirts, ballet flats instead of flip-flops, maybe some new jewelry?), and when I get back to Shipton in a month, I'll be totally ready for middle school! Since I'm awake, I'm starting right now. Downward-facing dog, here I come! Namaste, Rae.

3:48 a.m.

Ouch. I smashed my face into the wall and nearly kicked the window. I think I'd better open the bathroom door and try again. Also, I'm really stiff. But still . . . ONWARD!

Chapter 5

Stepping off the train into the dim predawn light, we can't help but feel lucky to be awake and experiencing this magical in-between time, with the sky barely starting to lighten over the buildings of Greensboro, North Carolina. The warm, humid air will be scorching later on, but now there's a touch of cool dampness on our skin. All of us, even Animal Planet, who is nearly asleep in Superwoman's arms, feel the excitement of a new beginning . . . a new day, a new adventure.

The Scribe can't wait to capture these first impressions. . . . We may still be in the United States, but we are far from home, and everything feels different already. She's madly scribbling in her journal—who knows what she's writing there?

4:00 a.m.

OMG. Mimi, in her excitement about getting off the train to explore the smells or whatever, didn't quite manage to tell us that we'd be arriving in Greensboro, North Carolina, at FOUR O'CLOCK IN THE MORNING.

Apparently the train stops at big-deal stations—like Washington, DC, and Atlanta—during normal hours, but at other, smaller stops during "off-peak hours," which is code for THE MIDDLE OF THE NIGHT.

I definitely need to learn to drink coffee.

Darrell the sleeping car attendant woke us up a few minutes before we arrived, just like he had promised. We had met him before bed last night and he was great, getting us all set up and offering complimentary bottled water (that Root quite loudly refused, asking why, in a country with clean and potable drinking water, anyone would purchase filtered tap water packaged in a planet-despoiling petroleum-based package). Luckily, Darrell just did his big HAHAHAHA laugh at that and told Root he was absolutely right, and it was a crazy world when people spent four dollars for something free. Then he re-filled our (recycled stainless steel) water bottles, told us all to sleep well, and said he'd wake us in time to get off in Greensboro.

So Darrell knocks on our door, and it goes something like this. I, of course, was awake, due to Mimi's bullfrog impression, and was working on my soon-to-be-daily yoga practice.

DARRELL:

(knock, knock!)

SARA:

(Squeak in surprise mid-cobra-to-warrior
pose) EEP! . . . Oh, um? Is it time to
wake up?

DARRELL:

Yes, ma'am! Greensboro coming up in nine
minutes. I have coffee for your mamas.

SARA:

(Tries to get out of the lunge, trips
over the yoga mat, and flies into the
wall. Horrible *CRRAAASSHH!!* when head
hits wall.) OWWWWWWWWWW!!!!!

MOM:

(waking suddenly) WHO'S THERE? Sara, are
you hurt?

MIMI:

(waking suddenly) IS SOMEONE BREAKING IN?

MOM:

(pulling off her eye mask, almost falling
out of her tiny bed) ARE YOU OKAY? GET
AWAY FROM THE DOOR!

SARA:

OW! Owowowow! My head!

MIMI:

(in a deep scary voice) DID SOMEONE HURT
YOU? WHO'S THERE?

SARA:

(rubbing head) It's just Darrell! I ran
into the wall! I'm fine!

DARRELL:

It's just me, ma'am. We're almost in Greens—

LADYBUG:

(from next door, sobbing) Mommmmmmyyyyyy!

Finally I turned on the light and managed to squeeze
the door open enough to grab the two coffees in dis-
posable cups (sorry, Root). Meanwhile, Mom was bellowing to Ladybug that everything was fine, we were
getting off the train. By the time the train slowed to a
stop, its long, low horn blasting, we were more or less
pulled together, crowded in the hallway with our bags.
The Texans were already there, of course, and Travis
the Cowboy Hat Wearer actually tried to chat, but I
glared at him so hard, he shut up. Who makes conversation at 4:00 a.m.?

We were the only ones getting off in Greensboro. On
the station platform I glanced back, and there were beady

eyes staring at us from the sleeper car windows nearby. Oh well. We never said we were stealthy.

Also, I have a massive knot on my forehead. I suspect in a few hours I'll look like a rhinoceros. Or a unicorn. At least I'll match my room back home. Once we got out into the light, Travis took one look at me and one of his eyebrows shot up so high, it disappeared under his hat. Awesome. Making fun of me is going to be a full-time job for him.

8:00 a.m.

Fun Fact!

Greensboro, North Carolina, was named after Major General Nathaniel Greene, whose forces fought against the British Army of Lord Cornwallis in the Revolutionary War. (Interesting. I always think about the Revolutionary War being up in Massachusetts, what with the Lexington Minutemen and Paul Revere and the Boston Tea Party. But apparently they were kicking British butt down here too.)

Not-So-Fun Fact!

Our Greensboro hotel closes its front desk between 2:00 a.m. and 6:00 a.m., so we had to sit outside on a bench. You know what there is to see and do in Greensboro at 5:00 a.m.? NOTHING.

Finally someone came on duty. She looked pretty surprised to see us, but when Mimi explained who we were and about the train, the woman said "Well, bless your heart" around a hundred times and scurried around to get our rooms ready. She asked if we had eaten, and when we said no, she insisted on opening the kitchen herself and getting us "a little bite to tide us over."

That little bite consisted of:

☆ Three eggs

☆ A massive bowl of buttery white mush called grits, which turns out to be oddly delicious

☆ Six strips of bacon

☆ Two sausages

☆ A biscuit covered in creamy gravy (Sounds gross, tasted *amazing*)

☆ Four pieces of toast

PER PERSON.

Of course, Ladybug couldn't eat a bunch of it, but she managed fine with bacon, sausage, and grits. We had planned to head right out and start experiencing the sights and sounds or whatever, but after that meal we all napped for an hour. Wow. Greensboro is looking up.

Fun Fact!

Greensboro was home to the first lunch counter to be desegregated. Part of it has been dismantled and is now displayed in the Smithsonian National Museum of American History.

Not-So-Fun Fact!

According to Laurel, even though segregation is over, black Americans are more than twice as likely to live in poverty than white Americans because of unfair income practices and other racial injustices.

We separated from the NTFs, thank goodness, who went off to research abandoned parking garages for Gavin's next thriller. Instead of *that* totally creepy outing, we spent the afternoon at the International Civil Rights Center and Museum, which, appropriately enough, is in the old Woolworth's building where that original lunch counter was. Mom started talking about how impressive these young people were and how she had marched on

Washington for equal rights for women when she was in college. Laurel fired right up and asked why on earth Mom could admire these activists and still get mad at Laurel for *her* protests. Mom puffed up and said while the environment was important, of course the stakes were much higher for individual rights, and besides, nobody was shooting at them in the 1990s, and I thought Laurel was actually going to lose it—turn green and bust out of her clothes like the Incredible Hulk—but then Ladybug started whining to go to the children's museum, which Darrell had told her about.

Mom looked like she wanted to stay and argue with Laurel, saying that if the only thing the kids were going to see was a children's museum, what was the point of traveling, but Mimi did her let's-reframe-this! thing and talked about the virtues of "a walkable city to experience as a family," and Mom laughed and hugged her, and they decided that the three of them could go to the children's museum while Root, Laurel, and I stayed here. Then Mom and Laurel hugged and acted like everything was normal, but I could tell Laurel was still slightly Hulk-ish.

Of course, before they left, Ladybug posed Bruce on one of the spinning diner counter chairs and took a photo. Can a Roman centurion be a civil rights activist? Why not, I guess?

After they left, Root, Laurel, and I walked around, looking over the exhibits. There's a video about the four college students who first sat down at the lunch counter in protest. They look pretty close to Laurel's age, and all they did was to sit down and politely ask to be served. It doesn't seem like a big deal—they're nicely dressed and sitting quietly in the photos—but I know it was.

I turned to Laurel.

"They must have been so mad that people were such jerks to them. I mean, look at them! They're just sitting there, all polite and normal! The world was so messed up."

Laurel ran her hands through her short hair, staring at the photos of the Greensboro Four. "They might have been mad. But they were probably scared. Like, pee-their-pants-level scared. It's easy to look at history and think that they knew right was on their side, but at the time a lot of people thought they were crazy. And they were black, which meant that people could spit on them, hit them, hurt them, and not get in trouble. Other people watching the violence would just cheer." Her eyes filled with tears.

I patted her back, which, admittedly, was pretty sweaty after our walk to the museum. Laurel has always been emotional. Not like Saanvi, who swoons and nearly faints and shrieks with laughter and so on. But . . . well, Mimi says Laurel has big feelings that need a way out. If Laurel thinks someone is suffering, or if something is unfair, she literally can't stand it. For example, Laurel once refused to go to school for over a week because her teacher had punished this boy Andrew, a really annoying kid who got on everyone's nerves. He wasn't even a friend of Laurel's or anything, but the thing was, he hadn't done whatever he got in trouble for, and she tried to stand up for him but wound up getting punished too. She was told she had to apologize to the teacher for yelling, and of course that was not going to happen. Instead she screamed and tore up her room, saying over and over that it just wasn't fair, until after a week Mom marched into the school and had a closed-door conference with the principal. Laurel went back to school without apologizing, but the next year she transferred to a small alternative school where she called her teachers by their first names and built yurts in the back field.

Anyway, seeing her crying at the civil rights museum wasn't all that surprising, but still, I felt bad.

"It's okay, Lo-Lo," I said, trying inconspicuously to wipe my damp hand on my shorts. "Things have gotten way better, right?"

She shrugged. "Have they?"

I stared at her. "We have an African American president! And segregation is illegal! And—"

She waved an impatient hand. "Of course that all matters. But, Sara, do you have any idea how unfair this country still is? Let me give you one example. You know how Root and I got arrested in May? For protesting the Arctic drilling? Well, my friend Ola was with us. And she's African American. And when we were all arrested, along with over a hundred other people, most of us were released immediately. But not Ola . . . She and four others were hurt pretty badly and kept in jail way longer than the rest of us. And all five of them were brown or black."

I didn't really know what to say. I just looked at the old photos on the walls, photos from history but from not that long ago.

Laurel sighed. "People thought that civil rights protesters were nuts, you know? That they were total idiots trying to change something that would never ever change. Even people who agreed in theory didn't think the protests would make a difference. They warned protesters not to bother, not to risk themselves on a lost cause."

I nodded, though I wasn't really sure what her point was. But she kept talking.

"And now, when we chain ourselves to the oil tankers or block the bridges, people think *we're* nuts. Heck, *Mom* thinks we're nuts! I mean, seriously, if an educated social activist like her doesn't support what we do, how do you think the rest of the world reacts? You can't imagine how many times someone has said to me, 'Look, I appreciate what you're doing, but big corporations and the government are never going to change.' But they *do* change, Sara! People *do* cause seemingly immovable mountains like segregation to crumble! And if we know that—if it's been proven again and again—well, how can we not keep trying? Who's going to tell us? Who's going to say *this* cause is worth fighting for, but *that one* . . . well, don't bother. Who can know that?"

By this point Laurel was almost yelling, and a few old men in suits nearby started nodding their heads.

"Preach it, sister!" one of them said, and the other banged his cane on the floor, kind of like applause. An old woman walking nearby nodded and said "Uh-HUH" as she passed.

Laurel took a breath and gave me a smile, but it was a watery one. "Well, anyway, you get my point," she said, and I admit, I was relieved that she lowered her voice a bit. Still, I put my arm around her. I love my sister, sweaty or not.

I wonder what it would feel like to be Laurel, so brave all the time. Even if I do every single thing on my Re-invention Project list (and who are we kidding, I won't be learning to surf anytime soon), I don't think I'll ever be as fearless as her. She blogs about this stuff sometimes, and every time I read it, I wonder how it feels to be so *sure* about things. I wish I were more like that.

Before we left the museum, I got a picture book at the gift shop about the four students who started the sit-in . . . nonfiction, of course! And I can read it to Ladybug. It's pretty fascinating. I know some of the stuff, but being down here and seeing everything with my own eyes makes it much more real. And scarier.

Sara,

I am trying to respect your privacy, but it would be really helpful if you could offer me a bit more insight and perspective on Greensboro than simply saying, "It's fine." As I recall, your take on New York City was "It's good."

Any chance you could share a bit more? You have so many wonderful insights! Remember when we went to the Metropolitan Museum of Art when you were four, and you asked why so many of the women in the paintings had their "nursing parts" out? Or last year at the aquarium when you called that one huge fish "the Super Duper Grouper"? I miss your wonderful voice!

Your loving Mimi

DEAR FROG I MISS YOU DO YOU MISS ME?? THIS POSTCARD SHOWS THE MUSEUM WHICH HAD TOYS AND A BALL PIT AND I TOOK A PHOTO OF BRUCE IN THE BALL PIT AND THEN THE GUARD GOT IN THE BALL PIT AND THEN HE TOOK A PHOTO WITH BRUCE. LOVE, LADYBUG!!!!!!!!

ALSO I ASKED MIMI AND SHE SAID THAT IS ENOUGH EXCLAIM POINTS. BUT I AM GOING TO ADD MORE!!!!!!!!!!!

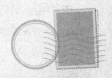

Frog Fletcher

14 Ructo Rd.

Shipton, MA

Chapter 6

Fun Fact!

Spartanburg, South Carolina, is where American forces defeated the British in a pivotal skirmish in the Revolutionary War. The victory was dependent on a local young woman, Kate Barry, who warned American troops of the British advance. (Huh! So there's a Southern female Paul Revere! Who knew?)

Fun Fact!

Notable figures associated with Greenville, SC, include Wayne Oates, the psychologist who came up with the phrase "workaholic."

Not-So-Fun Fact!

Mimi seems intent on redefining the term "workaholic" while trapped on a train with the rest of her family. Not sure how well the writing is going based on the amount of time she's been staring at her computer without touching the keys.

We're back on the train. At least this time we didn't wake everyone else by thinking Darrell was a criminal. Instead of Darrell we have Raymond as our sleep compartment attendant. Raymond is older than Darrell and bald under his cap. He said he's been working on this train since the days when dinosaurs would fall asleep on the tracks and the conductor would have to stop the train to wake them up. He also insisted on having his photo taken with Bruce. I like him.

So to recap, Greensboro was pretty cool, especially the museum and the food. The nice woman at the hotel was still there at dinner last night, and she insisted on serving up a "proper feed," an expression that was slightly terrifying, given what she called a "little bite" at breakfast. The fried chicken was amazing, and she even did a batch in cornmeal so Ladybug could eat it. Root said he was vegetarian, so she brought out a huge mess of mushy green (turns out they're called collard greens, and honestly, they tasted more like bacon than vegetables, but I didn't bother pointing that out to Root) and some beans and other stuff. By the time we stumbled up to our rooms at eight o'clock, we were all exhausted and went to sleep. I was sharing a bed with Ladybug.

This was how our bedtime routine went:

SARA:

Good night, Ladybug Li! Sweet dreams!
(tries to roll over and go to sleep)

LADYBUG:

GOOD NIGHT, WOOFY DOG! GOOD NIGHT! (flings
arms around me and squeezes)

MOM:

(from the other bed) Li-Li, sweets, let
go of Sara. Time to sleep.

LADYBUG:

Woofy Dog needs to sleep in a puppy bed!
Here! (starts building a nest on the floor
with the pillows, including the one from
under my head)

MOM:

No, love. Sara is going to sleep in the
bed with you.

LADYBUG:

NO PUPPIES IN THE BED!

SARA:

(pulling pillow back up) Lucky puppies
get to sleep in the bed with their owners. And I'm a lucky puppy. Good night!

```
            LADYBUG:

(pauses,  then)  Lucky  puppy?  That's  your
new  name!  LUCKY  PUPPY!  Good  night,  Lucky
Puppy!

             MIMI:

(snort-laughing)  Sleep  well,  Lucky  Puppy.
We  love  you.

             SARA:

(pretends  to  be  asleep,  even  though  the
light  is  still  on  and  Ladybug  is  making
Bruce  blow  me  kisses  good  night)
```

Anyway, it was good we went to sleep so early, because waking up before 4:00 a.m. again was brutal. Mom clutched her coffee with both hands like she was afraid someone would take it from her, and even Root, who is generally overly cheerful at all hours, looked a little pale. He said his stomach had been upset all night. Maybe I should have mentioned my bacon-in-the-veggies theory. Oh well.

Adding to the misery was the fact that Travis the Texan was still grinning like I'm the funniest thing in the world. I hate being laughed at. Even if it *did* turn out I had one of Ladybug's stuffed cats in the hood of my jacket. He looked like he was going to say something, but I stomped off before he could. Personally, I think anyone who tries to start up a conversation at four o'clock in the morning to make fun of a person should be slapped with a flounder. (And in case you're wondering, yes, I do know what it feels like to be slapped with a slimy bottom-feeding fish. Ask Laurel about the fight we had when she was in sixth grade.)

I just finished my yoga practice. I managed to get into pigeon pose without a horrible foot cramp this time, so that's good! I feel calmer already. I'm totally going to be mindful and centered by the time we're back in Shipton.

Mimi and Mom came back from the café car with more coffee. It smells divine. I need to *carpe diem* and try a cup. It's a small goal of the Reinvention Project . . . learn to drink coffee. I'm freakishly tall—it's not like anyone has to worry that it will stunt my growth. And if I want to be a writer, I'll need to start my unhealthy dependence on it soon. Plus, I'm sorry, but casually drinking coffee just looks cool.

7:15 a.m.

WHAT MADNESS IS THIS? How do people drink this stuff? It's like drinking Satan's tears. Good Lord. Any mindfulness I got from yoga is totally gone. My eyes won't stop watering.

Hi, all!

Hope you enjoyed breakfast. Mimi and I are working in the café car, so if you don't mind entertaining Lady-bug for a while, that would give us a chance to get a little work done. It would be a HUGE HELP, since Mimi set a goal to write twenty good pages, and she has ... less than that. (AROUND NINETEEN PAGES LESS.)

XOXOXO Mom

10:00 a.m.

Lots of time spent watching the world whiz by the window. We're on our way to Atlanta, due there sometime after noon. Outside the train are old run-down towns and endless fields, green and brown and green and brown moving in a blur. Sometimes we fly past tiny stations with nobody at them, just empty platforms that almost look like they're shimmering in the heat.

I'm not sure how this is what Mimi called an incredible opportunity for our family to reconnect. She caved after breakfast and let Ladybug watch a movie on her iPad, and Mom has been wearing her noise-canceling headphones and scribbling notes on some legal brief since the minute the train pulled out of the station. Laurel and Root are napping, and I'm writing in this stupid journal. We are about as disconnected as people can get when they are trapped in a steel box together.

Watching a movie with Ladybug. She's supposed to be watching PBS, but I hacked the movie-streaming site and we're now watching contraband Disney. Why are all the princesses such bobbleheads?? They look like lollipops. We're moving on from the bobbleheads and trying an animal movie. It has to be better than the dancing candlesticks. Though I admit I really kind of love that library. Ladybug's been adding Bruce into the dance scenes, which is pretty awesome.

Ladybug has, by my guess, taken roughly a thousand photos *a day* of Bruce. She says she wants to take a million photos of him and make a poster for school. That is going to be one big poster. Mom and Mimi gave her an old digital camera (okay, *my* old camera, complete with unicorn stickers), and she carries it *everywhere*. The click-click-click is constant. It's like having a mini member of the paparazzi in the train compartment with us, with Bruce as the world's tiniest media star.

OMG, the dad lion totally DIES in *The Lion King.* Are you kidding me? Ladybug and I are watching, and I'm thinking there's no way. . . . There's going to be some last-minute save, and she turns around and says (in a very cheery voice, I might add), "Mufasa DIES. Zachary at school told me." And now I'm sitting here trying not to blub. But seriously? What kind of sadist makes movies for kids where the parents die? I don't even know what to say. Maybe there's a good reason our moms never let us watch Disney.

I'll have to email my dad and ask him if he's ever seen these Disney tearjerkers. He *loves* movies, maybe because there's not that much else to do in Alaska. He's a doctor there. I barely ever see him, but we email and call a lot. And yes, before Mom met Mimi, she was married to my dad. They had two kids, me and Laurel, before Mom realized shortly after I was born that, as she puts it, she "would always love Dad for being a wonderful person but in my true heart, I knew I did not belong with him because I realized I was a Lesbian." The way she says it, you can see the capital *L.* (Saanvi would cringe, for sure.) Honestly, it's not like I *asked* for the play-by-play.

Anyway, Mom and Mimi have been together since I was around two, so Mimi's always been my other mom.

I don't really think about it much, except when, like now, we're somewhere totally new. Then I realize all over again that people notice us. I mean, we stick out for a lot of reasons: two moms, a Chinese sister, Laurel's pierced tongue and nose—plus don't forget that Ladybug is ALL CAPS LOUD, and Root is forever wandering over to peer into garbage pails and mumble about commercial compost. So having my moms get all kissy-face in public is just another embarrassing moment. Gag. (Vi says nobody's parents should be kissing in public, whether or not they're gay, and she may have a point.)

Laurel took Mimi's arrival in our lives pretty hard for a while. . . . She actually lived in Alaska with our dad for a year. But then she decided she didn't really like having moose in the playground and a 3:30 sunset in winter, and came home. Now she gets along better with Mimi than she does with Mom. Anyway, Mimi didn't have any other kids, though she obviously raised us, but when I was around seven, they decided to "have another child together," which, it turned out, meant adopting Ladybug.

I love my little sister very much, but I'm going to say, things didn't exactly get calmer and quieter when she arrived. (In case you didn't recognize it, that's called an "understatement." It's the opposite of hyperbole, which is when a writer wildly overstates things. If I were using hyperbole, I would say that having Ladybug in the house is like inviting a three-ring carnival complete with elephant and dancing bear and a team of Russian trapeze artists to move into the tiny bedroom next door. But that's not even major hyperbole.)

All this to say I have two mothers and a father in Alaska, and if I had the choice right now, I might take Alaska. Even with the moose.

Fun Fact!

Gainesville, Georgia, is called the Poultry Capital of the World because of the large number of poultry-processing plants.

Not-So-Fun Fact!

Root and Laurel have entered into a spirited discussion on the mistreatment of animals at large-scale animal farming operations.

LAUREL:

Of course I think factory farms are need-
lessly cruel and bad for the planet, but
there needs to be a plan for keeping
food costs low enough to feed the average
American, and not everyone can afford to
eat fancy organic chickens!

ROOT:

Nobody should be eating chickens! Then we wouldn't have this problem! They are sentient beings, and if we could rid ourselves of a meat economy, we could feed the world, heal the planet, and—

LAUREL:

Of course in a perfect world nobody would be eating chickens in the first place, but that's impractical and not a good starting place, since we aren't about to outlaw meat anytime soon. Plus chicken tastes good.

ROOT:

(wordlessly makes a kind of yowling yelping sound of frustration)

LAUREL:

(sticks out her tongue at Root)

At this point Raymond the Train Guy stuck his head in the open door to see what all the yelling was about.

Laurel and Root have agreed to disagree. Raymond gave Mimi his business card so she can interview him about life on the trains. He also took one more photo with Bruce and Ladybug. Ladybug is wearing his train hat. Good grief.

☆ ☆ ☆

OH, GIVE ME A BREAK. This was on my seat when I came back from the café car. Perfect. Now he's making fun of my writing.

Dear Rae—
   Girl, you sure like to write things down! I think you've written more in that book than I wrote for all of seventh grade. But then again, I'm not a big writer. Anyway, sorry you weren't around earlier to chat. But I guess we have plenty of time to get to know each other...almost a month! Yeehaw!
                              Travis

Chapter 7

Greetings from Atlanta! First stop, the World of Coca-Cola! Given that in our house soda gets the same kind of welcome as the mildew that creeps along our shower, this wasn't necessarily on my list, but according to all the guidebooks, it's a big deal. So here we go. Needless to say, we had to have a serious conversation with Animal Planet about the fact that, just because we're paying big money for tickets to look at Coca-Cola, it doesn't mean we're going to drink it. At least not after today. Not surprisingly, she's looking completely baffled by this logic. Can't say I blame her.

It is somewhat fascinating here. For instance, I didn't know that Coca-Cola used to be made with cocaine! (Not that this fact endeared the product to my health-conscious wife.) Also, I had no idea that Fanta Exotic, offered only in Uganda, is so . . . how can I put this? Disgusting? The Activist, who was already ranting to Tree over corporate evil, nearly spit hers into the nearby decorative ficus tree.

> MIMI: Double-check that Coke doesn't sponsor this fellowship, so as to avoid conflict of interest.

Fun Fact!

The core of Atlanta was burned to the ground by Union General Sherman as part of his march to the sea in the Civil War. (Okay, that's really not what I'd call fun. I mean, burning a city to the ground, even if it belongs to the enemy, seems a bit extreme.)

4:00 p.m.

I guess the fact that Atlanta was burned down explains why everything looks so new. I mean, there are huge skyscrapers in New York, and even in Boston, but there are also old stone and brick buildings and giant trees and stuff. Here everything looks shiny and modern. Even the subway, called the MARTA, is bright and fancy. So far we've been touring the city, checking out the "top family-friendly tourist attractions" that Mimi wants to include in her book. The first one was . . . wait for it:

The World of Coca-Cola, which is literally a museum about soda. It includes, and I'm not even kidding, exhibits like the Vault of the Secret Formula and Milestones of Refreshment. Mom is trying to be nice, I can tell, but her nostrils are flared and she's got those two lines between her eyebrows that only show up when she's trying not to stress about something. Of course Ladybug loves the whole thing—it's bright red, first of all, which is her favorite color—and keeps saying, "I LOVE Coca-Cola!" which makes Mom's eye start to twitch. Not a good sign. We did get a photo of Bruce with the giant stuffed polar bear figure. . . . I have no idea what the bear has to do with soda, but it seems to be a big deal. Except that Root then started in about the melting of the polar ice caps and the bears losing their habitats and drowning or starving, and Ladybug started to cry. So then Root sang a song—"Polly Wolly Doodle All the Day"—until she was smiling again. Let me pause for a moment to allow the image of Root, singing and clapping, to truly sink in.

Now let me find a way to someday forget it. (Fat chance.)

Hey, Saanvi!
  Thought you'd enjoy the sight of the Georgia Aquarium's shark tunnel, where you can walk through and watch tons of sharks swimming peacefully all around you. While we were there, a kid started screaming that the glass was going to break and they were all going to get out and eat him. I thought of you. But Root got down to eye level with the kid and told him how many sharks are killed annually by humans (between 100 and 270 million), and how many people are killed annually by sharks (5). The kid stared, then asked Root if he was a teacher. Root looked pretty proud.
                                        XOXOXO Rae

P.S. As if this trip weren't bad enough, there's another family of National Rail winners traveling the same route, and there's a thirteen-year-old BOY. Would you believe he wears a cowboy hat?? I KNOW.

Hola, Em!

Greetings from the Martin Luther King Jr. Center. We got to see the house where King was born. It's so weird to imagine him as a kid. Did he ever complain about having to clear the table or take out the garbage? Was he already different, like somehow he knew he'd be famous all over the world for his speeches and his peaceful fight for equality? I asked Laurel, and she said that he probably popped his zits in the bathroom mirror, and sat in his room practicing how he was going to ask out a girl at school. Weird to think about all that stuff. Anyway, I miss you TONS.

XOXOX Rae

P.S. How's the Reinvention Project going on your end? Email me!

Sara,

Seriously? All you have to say about the MLK Center is "It's fine"? You have a prodigious command of the English language. Why don't you throw me a few more words? Please?

Love, Mimi

There were tourists from all over the world at the King Center, and one of them started talking to Mimi. Well, of course Mimi went into the whole story of our train journey, and the woman, who was very nice and from Germany (she spoke perfect English but had a kind of hilarious accent), asked if she could take a picture of us, as we were a "wonderful image of an American family."

So we all lined up, Mom in her travel-practical capris and tank top, Mimi in a flowing sundress, Laurel in an Amnesty International T-shirt with a bandana on her head, Root looming tall and scruffy with his hemp shirt and sandals (really, people with such hairy toes shouldn't wear sandals), and of course Ladybug and Bruce front and center. Mom tried to make me crouch in front with Ladybug, but I kind of folded myself behind them instead. When the woman finished, Travis and Gavin wandered over (both in their hats, obviously), and she insisted on taking another one with them in it. That time I totally ducked down and tried to hide. At least the cowboy hats make good cover.

Big news! We're finishing up a "celebration" dinner, though the only thing I consider worth celebrating is the food. (Seriously. I've never in my life had fried chicken like this. Root had a salad that he had to return because it was *covered* in bacon.) Anyway, back to the celebration. Mimi got a phone call this afternoon, and . . . wait for it . . . *a publisher is interested in her book!* She's barely written ten pages, and yet some big shot New-York-Publisher-Type Person found out about it and contacted her! Mimi was dithering and blathering like . . . like, well, like a dithering, blathering fool.

> MIMI:
> I HAVE AN ANNOUNCEMENT! A very exciting
> announcement!

> MOM:
> (looks proud, holds Mimi's hand)

> LAUREL:
> Oh, God. You're not having another kid,
> are you? Because—

> MIMI AND MOM:
> (in total unison) No!

LADYBUG:

I WANT ANOTHER SISTER! FROG HAS THREE
BROTHERS, AND I WANT THREE SISTERS!
WOULDN'T THAT BE SO COOL?

MIMI, MOM, ME, AND LAUREL:
(in total unision) NO!

MOM:

(clearly trying to help) We have the perfect number of perfect daughters! It's
perfect!

LADYBUG:

We could be perfecter with one more!

SARA:

Did you know that *"Magna Soror"* is Latin
for "big sister"? Isn't that cool?

(pause as we all digest this)

MIMI:

(regrouping) Anyway. This is about my
journey to publication, as well as *our*
journey across the country! I got a call
today from a woman named Krista Beverly,
a *very* prominent publisher, and, well, I
guess the National Rail has done a big

```
publicity piece on the fellowship win-
ners, and, um, she read my blog, and,
well . . .
```

(blather and dither and more blather)

The upshot of all this is that a big-deal publisher is interested in Mimi's book and wants to see the first fifty pages "absolutely as soon as they're ready to be critically assessed," and Mimi might have a book contract before we even get home.

The Texas Twins were having dinner with us, and Gavin whooped and hollered and ordered a bottle of champagne for the grown-ups and Sprite (in champagne glasses!) for the kids. Travis of course was smirking away, probably imagining a bestselling book that details our life. For instance, tonight Ladybug quietly dropped her asparagus tips into my water until I finally noticed and yelled at her to quit it. (Her reason? She thought they'd look like alligators underwater. I can't even.)

Anyway, Travis and his smirk are the least of my concerns. The real issue? Apparently this Krista Beverly woman (and honestly . . . it sounds like two first names . . . maybe it was Beverly Krista, I don't know) wants it to be "authentic and include multiple voices to enrich the text." And what *that* means is that Mimi should try to include direct comments, thoughts, and words from the rest of us.

You know what words I'm offering? NO. COMMENT. I know.

I know I should be happy for her. But I feel like screaming into my pillow or something. I don't *want* to be written about! I don't want to have her poking and wondering what I think about every last thing! But of course I want her to get a book published! Just . . . not *this* book!

It's possible I'm a seriously horrible person.

9:00 p.m.

Back at the hotel. Everything has gone from bad to worse. After the "celebration" dinner where I pretty much inhaled my fried chicken and tried to look like I was happy for Mimi, we came back here and Laurel announced that she and Root were going out.

MOM:
Where are you going?

MIMI:
Ooh, there are some great blues clubs, if you want to listen to music!

LAUREL:
Actually, there's a huge protest—a "die-in"—in support of the Black Lives Matter movement.

ROOT:

It's tremendously important to connect the challenges of the global environment to the challenges of racial and economic injustice! In fact, I recently read a blog post about an urban garden that was growing its own hemp—

MOM:

WHAT??

Needless to say, that did not go over well with Mom. She started shaking her head so hard that her bun fell out and her hair did a fast back-and-forth whiplash thing. "Absolutely not!" she said, still head-shaking at top speed. "No way. Given the recent legal troubles you two have had, you are not going out to participate in a 'die-in'!"

Laurel was livid. She got all blotchy and red, which is what happens when she's mad. "Our 'legal troubles' were dropped! And this is important! What happened to marching on Washington? What happened to the courage of your convictions?!"

"I was an adult!" Mom yelled.

Mom rarely yells. Mimi and Laurel are the yellers in the family, while Mom and I tend to get icy and silent. But she was yelling tonight. "I was a *responsible* adult who was taking a measured risk! You—"

"I'M ALMOST TWENTY YEARS OLD! Last time I checked, that makes me an adult too!" Laurel yelled back. "I can vote, I can join the army, and I can decide whether protesting injustice is worth the risk!"

Mimi tried to get involved, which I could have told her would go badly. "Hey! Hey, now, you lovely, passionate people, can't we talk about this in a calm—"

"NO!" Mom and Laurel both yelled.

Laurel took a deep breath, in through her nose, out through her mouth. (Yoga breathing . . . I've been practicing.)

"I appreciate your concerns, and we'll be careful. Ready, Root?" she said, and they were out the door. She didn't even slam it, which is an improvement for Laurel, though it might have been that hotel doors don't slam.

Mom went into the bathroom. Those doors definitely DO slam.

10:00 p.m.

Mom and Mimi are arguing in that quiet, hope-the-kids-aren't-listening kind of way they do. We have a multi-room suite, and since Root and Laurel are still out somewhere, I'm in the living room, where they'll be sleeping. I wish I were old enough to go out too, though I have no idea if I'd want to go to a "die-in," which just sounds scary. Of course Laurel isn't scared, but I can't help wondering if

Mom's right. Anyway, I'd be too chicken for that, probably, but sometimes I honestly hate being twelve. It's like a bad version of Goldilocks. I'm too old to go to sleep at eight-thirty after story time, and too young to head out into a strange city and protest systematic injustice, whatever that actually means. I don't even know what would be my version of Goldilocks's Just Right on this trip. Having a friend would help, that's for sure. Anyway, I'm trying not to listen, but Mom's voice is getting louder and louder.

"Why didn't you back me up? Do you really think this is safe? Have you been reading the papers? People are getting into real trouble at these protests, and Laurel is so naive. . . . She's totally thoughtless about the repercussions of her actions!"

Mimi answered in a whisper. "She's not any more naive than we were, protesting outside the Supreme Court for marriage equality."

I silently scored one for Mimi. Our family had all gone to Washington, DC, for a rally that supported the right of all people to get married, and it hadn't really been scary at all. Lots of rainbow signs and kids on parents' shoulders.

"That was different! This is more . . . violent! It's riskier."

Mimi sighed, and through the open door I could see her turn away from Mom and go back to her computer.

"Laurel has to choose her own risks, love. We all do. And like it or not, she *is* almost twenty."

Mom snorted. "Twenty is *NOT* an adult," she said. "No matter what she thinks."

Then they were both quiet.

It's totally silent now, other than the occasional *tap-tap-tap* of Mimi typing. Tomorrow we're getting back on the train, after a few more hours of sightseeing in Atlanta. We have two days and another stop before we get to New Orleans, where we'll spend time being tourists before switching to a different train and heading up toward Chicago. Suddenly I have a weird wave of homesickness, a desire to be back in Shipton with Amos and Boris purring at the foot of my bed, and the salty sea air, and the creak and clank of the window air conditioner trying to cool down the living room. I want to walk into the kitchen and find something to snack on and call Em to see if she wants to come over for a movie, even though it's late.

It's less than a week since we left home, but somehow it feels like it's a million miles away.

Chapter 8

Back at the train station in Atlanta, waiting to board. Laurel and Root came home last night after I was asleep, but apparently they were safe and fine, and Mom and Laurel were extra polite at breakfast.

There are tons of people here, people who Ladybug keeps crashing into as she zooms around, riding Bruce on that stupid X-wing fighter. I don't even think she knows what it is. . . . She's never seen *Star Wars,* as far as I know. But anyway, she barely avoided landing Bruce on a dude in a business suit, and Mom finally snapped at her to stay close to one of us or else. Now Ladybug is pouting and Mom is pretending not to notice. Or maybe she really doesn't notice—it's hard to say. Mom's good at bluffing.

Two skinny old women are hooting and laughing so loudly near us that Ladybug's forgetting to sulk and is peering over, wondering what the joke is. I kind of wonder too. . . . They're laughing so hard, they look like they're going to fall down.

Well, that's interesting. As we were waiting to board the train, the Texas Turkeys came racing up, obviously rushing and running late. Gavin was panting and wiping his forehead with a giant bandana, while Travis bent over double with his hands on his knees. I guess Mr. Laugh at Everyone isn't in tip-top shape! *He* should be doing yoga. But then the two old women who had been goofing around caught sight of them and came barreling over.

"GAVIN ALEXANDER! I thought you were going to stand us up!" one of them shouted.

"Who would blame him? He was probably trying to find a way to shake you like a bad habit," the other one said.

They swatted at each other and kept trading insults while Gavin apologized and told them he and Travis were "ready for the shenanigans and couldn't wait to get them on board."

"Aunties, we wouldn't dream of doing this without you! It wouldn't even be worth the price of a ticket without your company," Travis said, which I would have thought was sarcasm, but he seemed totally sincere.

In fact, now that I think about it, he's always looking sincere. Hmmm. I assumed that giant grin of his was a scam, but maybe not. Nobody's that friendly. At least not in Shipton.

Anyway, Gavin called us all over and made introductions. Apparently these old women are Part Two of the NTFs. There's Miss Ruby, who is Travis's great-aunt, and Miss Georgia, Miss Ruby's best friend. They are literally almost ninety years old, but even after ten minutes it's clear they're total besties. . . . They joke and argue constantly, and reminded me so much of Em and Vi that I got kind of homesick, watching. This is how sad my life is. . . . I'm watching ninety-year-old women and feeling jealous.

As I said, INTERESTING. Suddenly Ladybug might not be the loudest thing on the train.

GIRLS! (And Root, if you're reading this!)

Once again we're in the café car, trying to work. Mimi's writing up our Atlanta visit, and I'm supposed to send notes to Governor Zacker about ... well, never mind. Point is: this is an OPPORTUNITY for you to bond as sisters! (And Root, as ... well, a Dear Friend of the sisters.) Please, unless it is an emergency, engage Ladybug and keep her OUT of the café car. ENJOY!

Love, Mom

P.S. We will bring back M&M's and Starburst from the café car. This is not a BRIBE. This is a reward and a celebration of all the BONDING you will be doing!

XO M

P.P.S. Travis is in here, looking a little bit bored. We have explained that you are otherwise occupied (SISTERLY BONDING) but that he should head back to see you if he wants.

2:00 p.m.

Fun Fact!

Travelers must reset their watches as they cross from the eastern to the central time zone. Those heading south (west) set watches back one hour. (This means we have an extra hour on this train. Oh joy.)

Fun Fact!

Alabama Power has seven dams on the Coosa River, making it the state's most developed river. Hydroelectric power has proven valuable to the citizens of Alabama but costly to some species endemic to the main stem of the Coosa.

Not-So-Fun Fact!

According to Root, construction of the dams on the Coosa River played a role in wiping out thirty distinct freshwater species, which was one of the largest extinctions in the past century. Ladybug is now crying, and Root is singing another round of "Polly Wolly Doodle All the Day," and now Travis has joined in on the chorus. Does Root not know any other songs???

We are sequestered. (Note: that's a vocab word from last year, meaning "isolated or hidden away." Cool, right?)

ANYWAY.

We are sequestered in the main seating area while Mom and Mimi try to get some work done. I guess this whole family-togetherness thing is not helping Mimi write. It's not exactly surprising. When did she think she was going to work, if we're all bonding and having meaningful conversations and taking in the sights and sounds of America? And Mom's taking a break from being a real, in-court judge to teach law school, which should mean she has time off, but instead she's forever on the phone with the dean of the law school or needs to "shoot a quick note" to the governor about Tort Reform or Jurisprudence or Corpus Seprestema (okay, I totally made up the last one, or maybe it's a Harry Potter spell, but you get the idea).

So Laurel and Ladybug and Root and I are playing Two Truths and a Lie. Which can be fun—it's a game where you tell three things. Two of them are true and one's made up, and the other people have to guess. But Ladybug gets confused. Example:

> LADYBUG:
>
> I've got them! Here goes! First, I love kittens more than anything. Second, I love puppies more than anything. Third, I want a mouse.

> LAUREL:
>
> Um . . .

> SARA:
>
> Okay, puppies! That's the lie!

> LADYBUG:
>
> (indignant) NO! I LOVE puppies! They're all true!

> SARA AND LAUREL:
>
> . . .

Yeah. Eventually she got the idea, but really, it was most fun when Laurel and Root played. I learned all kinds of things. For instance, here's one of Root's:

1) I used to belong to FFA (Future Farmers of America).

2) I hate the taste of kale.

3) I hate giant trucks.

And guess what? HIS LIE WAS #3!!!! Turns out he used to want to be a long-haul truck driver when he was a kid, and he still likes it when they honk their horns. He seemed deeply conflicted by the pollution they cause, since he still dreams of driving one someday. *And* he hates kale. Who knew??
FASCINATING.

2:30 p.m.

Oh FOR CRYING OUT LOUD. I found this on my seat after lunch. What's the story with this guy?
And OBVIOUSLY the lie is #3. He is seriously short.

Dear Rae,

    I see you're still writing away, so I thought I'd write you another note. Sorry you didn't feel like playing when I came over. That Two Truths and a Lie game is pretty fun. I had no idea your older sister was such a fan of death metal music! Since we haven't had much of a chance to chat yet, I thought you might want to learn a little about me, so here you go. Two truths and a lie:

1) My mom is a flight attendant living in Los Angeles.

2) I'm terrified of flying.

3) I'm the third-tallest kid in my grade.

               See you soon!

               Trav

Chapter 9

Fun Fact!

Bryant-Denny Stadium in Tuscaloosa is the home of the Alabama Crimson Tide football team, which has won 12 national championships, produced 18 Hall of Famers, and notched the most bowl appearances and wins of any college team.

Semi-Fun Fact!

Travis hates the Alabama football team with the fire of a thousand suns and can do a pretty funny version of their Roll Tide chant, which is actually hilariously rude. Not that I'm listening to him.

We're getting off the train again in a few minutes. Miss Georgia and Miss Ruby are arguing over something, and it seems to be escalating to poking and slapping.

Ah. The argument is over who peed on the seat in the train bathroom. . . . Now they're accusing Gavin, who assures them he "aims true like a Texan."

I am seriously going to throw up.

Though honesty compels me to admit that it *can* be hard to be neat, if one is trying not to sit on the public train toilet but instead squat over it, and the train abruptly changes directions. NOT THAT I'M ADMITTING ANYTHING.

So far all I can really say about Alabama from the vantage point of the train station is that it's Tarzan hot. I feel like I'm wearing a wet wool blanket. We're waiting for a van that's taking us to see the site of some ancient civilization called, and I'm not even kidding, Moundville. Seriously? That's the best name they could come up with? Anyway, after that the van is taking us to Eutaw, which—according to the guidebook's FUN FACT!—has 27 antebellum homes on the National Register of Historic Places. How will I contain my excitement?

• • • • •

LIFE IN THE GREEN LANE

What does it mean to be a tourist in places that were on the wrong side of moral history? Today my family and I are deep in the American South. First we checked out Moundville, a site so ancient that a whole thriving civilization rose and declined long before the Europeans even showed up. In fact, this busy, complicated community, with its city plaza and skilled craftspeople, nobles, and commoners, was abandoned long ago. Historians are unsure how the people who lived there relate to the historic Native American tribes of the region. Wild, right? Hard to describe but very cool.

Though maybe ancient Moundsville's not as hard to imagine as the fancy antebellum mansions we went to next, so perfectly preserved, you can imagine chilling out on the porch, maybe sitting down to dinner with the family in the dining room, or curling up with a good book in one of the off-the-hook cozy-looking bedrooms. (HELLO, featherbed!) These houses look fresh and tidy, including the original slave quarters on display for all to see. Yep, that's right. Slave quarters. Where people owned as property were forced to live.

Which is more bizarre? Giant bumps in the ground that held sophisticated culture over five hundred years ago? Or perfectly preserved buildings from barely two hundred years ago where people owned other people as slaves? Put it another way: My great-great-great-grandparents were alive when some of these houses were built. Family members I have pictures of, who my great-grandma told me all about . . . they were alive for this. Makes it seem pretty recent, when you think about it. A lot's changed in our world since then, of course. But not everything. Not enough. And today we still have to work hard and fierce to push back the injustice that wants to creep up like the kudzu that grows everywhere down here.

Is it scary to fight back? Maybe sometimes. But when well-meaning people tell us to be careful for ourselves, not to take risks to protest injustice . . . well, that's when injustice grows and wraps its tickling vines around communities, cities, and the whole country. History isn't over yet, kids. We still have to go to work, no matter what some people think.

Peace, Laurel

Oh, Moundville. It definitely lived up to the name, in that there are big mounds of earth poking up out of the ground. But honestly, I think they could get more tourists if they gave it a catchier name, like the Ancient City or the Buried Cove of Magic. We all stared at them for a few minutes, but really, how many things can you say about a mound of dirt, even if it *is* historical and important? I think Mom felt bad for how grumpy she's been, because she was trying to be all upbeat and cheery, making up a story for Ladybug about a little girl who might have lived there hundreds of years ago, but Ladybug was hot and mad and said that she and Bruce needed lemonade. So we left. The NTFs stayed in the visitor center, which I have to say was probably a good idea. I can't really imagine Miss Ruby and Miss Georgia slogging through that heat to stare at a mound of dirt, no matter how ancient.

Now we're in Eutaw, which does indeed have lots of fancy old houses. We're staying at one that was turned into a guesthouse, with a rainbow pride flag over a porch that's painted and decorated nearly as bright as the flag. It's owned by two men who seemed scary uptight at first but turned out to be chatty and friendly and *excellent* cooks.

They have three dogs: Lulu, BooBoo, and KooKoo, and they let Ladybug take a photo of the three of them wearing their dressy rhinestone collars, with Bruce balanced in front of them. When we first arrived yesterday, the two men got us "a little bite," which I now know means an epic amount of food. They brought out sweet tea, three different kinds of cake, and a spreadable cheese thing that was actually delicious. Ian, one of the owners, said it was his own pimento cheese spread and it was so good, it was almost illegal. He's not wrong.

Travis tried to get me to talk to him about what I was writing in this journal, but I gave him a kind of vague non-answer and kept writing, and finally he wandered off to play checkers with Ladybug.

Yeah. I know that wasn't the nicest thing to do. But . . . gah! Between his nosiness—okay, I mean friendliness— and Mimi constantly creeping up and asking if I can "share a little more about the experience," I'm ready to become a hermit. Still, I feel kind of bad. Though by the way he's hooting and cheering, it must be a pretty good checkers game. Travis is hard to figure out. I'm still not sure if he's making fun of me with that giant smile. It's weird to smile like that all the time, right? If he's not scamming, he's the friendliest human being I've ever met. Who are we kidding? He's probably glad not to be talking to me anyway.

We booked two rooms, but since they had a late cancellation, they said we could take a third room.

Ladybug and I had a room to ourselves. Never before has sharing a bed with my sister felt like a luxury. But, boy, was it. Not only was it a break from Mimi's bullfrog noises, but we were also in a giant canopy bed that was so tall, there were stairs to get into it. New book title: *The Girl Who Refused to Get Out of Bed.* Because . . . yeah. SO GOOD! Also, I can do my morning yoga without having to stretch halfway under a bunk in one direction and halfway in the bathroom in the other. It makes half-moon pose *much* easier. Last time I tried it on the train, I accidentally flushed the toilet with my foot.

Noon

After breakfast—another "little bite" that included gluten-free waffles with whipped cream and homemade peach-and-rhubarb compote . . . I mean, seriously!—we went out to tour the old houses. Turns out "antebellum" means they're from before the Civil War. Which means they have slaves' quarters. Which . . . honestly, makes me feel gross. I know no one's living in them now, and they're kept for authentic history reasons, but still. Root says those who don't know their past are condemned to repeat it, and that it's important to keep "America's dark atrocities"—he actually said that—in our minds so that we can be our best selves as a country.

Sometimes I don't know what to make of Root. I

mean, he's tragically earnest about every single thing—I don't think I've ever heard him use sarcasm, which is practically Laurel's second language. But he's always trying to convince some stranger to join an environmental cause, or rushing off to throw out garbage he sees on the train platform. He makes me think of that old poster my Nana had up in the bathroom, with a girl walking down a beach where tons of starfish were stranded up on the sand. The girl starts throwing them back into the water, and a man walks up and asks why she bothers, since there are too many for her to possibly make a difference. And the girl takes another one, throws it into the sea, and says, "I made a difference to that one!"

Root's like that girl, I guess.

Almost time to go back to the Tuscaloosa station and get back on the train. Travis and Ladybug and Laurel seem to have some big plan for a game called Telephone Pictionary. Whatever.

2:00 p.m.

UGH! What is up with him? Another note. It's hard to tell. . . . Is he being sarcastic about my hand being tired?? I will NOT answer him. He's clearly a *caudex*. (Also, that's so weird about the shinbones.)

Dear Rae,

I didn't get a note back from you, but that's okay. Maybe your hand's too tired after writing in your journal all day long. You sure write a lot. I don't enjoy writing by hand—I'm more of a computer guy—but I thought you might be really antsy wondering about my Two Truths and a Lie.

So here you go: the lie was #3. I'm actually the FOURTH-tallest kid in my class. There are only six boys in my whole class, and I guess we're just a short crop. I actually ran an analysis of our class heights once, and our particular class had the shortest mean and median of the whole school. Also, when I presented my results, the one boy bet me ten dollars that he'd be taller than me by the next week, and he was! He grew an inch, measured when he was in bare feet. I asked him how he knew, and he said his shinbones always tingled before he had a growth spurt. Interesting, huh?

See you soon!

Trav

DEAR FROG IT IS ME LADYBUG AND I AM IN A FANCY HOUSE WITH THREE DOGS. THEY HAVE DIAMOND COLLARS BUT MOM SAYS THEY ARE NOT REAL DIAMONDS. I TOOK A PHOTO WITH BRUCE AND THEY SAID IT WILL GO ON THEIR WEBSITE!!!!!!!!!!!!!!!!!!!!!!!!!!!!

XOXOXO LADYBUG

P.S. The dogs didn't say that, the owners did. Hope your family is well! Miranda

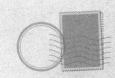

Frog Fletcher

14 Ructo Rd.

Shipton, MA

Chapter 10

Oh, Animal Planet! You are definitely creating a new game. It's called How Close to Missing the Train Can We Get?

The landscape out the train window blurs by, distant and wild, until the whistle sounds and we slow to a stop in yet another tiny town. These are short stops, just a few minutes, and we are all excited to venture out into the hot new air. We stretch our legs, take mental snapshots of deserted platforms, old-fashioned buildings, and the odd, lonesome traveler boarding the train. But you, Animal Planet, see each of these stops as a rigorous training opportunity, a chance to get down and run, run like the wind, wherever and however you can.

You run into the building.

You run past the building and out to the weed-choked parking lot, where there's usually one ancient pickup truck covered in dust.

You run across the platform to the other side, where someday a train will arrive to take people in the other direction.

And when the whistle blows again, telling us the train is ready to leave, you run even faster! What a fun game! I can tell that the conductor really loves it too.

Luckily, Tree ran track in high school. So far he has a perfect record for grabbing you before the train actually starts moving.

> MIMI: Do NOT let Ladybug get out if the stop is less than three minutes! Make sure to thank the conductor for waiting . . . maybe send note to National Rail apologizing for the delays.

Fun Fact!

Meridian, Mississippi, was established in 1860 at the junction of several rail lines, but it burned to the ground at the conclusion of the Civil War. (Again with the "burned to the ground"! That appears to have been a big thing in the Civil War.)

Fun Fact!

Laurel, Mississippi, is the birthplace of Lance Bass, member of the noted boy band 'NSYNC. (Okay, I can't even. First of all, when Mom read this, she actually busted out with an old 'NSYNC song, which was both astonishing and embarrassing. Pop music is more Mimi's thing, but apparently Mom was a huge fan back in the day. WHO KNEW? And second, "noted boy band"? Maybe a million years ago! The only reason I've heard of them is because there was Retro Night at school last year. Again I ask, who writes these things??)

Not-So-Fun Fact!

Three middle-aged women who are traveling to New Orleans to celebrate their "Divorceiversary" joined Mom in singing. What a group of *stultissimi*! New book title: *The Girl Whose Face Lit a Train on Fire.*

I wonder what Em and Saanvi are doing right now. I don't even remember what day it is until I look at a calendar, and since we haven't had WiFi lately, I haven't checked email since Atlanta. One thing I can absolutely guarantee they aren't doing? Watching entire buildings turn green with kudzu, this fast-growing vine that's taking over the South, while listening to a bunch of ladies singing "I Want You Back." In all honestly, I don't know what's scarier. But this kudzu is wild. . . . If you stood still for a few hours in one place, it would wrap you up and smother you. Abandoned cars, telephone poles, piles of garbage, and even old houses are all overgrown. Not covered like a plant might wind around a tree at home, but covered like someone took a blanket and laid it over top. It looks like something out of a science fiction story.

We're almost in New Orleans, which I can't decide if I'm excited about or not. On the one hand, we get off the train for a few days, *and* we're done with the *Crescent*! One train down, three more to go! On the other hand, all I really know about New Orleans is music and partying, and as I said before, the Goldilocks thing is really annoying. Not like I'd want to be out partying until one in the morning, but there's something kind of lame about walking around with a six-year-old calling you Woofy Dog when everyone else is having a wild time. And YES, of course I realize there is another person here my age, but I DON'T CARE. Just because he's on the train doesn't mean he's suddenly my new best friend. Though, speaking of best friends, Miss Georgia and Miss Ruby played a joke on Mary Sandra, our current train attendant. They called her over, sounding all panicked, and asked if the air-conditioning on the train was running, because they felt like it was "oppressively hot" and getting hotter. When Mary Sandra said, "Yes, darlin's, of course it's running!" they immediately bust out into these loud cackles, and shouted, "WELL, THEN YOU BETTER GO CATCH IT!"

Seriously.

I don't think I've heard that one since kindergarten. . . . Even Ladybug and her friends are too sophisticated for it.

But it was actually pretty funny—Mary Sandra looked totally freaked out for a minute, then laughed so hard, she had to sit down and slap the back of the seat a few times. That made Miss Georgia laugh even harder, and she almost fell off her seat when the train took a curve, which had Miss Ruby sobbing, she was cackling so hard. I wish Em and Saanvi were here. . . . Though hopefully we'd find better jokes than that. (Who am I kidding? Our jokes aren't any funnier. For reference? We once laughed for an hour in Vi's room because of the way her voice squeaked on the word "underwear." So who am I to talk?)

6:00 p.m.

Fun Fact!

Picayune, Mississippi, has become home to many who moved north from the Gulf Coast and New Orleans, searching for a safer place to live after Hurricane Katrina. (There is nothing particularly fun about this. . . . I continue to wonder about whoever wrote these!)

Fun Fact!

A 6.2-mile-long trestle bridge carries the *Crescent* across Lake Pontchartrain, the second-largest saltwater lake in the US. (Okay, this really is a fun fact, because the tracks we're on are narrower than the train, which means if I stare out the window, all I see is water rushing by. It looks like we're flying over the water, and I can't help thinking of the Harry Potter movie (none of them were as good as the books but they were still pretty good) where he's riding his broom-stick really low over the water and skims his hand on the surface. This isn't quite that cool, but it's close!)

Mom just sidled up to me and asked what I want to do in New Orleans. I wasn't sure. I know we're going to hear some music at one of the places that allows kids, and of course eat some famous food, like beignets, which are a kind of donut-ish thing, and po'boys, which are fancy sandwiches, and so on. But other than that I didn't really know.

"Are there any famous writers from New Orleans?" I asked finally. Maybe I can at least try to get some inspiration for a story.

Mimi, who I guess was listening, jumped like she'd sat on a tack. "Are there any writers? New Orleans is known as one of the most literary cities in the country! Why, everyone from Mark Twain to Ernest Hemingway wrote here. We can take a literary walking tour of the city, if you want!"

I smiled. Finally something that fit—Goldilocks never had it so good. "Perfect. Do you think everyone needs to go? I mean—" I backpedaled, not wanting to sound mean. But the thought of trying to get into the literary spirit while Ladybug took photos of Bruce and Root wandered off to assess the bee population . . .

Mimi must have been thinking some of the same things, because she pushed her hair out of her eyes and nodded thoughtfully at Mom. "Maybe it can just be the three of us. A special date," she said, and I admit it, I might have felt a little guilty, but not enough to suggest we should invite everyone else.

Fun Fact!

Note the aboveground cemetery as the train enters New Orleans. The land above the water table isn't deep enough for there to be belowground cemeteries. (If I'm understanding this correctly, dead bodies are sitting above the ground in stone boxes, because if they were buried there, they'd be underwater? Okay, that is CREEPY.)

Not-So-Fun Fact!

The force of Hurricane Katrina literally raised the dead from their resting places, as coffins were ripped up and sent floating around the Gulf

Coast. (Okay, YIKES. That's the creepiest thing I've ever heard.)

We're here. There are roughly a million people wandering around outside the hotel, singing and dancing on the sidewalks. Every bar and restaurant has open doors with air-conditioning blasting out into the steamy street, which of course has Root freaking out over energy loss. People are crammed in all the doorways, half inside and half out, laughing and shouting at people walking by. Every door has different music pouring out along with the air-conditioning; one has some guy singing about wasting away in Margaritaville, the next has tons of trumpets and saxophones and other horns, while across the street some country-western song has people stomping and cheering. Gavin looked a little too excited about that one. He started singing along, with Miss Ruby and Miss Georgia and Travis joining in on the chorus. I would say it was horribly embarrassing, except literally no one even noticed. This place is WILD.

We finally got into our guesthouse, a tiny brick building on a side street around the corner from all the action. It looks kind of dingy on the outside, and the light next to the door was out, which had Ladybug grabbing Mom's hand and asking about monsters. But inside it's all bright and kind of fancy, and there's a big garden in the middle of the building that you can't even see from the street. Mimi said it's called a court-yard. Mom asked right away if there was some kind of street fair or event going on, and the woman behind the desk laughed, and said, "Lawd, no, darlin'! You just in N'awlins now!"

Then she walked over and planted a big kiss on Mom's cheek.

Mimi whooped and asked where she could get herself a feather boa like the one the desk woman was wearing.

Mom looked tired.

Chapter 11

DEAR FROG WE ARE IN NEW
ORLEANS!!! THERE IS A WOMAN WHO
LOOKS LIKE MISS DIANE BUT SHE HAS
NO SHIRT ON JUST A BATHING SUIT
AND A FUNNY HAT!!! I TOOK A
PICTURE OF HER AND BRUCE AND
SHE TOOK A PICTURE TOO AND SHE
ALSO KISSED ROOT. LOVE, LADYBUG!!

Frog Fletcher

14 Ructo Rd.

Shipton, MA

That was no bathing suit. Wow. This place sure is nuts. . . . Poor Root is so red, he looks like his poncho.

August 12—9:00 a.m.

It looks like a totally different city than it did last night. The street cleaners are out in carts and trucks and on foot, basically hosing down the whole garbage-and-beads-and-grossness mess from the street and making it all gleam and shine in the early morning sun. It's already hot, like hottest-day-of-summer-in-Shipton hot, but compared to yesterday it actually doesn't feel so bad. The rest of the family and the NTFs are doing their own tour this morning—uptown to Tulane University and the zoo—so Mimi and Mom and I walked down to this famous restaurant called Café Du Monde to have beignets. Apparently this place is known for café au lait, which is really warm milk with a little bit of coffee. Sounds kind of gross, but I figured it couldn't be worse than the black coffee on the train. I'm still traumatized by that.

The waiter is movie-star gorgeous, with slicked-back hair and a tattoo sticking up out of his shirt collar. He has an accent too . . . not a Southern accent but exotic, from overseas somewhere. Mom just had to snap her fingers in front of my face to get me to focus. I guess I should put this away for now.

1:00 p.m.

UGH. That went from awesome to bad really fast. I guess I should start back at the café.

Once we'd ordered, Mimi leaned in and, as expected, started asking questions.

"Say-Say, I'm so eager to hear what you think of it all! Now that we finally have some time, can you share a little of your impressions so far?"

I know what she wanted to hear. She wanted me to tell her that the trip is amazing, that I'm loving it, that it's the best idea she's ever had. She wanted lots of details so she can cram them all into her book.

But I couldn't do it. "Rae? Please try to remember," I said.

Mimi's face kind of froze in her smile, but before she could answer, the waiter came back.

I tried not to stare, but wowza . . . he was pretty dazzling.

Of course things had to go wrong.

Mimi was babbling away to Mr. Handsome, Mimi-style, asking where he was from and how he liked New Orleans. He told her he's from Ukraine, over in the United States on a student visa but hoping to stay. Then Mimi asked what he's studying, and as they blathered, I started in on a second beignet. . . . They're really delicious. Suddenly I heard my name and inhaled powdered sugar, choking as it hit my windpipe.

MIMI:
Our middle daughter, Sara . . . sorry! I
mean Rae . . . is a writer too!

MR. HANDSOME:
(smiling at me) That's wonderful.

SARA:
(keeps choking on the sugar, tears streaming down her cheeks as she coughs and
coughs)

MOM:

Sara! Rae! Are you okay?

MIMI:

(whacks me on the back)

MR. HANDSOME:

(rushes to grab water) Here! Drink this!

WATER:

(spills all over the table and Sara, ice
cubes bouncing off her lap)

SARA:

(Kicks legs out as icy water hits, tip-
ping the table. The untouched café au
lait goes flying.)

"AIIIEEE! Sorry! I'm so sorry!" The poor waiter looked distraught, almost ready to cry, reaching across the table to the napkin dispenser and handing me napkins like he was putting out a fire.

At least getting doused seemed to help with the choking. I put up my hands. "I'm fine! It's fine! Seriously. It's . . . um, refreshing. I'll be much cooler now. Really."

He paused. "Really? You are not angry? I am *so* sorry. I will pay for your breakfast, if you—"

Mom spoke up in her everything-is-under-control voice. It's surprisingly effective. Maybe it's a judge thing.

"Don't worry in the slightest. She won't melt," she said, and everyone kind of calmed down a bit.

"Yes, Sa—*Rae* is an intrepid traveler. She'll file this away under 'something to write about,'" Mimi added. "Now, you save your money—writers usually don't have enough of it! And if you're able to take a break, come join us for a beignet. You can tell us all about your experiences in the city!"

And that is how I wound up eating breakfast with a gorgeous Ukrainian writer while looking like I peed my pants.

We talked about his favorite places to walk in the city, and what bookstores had the best collection of signed books, and what he thought of the United States. By the time we left, my shorts were mostly dry and Mimi and he had exchanged emails so he could ask her for letters of introduction to some of her publishing friends.

As we left, he bowed low and kissed my hand, which probably still had sugar on it.

"I look forward to following your writing career," he said, "and I wish you luck."

SWOOOOON.

Of course, moments later, Mimi ruined it.

We were walking toward some building where William Faulkner wrote, and she got all Mimi-ish, stopping and hugging me in the middle of the sidewalk.

"I'm so excited to be able to share this with you!" she

gushed. "This is *exactly* the kind of experience I hoped we'd stumble upon . . . handsome waiters and silly mishaps and inspiration and history, all mixed together! And you know what would be amazing? If you would write up this vignette"—she actually used the word "vignette"!—"and I included it in the manuscript! Wouldn't that be awesome?"

Well. That pretty much killed my good mood. I . . . I'm not proud of it, but I snapped.

"My life isn't your property!" I shouted. "And I don't really want my 'vignettes' to be in your book, whether I write them up or not!"

She looked like I'd slapped her or something, which of course made me even more frustrated. How did *she* get to be the one who was mad? So I kept talking. "It's not like I'm stealing from you! I'm allowed to have my own life, right? Or was I supposed to give that up, along with my summer plans and my friends and everything else?"

Then Mimi got all dithery and defensive and blathered that "a trip like this is a privilege, not a burden" and "of course everyone deserves privacy" and "everything that happens is everyone's story" and "the keystone of this project is the details of the family" and "my perspective is not your perspective" until Mom finally cut her off.

"There's plenty to write about without sharing specifics of Sara's life, if that really bothers her," she said, once again using the all-in-control voice. "Right?"

Mimi didn't say anything at first, and pulled her sunglasses over her face so I couldn't really see her expression.

"Miranda?" Mom said, touching her arm. "Are you all right, love?"

"Of course," Mimi said, and her voice was supertight. "Sure. That's fine. Though, if you want to know the truth, I can't really say *what* I'll write about, with or without Sara's insights. I've barely written a decent page since the trip began. It would be great to have it feel like a team effort. But that's not Sara's—sorry, I mean *Rae's* problem. It's mine. So never mind. Let's just go see the literary sights. Okay?" She tried to smile, but it wasn't a very good one.

I didn't say anything, because I couldn't think of anything *to* say. It's *not* my problem her writing was going badly, is it? And as for a team effort . . . give me a break! Still, she looked so stressed. I felt really bad, then felt even more annoyed that now I had to feel guilty on top of everything else.

Needless to say the rest of our "special date" was pretty silent.

2:00 p.m.

The others are back from their adventures. Ladybug's sulking and refusing to talk to anyone. So now we're all in a bad mood.

Ah. Apparently Ladybug tried to climb one of the trees in the Amazon jungle exhibit to take a photo of Bruce with a macaw. A very stern guard made it clear that Ladybug—and Bruce—are no longer welcome at the zoo. Awesome.

Mom was *not* impressed. She pretty much exploded on the spot. "Laurel, are you serious? You let her take off and climb into an exhibit? Do you realize these are wild animals, and that she could have been badly hurt? I expect more from you, honestly."

"She was fine!" Laurel said, looking annoyed. "You know her—she ran off before I could even grab her. But it was no big deal, just an over-empowered security guard who was way too happy to intimidate a little kid. Do you know those guys carry guns? I mean, what's that about?"

"It doesn't matter that she's fine! This is typical of the kind of risky behavior we keep seeing from you! She was running loose with wild animals! Just because there weren't consequences this time—" Mom was pacing around at this point, but Root stood in front of her, his hands up as though directing traffic.

"Actually, Carol, there were only macaws and parrots. Oh! And one very sleepy anaconda, but Ladybug was nowhere near it."

At this, Mom stormed out of the room. Even more awesome.

LIFE IN THE GREEN LANE

So I'm sitting in this pretty awesome café in the French Quarter in New Orleans, and I asked my server, "Do people still talk a lot about Hurricane Katrina and all the damage, or have they mostly moved on?"

I was curious, see, because my environmental science professors are interested in how natural disasters like hurricanes and tidal waves and wildfires are getting worse with the changing climate. And because people usually get freaked out and donate money when something terrible happens, but then they forget about it and go back to driving their giant SUVs and drinking bottled water and cranking their air-conditioning up when they're hot.

But my server hesitated, and I could tell, in that second, she was deciding if it was worth it to educate me, or if she was going to give me a quick answer and move on to the next customer. Trust me, I know that look. . . . I probably have it half the time I'm slinging coffee at the student union and someone asks me about my Ban Fracking button.

"Lay it on me," I say. "What's it like all these years after the hurricane?"

She shook her head, really slow, and said, "See, that's just it. It WASN'T the hurricane. Katrina wasn't the problem. Or at least, not the only problem. We're not talking about a natural disaster, no, ma'am."

I squinted at her. She looked pretty chill, with some New Orleans Community Garden T-shirt and a cool tattoo, but this place is full of . . . well, free spirits. For all I knew, she thought aliens had come down and caused the flooding.

But her story didn't have aliens. Instead it had . . . engineers.

"What you're asking about was the flooding from when the levees—the big walls that are supposed to keep the sea back—when they broke," she explained, putting down her coffee pot and leaning on my table. "And they broke because they weren't built right. And weren't fixed up right as they got old and worn. Or maybe they broke because someone wanted them to break. Or maybe because someone made a mistake. But the point is . . . and here's where you need to listen . . . the damage to our city wasn't from a natural disaster. Not really. Sure, the hurricane started it. But those levees . . . those were human problems."

She crossed her arms and kept going.

"And I'll tell you one more thing that's not natural. The way the government responded? The number of people who were left without help? Well, make no mistake there either. Natural disasters don't 'naturally' choose the poorest and brownest people to hurt, do they? Nope, Katrina just put a spotlight right on all the injustice that was already here."

Wow.

So there you have it. New Orleans, the Crescent City, where so many people lost their homes and everything they owned in the world. Maybe not a natural disaster. Maybe people, once again, are just messing things up.

This is the thing of it. It's easy to get overwhelmed by how much is outside of our control, or to decide that our personal safety is way more important than the greater good of our world. Even some very good people who I love and admire (not that I'm naming any names) can tell us to play it safe, not to take risks, not to stand up for what's right.

But we have to stand up.

I don't know, man. But if this were my city, I'd work pretty hard to protect it. It's a cool place, that's for sure.

Peace, Laurel

Ladybug in New Orleans . . . how best to explain this? Basically, picture this scene:

LADYBUG:

(on a busy sidewalk) Look at that cool guy! He's playing music! Let's go listen!

MOM:

Love, we've only gone half a block. How about we—

LADYBUG:

(runs over to musician and starts dancing)

MUSICIAN:

(playing jazz trumpet or rock guitar or classical violin or African drums or whatever, starts playing louder) Hey, girl! Get your dance on!

LADYBUG:

Whooohooo!

MIMI:

Whooohooo!

MOM:

(glances at her watch, then at the guidebook she's holding)

ROOT:

(bobbing his head slightly out of time to
the music) This is beautiful, man. Music
is our common language.

Now repeat this scene four hundred times all over the city. We never got uptown, we never got to the big park, we never got to the children's museum. We walked a half block, listened to music, walked another block, listened to music, stopped to get ice cream or Popsicles because we were so hot, stopped again to hear more music, and so on. And of course every place we went, Bruce came along.

By the time we got back toward the hotel, word had spread and a group of street performers actually asked if she was the girl with the little Roman dude, and would she take a photo with them! Of course she did, and they did a special juggling routine just for her, ending with Bruce being sent through a flaming hoop.

New Orleans is seriously amazing . . . way too much fun for everyone to stay mad. Laurel and Mom bonded over some triple chocolate mocha dessert, and even Mimi and I were having such a good time listening to music, we forgot to be annoyed with each other. A lot of the sightseeing was with the NTFs, but I am doing my best to continue ignoring them. Not in a rude way, of course, just in a "I think I'll talk to Laurel" or "I think I'll walk with Mom" or "I think I'll put my earbuds in and pretend I'm listening to music even when I'm listening to everyone else talk" kind of way.

That's not rude, right? Anyway, even if it *were* rude, I don't think Travis notices. I've never met anyone who can chatter on the way he does. He doesn't seem to need answers, either. He blathers on and on, sometimes saying "Isn't that right, Daddy?" or "Do you remember that, Auntie G?" and they'll chime in. Then he'll chatter some more. It's oddly fascinating how much that boy can talk. And honestly, while I was sure he was judging my family when he and his dad first got on the train, the more I see his aunties, the more I think he's probably not judging anyone. Those women are all-around wild, and oddly, Travis doesn't seem to be even a little embarrassed by them. Even when they're crashing into postcard displays or taking selfies with street musicians. Maybe that giant smile of his *is* 100 percent legit. Weird.

Of course even as we're all hanging out having fun,

Mimi has been keeping her super-polite I'm-hurt-but-trying-to-rise-above-it voice going with me ever since I blew up at her. I feel bad about that, but not bad enough to say I've changed my mind. My stories are MINE. Is that horribly selfish? Gah! This trip feels like it's going to last forever, and we've only been gone a week.

I decided to check in on my Reinvention List, to see how it's going:

☆ Learn Latin (Started strong, but wow, there are a lot of verbs. Must recommit.)

☆ Learn to surf, at least the basics (Obviously this is going nowhere.)

☆ Practice yoga every morning to develop Inner Peace and Mindfulness (Hmmm. Not bad, considering. I hit my nose and got a nosebleed when I tried turtle pose, but otherwise I'm getting there.)

☆ Change hair (*Note: this is Vi's idea. I've been growing mine for four years, and I'm definitely not cutting it, but dying the ends . . . that I can do.*) (Nothing yet.)

☆ Start wearing dark gray or navy-blue nail polish (*and try not to pick it off in ten minutes*) (*Note: this is Vi's idea too. We'll see.*) (I colored my nails in with mom's Sharpie. Does that count?)

☆ Read at least five nonfiction books (Two down . . . Loving *I Am Malala!*)

☆ Pick a signature social cause to care about (*Note: This one's Em's idea. I have lots of causes I care about, but apparently we each need a "signature cause."*) (Maybe the environment? Laurel's got me pretty worried.)

☆ Eschew with a firm hand all old camp, soccer team, and dumb club shirts and sweatshirts, even if they are soft and cozy (Since I didn't pack any, I am totally nailing my new style! Still, I miss my old Hidden Valley Camp T-shirt.)

☆ Consider jeggings (Not sure this one's going to stick.)

☆ Drink coffee (Nope.)

☆ Rebrand myself as Rae, not Sara (Hmmm . . . So far Travis is the only one who remembers every time, and how useless is that?)

☆ Work on a novel, or at least figure out a good story (Nothing. Haven't written a word. Phooey.)

Chapter 12

GOOD MORNING, party animals! I hope you had fun last night. We enjoyed watching the world go by on the street until someone threw up next to Mimi's purse and we decided to head in. Don't forget that today is the SWAMP TOUR. Root, I respect your concerns about chemical sunscreen and bug spray, but I really think you may want to reconsider for today. After all, you're still peeling from the sunburn in Atlanta. I don't think skin is supposed to turn that color.   Love, Mom

August 14—8:00 a.m.

I might have to rethink the whole college in New York thing. The food, the music, the funky people from all over (not to mention the gorgeous Ukrainian waiters) . . . this would be a great place to go to school. There's this amazing feeling here, even walking around the streets. That sounds kind of dumb, I guess . . . but it's hard to describe. Everyone is an artist or a musician or a dancer or a tattoo designer or something, and they're all singing along with the street performers or dancing around while they're waiting tables or telling us the plot of their novels while driving us around. I don't know. . . . Obviously people here must do their laundry and drive to supermarkets and watch dumb TV shows, but it seems so much . . . cooler than all that. Like, who would stay in watching *Cupcake Wars* when they could wander down the street and get amazing pastries in a tiny shop with a basket of kittens by the door and a sign that says "Free Purrs. Take What You Need!" (Of course Ladybug lost her mind and planted herself on the floor right by them, letting the kittens climb all over her and posing Bruce on their backs. Then Laurel grabbed Bruce and pretended that this one tiny orange kitty was a lion and Bruce had to fight it off in the Colosseum, which got a lot of attention. By the end everyone in the café was laughing and cheering for Bruce.)

Anyway, New Orleans feels like another country, where you don't need a passport and can understand the language. I love it. It would be so easy to do the Reinvention Project here—if I lived here, no one would even notice if I dyed my hair, and maybe I'd learn how to read tarot cards and get henna tattoos on my hands! It's really easy to be someone new here, I think.

I sent Saanvi and Em an insanely long email last night with photos from our day, including the kittens and one of Ladybug, Erik (Handsome Waiter Guy), and Bruce posing with a bunch of Café Du Monde beignets. (We went back with the whole family.) Vi wrote back within seconds, saying, "I know what I want as a souvenir! Don't bother to wrap it!" She makes me laugh. Imagine if we all went to college here! I might even get a tattoo.

However, as much as I love New Orleans, all good things come with their burdens, and today we're heading out of the city and into a *swamp*. I have some real misgivings about this spend-a-day-in-a-swamp idea. Mom has even more misgivings. She actually said she thought it would be better if we avoided places with killer alligators and endless mosquitoes, given Ladybug's habit of dashing off. But Mimi looked stricken, and mumbled something about "a new environment" and "beating writer's block." Then Mom looked worried and sympathetic, and said it sounded "very exciting and would be just the thing to energize the creative process," and that was the end of it.

Mimi looked more cheerful again, and I admit I felt bad that she's having such a hard time, so I didn't even complain. Much. In an hour we'll head out in a van for the bayou, which I believe is the Cajun word for "swamp." We're supposed to meet the NTFs, who apparently have been researching still more likely murder sites for Gavin's next book. I don't even know what to say about that.

Where to begin talking about the swamp? And the bayou? And the Cajuns?

I guess we'll start with what I *didn't* know, which was pretty much anything. When our tour guide, Jock Cormier, picked us up at the hotel, he asked us what we knew about the Cajun culture. Mom started talking about the French settlers kicked out of Nova Scotia in Canada and settling in Louisiana in the 1700s, and then Mimi started in on how Cajun culture is a blend of French Canadian, Native American, other immigrant groups like Germans and Irish, and African and Caribbean slaves, all living and intermingling and intermarrying over hundreds of years. Poor Root kept trying to interrupt her to say something about how Cajun French is closer to original seventeenth-century French than anything currently spoken in France, but Mimi steamrolled over him.

Finally Jock interrupted her. "You get a gold star, darlin'. But you missed the most important thing 'bout us. We love good food, we love good music, and we love us our bayou!"

And with that he whooped and hit the gas, flying onto the highway, out of New Orleans through the countryside toward the swamp. Miss Ruby and Miss Georgia gave a kind of YEEEEHAWWWWWWW yell, and Gavin whistled with his fingers (something I've always wanted to do but usually just wind up drooling all over my hands), and off we went.

Trying to write about the bayou makes me doubt I'll ever be an author. I don't think I'll even get close to describing what it's like. We got on a small metal motorboat with a loud whiny engine and headed out into a swampy area, but it's like nothing we have up north. What I call a swamp at home is a muddy little pond with frogs and maybe some dead trees or even a beaver dam. This was like something out of a fairy tale, or maybe a horror movie. . . . Imagine giant trees with roots that stand up in gnarled tangles above the water, while vines twist and hang all over them like they wanted to swallow the trees whole. Then the moss hangs off the branches like super-sized cobwebs in some abandoned attic, and the heat is so steamy that it feels like the whole place is out of another world, where dragons or wraiths or zombies or swamp princesses are just out of sight. Oooh! *The Swamp Princess* . . . That would be a cool title. Or even *The Swamp Princess and the Zombie.*

Anyway . . . what was I saying? Oh, right—the amazing scenery. Even Ladybug was struck dumb, between the heat and the eerie landscape. Travis kept shaking his head and whistling low, saying "Dang. *Daaang,*" again and again, like a quiet chant. It was hard to remember how close we were to the city.

So after a while we got used to the creepy trees, and

Jock told us all about the land and the people who lived there, and then he started making these weird noises, and I honestly started to freak out, thinking that he had lured us out there to kill us.

But don't worry, he was just calling the alligators! YES, THAT'S RIGHT. HE WAS CHATTING WITH HIS BUDDY, THE EVIL REPTILIAN GATOR KING. Good grief . . . this trip was not for the faint of heart. Mom grabbed Ladybug so hard, she squeaked, and even Laurel said, "DUDE. That's legit," in the kind of voice she uses when she's seriously impressed. The alligators come when called, it turns out, not because Monsieur Cormier is a murderer who feeds tourists to the gators, but because he feeds them marshmallows. Yep, good old Campfire marshmallows like we have at cookouts. Apparently alligators love them.

Then Jock told us all about an invasive species called nutria, which are basically giant rodents that look like beavers with rat tails, which ARGH, SOMEONE GET ME BRAIN BLEACH! These things are destroying coastal Louisiana, eating all the wetland plants and stuff, so a few years ago the government got involved.

"It went like this," Jock said. "The Feds started offering good cash money for turning in nutria tails, and many a swamp Cajun made a pretty penny that way!"

"Why only the tails?" Laurel asked.

Jock burst out laughing. "'Cause nutria's good eating,

if you want to put it in the stew pot!" he said. "Consider it a form of recycling!"

I. Cannot. Even.

Ladybug was pretty excited about the whole thing. She broke free from Mom and peered over the edge while Mimi held on to her collar. All we could see of her was her bum, sticking up as she stared into the water. Then she popped back up, all excited.

"Snake!" she called. "Mr. Jock, I saw a big snake!"

Laurel blanched a little. She's super-crazy-brave about almost everything, but not snakes. She got kind of pale, and I could see she was trying not to look into the water. "Are there snakes here? Seriously?" she asked.

But Jock grinned. *"Mais oui,"* he said, then gave a little wink and cupped his hand around his mouth like he was telling us a secret. "That's French, y'all, in case you were wondering. Course you saw a snake, because . . . did you forget? We in the bayou now! We got all kinds of snakes. What'd you see down there, princess? A cottonmouth? A coral snake? Rattler?"

Laurel looked like she was going to barf at this point, and even Mimi, who was the most gung-ho about this whole tour, stiffened up.

"Jock, honey," she said, and she had that I'm-not-upset-I'm-just-curious voice she uses when there's a massive kitchen disaster at home. "How safe—"

But Jock started laughing and promised no snake could

climb into the boat and we were safe as kittens. Then he talked about snakeskin belts and illegal poaching until we all felt bad for the snakes and even Laurel relaxed a little.

Travis turned to his dad and whispered, "There are more things that can kill you here than even in Texas!"

Remind me never to go to Texas.

For all his goofing around, Jock really knew a ton. He showed us an eagle's nest and some rare endangered type of turtle, and he got Root all fired up by talking about alternative energy sources. Even though I was literally dripping sweat and the mosquitoes were buzzing and whining like nuts, I have to admit, it was pretty awesome. I felt like I was a million miles away from Shipton.

We're sitting back at the dock now, waiting. Jock says he has one last surprise for us before we leave. I really hope it's not another alligator.

8:30 p.m.

It was another alligator.

But a baby one! And it turns out baby alligators are actually kind of cute. Laurel even held it, and Jock talked more about conservation and endangered environments, and pollution, and then Ladybug took a photo of Bruce and the baby alligator.

Then the party started.

Cajuns know how to throw a serious party. Jock's final

surprise was a *fais do-do,* a kind of dance party/feast that his wife and her sisters and their kids and maybe some cousins—it was hard to tell who everyone was—cooked up, and a live band played a kind of music called zydeco, which was the most foot-stomping, toe-tapping, sing-along music I've ever heard. I wonder what Saanvi, who's a total music snob, would think about zydeco. It's not anything like hip-hop, but wow. People played accordions and guitars, and there was an old guy with a beard wearing a metal chest plate, which was actually an old washboard that he whacked with drumsticks like it was a wearable drum. Then there was a teenage girl, probably not much older than me, and she played the fiddle like someone had lit her on fire. People were screaming and stomping their feet, and her hair was flying into her eyes, her dress strap fell off her shoulder, and she just kept going, and one of her fiddle strings broke, and she whooped and screeched and played on without it.

Anyway, Jock ended the festivities by teaching everyone some dance steps, which involved Miss Ruby and Miss Georgia pushing and shoving, then giggling so hard, Jock had to hold them both up. Finally they got the hang of it. Then it was Mom and Mimi, Travis and Miss Ruby, Gavin and Miss Georgia, Laurel and Root, and Ladybug and Jock all dancing away in pairs. Mimi of course blathered loudly about how this was *just* the sort of spontaneous joy that travel brings, and how she couldn't wait to write about it. Needless to say I politely declined when she invited me to dance with her and Mom. That's all I need—a play-by-play of my totally pathetic inability to follow any steps. (Seriously. Ask Em. . . . I can't even do the most basic dance moves she tries to teach me. I'm a mutant when it comes to dancing.) Not that I was paying much attention, but Travis is *not* a dance mutant. . . . He's more like a dance savant. He was the first to pick up all the steps, and he and Miss Ruby were pretty impressive. It looked fun, honestly.

Right before we left, Jock balanced Bruce on top of the giant wooden carved alligator statue and took a photo with him. By the time we all got into the van to head back to New Orleans, my tongue was burning from all the spices in the gumbo, my hands were sore from clapping, and I was singing along with the chorus of the last song, *"Allons Danser."*

It's too bad I didn't learn the dance steps. Not that watching wasn't good too. It was. Totally.

10:00 p.m.

It's our last night in New Orleans. Tomorrow we get on a new train, *City of New Orleans,* and take it to Chicago. The *Crescent* feels like a million years ago.

I don't really want to leave. Even though I'm hot and my stomach is a little sore from all the food and Mom has gone back to being grumpy (she and Laurel fought again . . . not even sure what about this time), even so,

I don't really want to get on another boring train with a boring dining car and my boring life.

Here I can pretend that my world is far more exciting than it actually is.

Another note! What is his story? I'm going to write him back and tell him to stop. But in a nice way. Obviously.

Dear Rae,

Sorry we didn't get a chance to chat much on the bayou tour today. It sure was interesting. Do you know that Texas has the second-highest number of venomous snake species of any state in the US? Arizona has a few more, by last count. Not sure where Louisiana falls on the list, but it must be up there. I noticed you didn't want to dance, which is too bad. Maybe something was wrong with your ankles? I'd be happy to do some strengthening exercises with you, once we're back on the train. Just say the word.

See you soon!

Trav

P.S. I noticed your Latin textbook at breakfast today. It so happens I've been studying Latin the past few years, just for fun. Happy to study together if you want. T

134

Dear Travis,

   Thanks for writing. But there's no need to keep doing it. I'm pretty busy with this summer journal assignment, and, well, other things. But thanks for the warning about Texas. I'll be sure to stay away.

                                        Rae

P.S. My ankles are fine. Thanks for asking, I guess.

Dear Rae,

   Thanks so much for your note! It was nice of you to write back. Glad to hear your ankles are plenty strong. I'll look for you next time for some dancing.

                              Trav

FROG I SAW ALLIGATORS!!! LOTS
AND LOTS OF THEM AND THEY ATE
MARSHMALLOWS THEN WE LEARNED
HOW TO DO CAGE DANCING I MISS
YOU LOVE, LADYBUG!!!!!
   P.S. It was actually Cajun
dancing. There were no cages.
Tell your dads we say hi!
Warmly, Carol

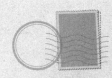

Frog Fletcher

14 Ructo Rd.

Shipton, MA

Chapter 13

Getting back on the train somehow seems ridiculously hard this time. Laurel nearly missed it because she was getting her palm read, Ladybug was crying about saying goodbye to the kittens at Purr Café, as she named it, and Mom was on a work call on the platform, trying to keep the phone on mute so the lawyer on the other end couldn't hear Ladybug wailing. When we loaded all our bags and ourselves onto the train, everyone was mad: Mimi was mad that Mom wouldn't get off the phone; Root was mad (though he calls it being "bummed out, dude") that Laurel seemed more into the palm reader, a tall, dramatic-looking girl who wore scarves and a nose ring, than hearing his newest idea, which seemed to involve on-train vermiculture, which is another word for worm-based composting. (This means keeping buckets of worms on the train and dropping all compostable food into the bucket. I . . . I don't even have enough words for all the reasons I think this is a bad idea.) Anyway, he'd been talking about it with a group of musicians who'd recently converted their tour bus to run on used restaurant cooking oil, and he was all fired up.

Finally we made it. The NTFs arrived at the very last minute, looking a little frazzled. Miss Georgia's face was pinched, and there was none of the usual loud laughing and goofing around. Travis kept trying to help her, and she yelled at him, kind of meanly, I thought. But he kept helping like he didn't even hear. They settled into a bunch of seats near a bathroom and kind of kept to themselves, which was a relief. I wonder what's wrong, though. Not that I need to know, obviously. I mean, it's their business, not mine.

The train was icy cold, air-conditioning blasting away any last memories of New Orleans fun. We ate cruddy stale gluten-free crackers from Mimi's bag and stared out the window as the city disappeared. We're on the train until Memphis, Tennessee, where we arrive late at night. Hours and hours of watching the kudzu wrap around buildings as the Big Easy gets farther and farther away. Goodbye, zydeco music, alligators, beignets, Erik the Adorable Ukrainian. I'll miss you!

1:30 p.m.

I forgot how boring the train is. Mimi fell asleep and is snoring. . . . There is no bullfrog in the world that makes a noise like she does.

Fun Fact!

Jackson, Mississippi, was named for Andrew Jackson, and was invaded by General Sherman during the Civil War and . . . wait for it . . . was burned to the ground. Honestly, the burning to the ground is getting really old.

4:00 p.m.

Fun Fact!

McComb, Mississippi, enjoys the distinction of being the Camellia City of America. No city can boast a greater variety. (No, really, this is considered a fun fact. I think the people writing this are getting desperate. I know how they feel.)

Fun Fact!

Brookhaven, Mississippi, is the childhood home of Robert Pittman, founder of MTV.

Not-So-Fun Fact!

The mention of MTV appears to have reinvigorated Mimi, and she's reminiscing about her youth and music videos and some song about getting "your money for nothing and your chicks for free."

Laurel apparently doesn't like that song, and they're now in an argument about feminism.

LAUREL:

Just because you're a lesbian doesn't mean you get to call women "chicks."

MIMI:

Honey, I was a feminist back when you were begging for the deluxe Bratz doll set with matching eye shadow kit. Shush, now.

Honestly, I think they each have a valid point on this one.

Huh. I was walking by Travis's empty seat on the way to the bathroom, and he had left his stuff all over the table. I guess I *could* have walked by, but I was kind of curious. He wrote, "Auntie G is feeling pretty rotten, which is to be expected under the circumstances." I wonder what that means? What circumstances?

Also, he wrote, "That girl is still top-level prickly. But I'll keep chatting away. It'll either warm her up or make her mad, and both are pretty fun."

PRICKLY. DOES HE MEAN ME?? OMG.

9:00 p.m.

We're almost in Memphis. This train ride was more boring than usual, probably because Ladybug, Laurel, Root, and Travis spent the whole time playing games while I read. Not that I want to play games—I'm so done with Ladybug's "rules." The last time we tried to play Twenty Questions, it went like this:

SARA:

Okay, Ladybug. Your turn!

LADYBUG:

I'm thinking. . . . I'm thinking. . . . I'm thiiiiiiiiiiinkinnnnnng. (keeps thinking for ten minutes)

LADYBUG:

(finally) I have it! BUTTERFLY!

SARA:

. . . Um. Butterfly?

LADYBUG:

YOU GUESSED IT!

Seriously.

So just because Travis is laughing his huge TEEHEE-HEEHEEHEE laugh and Laurel is snorting and slapping the table does NOT mean that game time is fun. It just means they have a pathetically low bar for amusement.

Meanwhile I'll sit here and count the number of seats in the train car. In Latin. *Unus. Duo. Tres. Quattuor . . .*

The Scribe has taken writing to a new level. I confess I'm jealous. She scribbles in her notebook all day, looking for all the world like her hand can't move fast enough to get the words out of her brain and onto the paper. I find that unimaginable at the moment. All this lovely togetherness means that I am not actually writing. But as I am forever telling the kids, LIFE IS A JOURNEY! AND THE JOURNEY IS THE REWARD! WE ARE LIVING IN THE MOMENT, PEOPLE!

Of course the moment, for the Scribe, appears to be seeing how few words she can say out loud. Sometimes she glares at me so hard, I expect the chair behind me to burst into sizzling flames. Ah, the disdain of a twelve-year-old . . . if we could channel it, we could power a small city. (Which would probably delight Tree and the Activist, who seem intent on pestering Superwoman to convert our minivan to biofuel when we get home. Which means we would be driving around smelling like french fries. . . . I think not.)

Meanwhile, other than the surly Scribe, the cross-generational Love Train is working beautifully. The Activist and Animal Planet (and Tree, dear Tree, who is more patient than everyone else on this trip put together) have reconnected through endless games, inviting our new friend, Cowboy Junior, to join in. Unlike the Scribe, Cowboy Junior does not seem afflicted with a terminal case of adolescence. How refreshing.

MIMI: Figure out how to get Sara to talk to that poor boy! Maybe a bribe? Why is she so self-conscious? Consider a heart-to-heart on body image and teen self-esteem.

Chapter 14

Fun Fact!

Memphis is known as the birthplace of a style of music known as the blues, and was home to blues musicians like B. B. King, Muddy Waters, and Robert Johnson.

Fun Fact!

Memphis is also home to "the King"—Elvis Presley.

Not-So-Fun Fact!

Elvis fans apparently have no shame and will parade around in public wearing monstrous Elvis-covered articles of clothing.

Not-So-Fun Fact!

Most people here look like "late Elvis"— really fat, long sideburns, bad jumpsuits—not "young Elvis," who, I have to admit, was pretty darn cute.

Memphis is LOUD. And bright. Just getting from the train station, we've seen more Elvis stuff and weird music souvenir stands than you'd think any city needs. Luckily, we're taking a taxi, because Ladybug is fast asleep, clutching Bruce and occasionally muttering something about dancing cowboys. (I blame Travis for this.) Root is being heroic and carrying her. (I should clarify, this is heroic not because she's heavy: the rest of us are hauling all the bags, which weigh a lot more than a six-year-old. But there was a little mishap with the ketchup at dinner, and Ladybug's pretty sticky. Plus it looks like she's been stabbed. To Memphis's credit, no one seems to notice that we're walking around with a comatose red-splattered kid. On second thought, maybe that doesn't say anything good about Memphis. I mean, isn't this the kind of thing someone should notice? Good grief. Remind me not to get stabbed here.)

What was I saying? I am seriously tired.

We managed to avoid the NTFs only because they had plans to head "DI-rectly to the Blues Palace," where some famous musicians were playing. Thank the Lord for small favors. Anyway, we've finally gotten to the taxi stand, but not surprisingly, there has yet to be one large enough for the six of us plus luggage. Root's trying not to complain, but Ladybug just flailed in her sleep and knocked his glasses right off his face. Luckily, they didn't break. Unluckily, she also managed to smear ketchup onto his face, so now *he* looks beaten and bloodied. No wonder the cabs aren't stopping.

Well, that was amazing. Mom and Mimi were in one of their muttered conversations, trying to figure out if we should split into two groups, when a GINORMOUS stretch limousine pulled up. The side window opened and . . . I guess this is what happens in Memphis . . . Elvis leaned toward us.

"Where y'all headed, darlings?" he asked, lowering his sunglasses just enough to peer over them. (Note: was almost eleven at night and dark out.)

Mom of course tried to tell him we're not interested, but Mimi didn't miss a beat. She opened the back door and started flapping at me, Laurel, and Root to start getting in.

"Peabody Hotel, please! And can we request some 'Jailhouse Rock' on the way?"

And that is how we arrived at the fanciest hotel I've ever stayed in: the limo's disco lights flashing, and the driver, complete with microphone, belting out old rock and roll. Ladybug woke up of course, but took it all pretty well. In fact, she managed to get Bruce to perch on the driver's shoulder when we stopped at a red light. The best part? When we got to the hotel, no one seemed to find it strange that a bloodstained (okay, ketchup-stained) kid with a Roman centurion was posing with an Elvis impersonator and his limo. They welcomed us in, nicely offered Ladybug and Root a couple of wet wipes, and sent us up to our room.

This place is really NOTHING like home. Maybe that's okay.

August 16–6:30 a.m.

I'm not allowed to sleep in, even though this is one of the fanciest, biggest, most comfortable beds ever. The place is huge. Even better? Ladybug, after (finally!) getting cleaned up, was whiny and refused to go to bed with me, so she slept with Mimi and Mom, and I got a whole giant bed to myself! And Mimi didn't even snore . . . maybe because Ladybug was pushing her out of bed all night. Welcome to my world, Mimi. Anyway. Best. Sleep. Ever.

We're up early because we're trying to beat the crowds at Graceland. Even Mimi, who's been obnoxiously psyched about everything, couldn't make it sound fun to stand in long lines for Elvis Presley's house. But apparently one cannot come to Memphis without making the trip. I, personally, could DEFINITELY come to Memphis and not get up at the crack of dawn just to see some stupid house, but I don't get a vote. I am trying. Really, I am trying not to be Veruca Salt, but this stinks.

Apparently we're also rushing because we have to be back at the hotel by a certain time. I have no idea why. . . . Our train doesn't leave until late tonight. Mimi says there is a surprise for us. Oh good—maybe it's MORE Texans in cowboy hats.

HALLELUJAH AND PRAISE ELVIS! There's been a reprieve.

Mom took one look at my face and suggested that she and I "take a rain check on Graceland" and spend some "one-on-one time" together.

Mimi looked a little disappointed, but Ladybug was so excited to see where the King lived, and Mimi cheered right up. They all left around seven-thirty, and Mom and I immediately looked at each other and climbed back into our beds. I think I was asleep before they got to the lobby.

Mom woke up first and was sitting in the fancy living room area, working, when I finally resurfaced from under my fort of silky sheets and soft, cushy pillows.

SARA:
I feel like a truck hit me. What time is it? What do you want to do now? Should we go out and . . . I don't know . . . sightsee or something?

MOM:

(looking a little guilty, but with a big
smile) Room service?

AND WE DID! We actually ordered room service and along came a knock on the door, which I answered, feeling totally self-conscious and idiotic. What are you supposed to do when someone shows up at your door and you're still in pj's and have crazy bedhead and probably dried drool on your cheek? I just stood out of the way, pretending I was really interested in the wall. New title: *The Girl Who Pretended to Be a Statue.* Gah.

Once the hotel person finished wheeling in this fancy cart with a white tablecloth, and taking off the silver covers on all the food, and pouring steaming coffee into one cup and steaming hot chocolate into the other, and pulled up the chairs and unfolded our napkins and asked politely if we needed anything else, he left. We looked at each other.

"Well!" Mom said finally. "Shall we eat?"

It was the best breakfast ever. Mom asked about Emily and Saanvi, and what the news was from home, and we talked about the book we're reading to Ladybug, about a girl at the end of the nineteenth century who's fascinated with Darwin but has to do stupid girl things instead of study science. Sometimes I forget how cool Mom can be. When she's listening to you, she's *really* listening, so hard, you can almost see her processing what you're talking about. Between work and Ladybug, and Laurel being home (with Root, no less), and the ongoing conversations about Mimi's writing career, I can't remember when it was just the two of us.

I like it.

Then I tried to ask if she actually liked this train trip, and what she thought about the stupid NTFs. I kind of hinted that not only was Mimi forever peering at us all under a microscope for her book, but we also now had two nonagenarians (note: that's a fancy word for "people who are in their nineties") and a short kid in a cowboy hat and his dad, and it was reallyreallyreally annoying. But she shut me down. Instead she gave me a lecture.

"You need to give things—and people—a chance," she said. "You make such fast judgments, Say-Say, and then BOOM! Your mind is made up. Be a little more open to the possibilities that new experiences bring."

"Laurel's always willing to try new things, and you get mad at her," I pointed out, which might have been a mistake. Mom looked like she'd sucked a lemon.

"Your sister," she said, putting her coffee cup down so hard that some slopped over the edge onto the white tablecloth, "is far too cavalier with her safety! That is NOT what I meant at all."

"But she's open to possibilities," I said. "She's brave

about everything! And she gives everyone the benefit of the doubt."

Mom folded her napkin again and again until it was the size of a phone. "There's brave and there's reckless. Don't get them confused." She stood up fast. "Why don't you shower while I finish up my work? We should get out and enjoy the day."

After breakfast, I took the world's longest shower, since for once no one was banging on the door telling me to hurry up. It was pretty awesome, with two jets and tiny fancy soaps and shampoos and stuff. Of course I used body lotion in my hair, thinking it was shampoo, and had to rinse it a few million times, but at least I smelled good. As I stood under the steamy water, I wondered what it would be like to be Laurel, and to be so brave about *everything*. Even when we were little, she was braver, and now she seems like a different species. I bet she never needed a Reinvention Project. She probably barely thought about cutting off her hair, or marching in giant protests, or wearing her cool braided necklaces. . . . She just did it. Thinking about her made my whole list feel kind of stupid. I mean, I'm trying to figure out if I can manage gray nail polish, and she's fighting to save the earth. What's the point, really?

Still, maybe I'll see if we can stop in a drugstore later today. Vi's right . . . the nail polish would be cool. If I can ever get this Sharpie off.

DEAR FROG WE ARE IN MEMPHIS AND MIMI TOLD ME
THE KING LIVED HERE AND WE WOULD SEE HIS HOUSE.
BUT GUESS WHAT??? HE WAS NOT A REAL KING AND
THERE IS NO CASTLE!!! I AM MAD AND AM NOT TALKING TO MIMI. THIS IS A
POSTCARD OF THE HOUSE BUT IT WAS DUMB!!!!!!! LOVE, LADYBUG AND BRUCE
HE IS MAD TOO.

P.S. Miranda here—sorry for the angry letter. I guess we
shouldn't have called Elvis "the king" without explaining. Something
to keep in mind if you Fletchers ever take a trip down here.

Ladybug was NOT impressed with Graceland. I'm
even more relieved that I didn't have to go. On the other
hand, the NTFs apparently had a ball. . . . They came
back carrying a life-sized cutout of Elvis Presley. You
know, the kind that you can prop up, with a built-in
stand? Miss Georgia and Miss Ruby could barely stand
up, they were giggling so hard when they came into the
lobby. I was sitting by the fountain trying to read, but
it was hard to keep my eyes off them. Of course Travis
the Can't-Take-a-Hint came up and peered over my
shoulder.

"Howdy there, Rae," he said, plopping down next to me
on the couch. "You getting some good reading done? It was

too bad you didn't come along to see Graceland. Though you know? Hard to say if you would have liked it."

I wanted to roll my eyes, and only managed to restrain myself by great discipline. How would he know what I like or not? But I nodded. "I wasn't too sorry to miss it. I'm not a big Elvis fan." My eyes went back to Miss Georgia and Miss Ruby, who now had the giant Elvis on the fancy luggage cart and were wheeling him around.

Travis laughed, a ridiculous TEEHEEHEEHEEHEE laugh. "Me neither! Not my kind of music, for sure! But it was interesting, even so. For instance, did you know he had a twin who died at birth? Wonder if they were identical. Can you imagine if that kid had grown up? An identical second Elvis?"

I had to admit, that *was* pretty cool. "He probably would have been some kind of ultra-shy nerd who *hated* attention. And of course he'd get attacked by fans thinking he was Elvis."

Travis laughed even louder, until I was laughing too, partly at how goofy he sounded. Seriously, it sounds like a cartoon. Anyway, we went back and forth, imagining this poor dude—in our version he was a herpetologist (that would be a snake scientist, in case you didn't know)— who would get mobbed every time he went out in public.

"No! Please! Don't tear off my clothes! I'm *Rupert* Presley!" Travis said, giggling. "You're looking for my brother, Elvis! I'm Rupert!"

"He'd probably keep a snake on him at all times," I said. "He'd wrap his favorite boa constrictor around his neck and train it to hiss."

It was actually pretty amusing, but then Mimi sat down, asking what was so funny and chatting away with Travis about the tour guide at Graceland. I went back to my book.

It's not like I wanted to talk to him anyway. I was being polite. I should probably make a sign that says MIHI MOLESTUS NE SIS!

When one is traveling with Animal Planet, of course one considers when and how to build in animal sightings during any trip. And for this journey I knew we would absolutely have to commit to the world-famous (in Memphis, at least) tradition: the daily parade of the Peabody Hotel ducks. Yes, dear readers, you read that correctly! This grand hotel, which embodies Southern hospitality, also embodies all that is weird and wonderful in its hometown. For nearly ninety years the hotel has been home to a small group—or flock, if we're going to be precise—of waterfowl. These birds live the high life in a customized home on the hotel roof and visit the lobby daily. The sight of these handsome fowl marching with a fully liveried "duck master" is going to blow Animal Planet's mind! Moments like these are hard to explain, because they are unique to parents: the feeling of excitement for something you care nothing about, because you know it brings joy to your children. There's probably a German word that means exactly that, but I call it parenting.

Just when I thought Root couldn't get any weirder. UGH. Consider this draft of his "apology letter" as Exhibit A. At least we were already leaving . . . we didn't get kicked out.

To the staff at the Peabody Hotel:

I'm totally, completely sorry about the whole "duck fiasco." When we got to the lobby and I saw all those hundreds of tourists freaking out over ducks walking right through the middle of the fancy floor, I really thought: "That is NOT CHILL." I mean, these are wild creatures, right? And they're parading around a marble lobby, surrounded by screaming fans with cameras and stuff. The ducks even have security! Dudes. That didn't seem right to me.

But I get it, man. I overreacted. I just . . . I don't know. Maybe it was all the refined sugar in that fried dough I had at Graceland, but I felt this rush of energy, like those ducks NEEDED me to get them out of there. I swear, and I know Judge Johnston-Fischer also assured you, I didn't want to hurt them or cause them any more trauma. I mean, hanging out in a crowded lobby was probably traumatic enough, you know? I figured I'd help them get outside, where they belong.

Now that I know the whole story ... how the ducks only stay with you for a little while before going back to the wild, and how they have a pretty sweet duck home on your roof ... well, I guess it's all cool. And sure, it's definitely all about your point of view. I mean, I can see how having a ninety-year history disturbed by a random stranger could be pretty freaky. (Though, for the record, I don't really think "ecoterrorist" is fair. I was just trying to get the ducks outside.)

Anyway, I want to apologize. You guys were totally rad to drop the charges and let us check out without the police escort. And we really do appreciate getting that photo of the ducks with Bruce.

Peace,

Root

Chapter 15

Back on the train just in time for bed. We saw the NTFs as we were boarding. . . . Miss Ruby was carrying the life-sized Elvis, and Miss Georgia was lagging behind, holding on to Travis's arm. I hurried into our roomette before they caught up to us. Mimi gave me THE LOOK, but I don't care. We didn't exactly blend into the crowd, and I kind of wanted to distance myself from the rest of them. No matter what Mom says, people DO pay attention to us, what with Ladybug flying Bruce on a Graceland helicopter, the Elvis cutout, and of course Root, who has several bandages from where the ducks attacked him. Also he's wearing a few of his new purchases, which include a *new* poncho, a hemp satchel that looks suspiciously like an ugly purse, and a "Peace Begins at Home" T-shirt that some volunteers were selling at the train station. Sometimes I really, really, *really* wish I'd hopped on a different train, like one to Alaska.

This is ridiculous. I can't sleep. Not only is Mimi bull-frogging away, but Mom has started falling asleep to some white noise ocean sounds on her phone, and apparently the headphones have come off. Now the whoosh of waves is loudly crashing through our tiny room.

If I sit up, I can move the shade a little and peer out the window. It is crazy dark out, so dark that even as we race by, I can see stars and a fingernail-clipping moon whizzing in and out of the trees. Every once in a while we pass a house, black and inky against the almost-as-black sky, and a few minutes back we passed one with a porch light on. It looked so bright in the night, brighter than Memphis or even New York City. But it was only one tiny porch light. There was someone sitting on the porch too. We went by way too fast for me to see much, but someone was out there, watching the train go by. I wonder if he or she could see me peeking out the window.

I wish I had waved.

Laurel would have waved. Heck, Laurel would be halfway through her Reinvention Project list by now, not avoiding Latin verbs and stuck in turtle pose in yoga and too chicken to even wear the cool yin-yang tank top she packed. Laurel would *never* sit around and endlessly mull over a stupid list. What's wrong with me?

I won't be that person either. Not anymore. Enough

with waiting around . . . *Semper Audax* is going to be my new motto. Starting Right. Now.

Well, starting in the morning, I guess.

But wait.

I *could* start now. I mean, really commit to this whole thing in a . . . what did Laurel say when she shaved off her hair? She called it "an outwardly visible way to show my commitment to shaking up the status quo."

Maybe *that's* what I need! There's no real reason I can't dye my hair in the bathroom, right? I mean, Mimi and Mom are both sound asleep, and by the time they wake up, it'll be done. And I know it's just hair dye, and it's not going to change my life, let alone change the world, but still. It's *something different*. It's an outward commitment to my Reinvention Project. Something visible and obvious that no one can miss that says Sara—I mean *RAE*—Johnston-Fischer is definitely a different person than she was before this summer! *Carpe diem!* Let's do this!

2:15 a.m.

I'm taking the fact that I got the hair dye out of the suitcase under my bed without waking anyone as a good sign. And really, all I need is water, which I can get from the sink, and a clock. As long as I don't leave it on longer than twenty minutes, everything should be fine. Mom and Mimi will have to learn to live with it. . . . It's only a few inches of hair. I can't wait until we have Internet again and I can send Vi and Em a photo of the finished product! I wonder if they've done theirs yet. . . . Maybe I'll be the first!

Wow, this stuff smells awful. It's making my eyes water. Also, it's harder than it looks to make it even. I started with around two inches, but then the train lurched and I went up higher on one chunk of hair, so I had to do the rest of it higher to make it match. Then I went higher on the *other* side, so I had to even up the first side. But I think it's even. Or even-ish, at least. I can't really tell, since I can't see the back or sides very well. And of course I can't keep a shirt on, since it would turn blue, so I'm wrapped in a bunch of train towels. Still.

    I. Am. Doing. It!

    OHMIGOD. What was—

Oh no oh no oh no oh no oh no. This cannot be happening. THE FREAKING TRAIN BROKE DOWN AND I AM STUCK. WITH BLUE DYE IN MY HAIR.

    I was writing and waiting to rinse it off, when the train gave a crazy lurch, then another one, then the power went out, including the air conditioner and the water and EVERYTHING. I fell off the toilet, where I'd been sitting, and my hair flung over my face, and the tub of blue dye went everywhere, and Mimi fell off her bunk and everyone started yelling and screaming at once. DID I MENTION THE STUPID DYE IS STILL IN MY HAIR? It's supposed to stay on twenty minutes. Twenty minutes, and no longer. And it has been forty-five minutes. FORTY-FIVE. I have no idea what will happen. Will it be a *brighter* blue? Or paler? Who knows?

Mom and Mimi don't even know yet because the power's off and it's still totally dark, except for the tiny emergency lights on the floor. Mom did say, "What's that smell?" but Mimi said it must be related to the train, and that was the end of it. I'm writing on the floor, using the emergency light to see the page, so who knows if I'll even be able to read this? But who cares??

WHAT AM I SUPPOSED TO DO? We don't even have bottled water, because our refillable water bottles are in the other compartment—thanks, Root—so I can't sneak into the bathroom and pour it over my head.

I am so dead. Of course who knows where we are and if we'll ever get moving again. It's insanely hot in here, so maybe we'll all pass out from heatstroke and they'll find the train years from now with a bunch of skeletons and a box of blue hair dye. Okay, I know we're not actually that far from Chicago and we're not about to be abandoned here, but . . . this is almost worse. This is bad. This is reallyreallyreally BAD.

Train just started moving. Now the conductor's talking through the speakers, telling us all we'll be making an emergency stop while they "assess the extent of the damage."

I too will be assessing the extent of the damage . . . *on my head*. I AM SO DEAD.

Oh, this is really really really bad.

Really bad.

When we finally got out at the station, the lights hit my hair, and Mom screamed. Actually screamed.

"Sara! What's happened? You're—you're . . . What *have you done?*"

That's when I reached up to pull a piece of hair toward me, and it came off in my hand. I grabbed another piece, and again, it just . . . dissolved. It wasn't blue. It was kind of a pale white, but more to the point, it was *gone,* crumbling in my hand.

THE HAIR DYE HAD EATEN MY HAIR. RIGHT OFF MY HEAD.

"Water!" I yelled, running onto the platform. "I need to rinse it off!"

Mom caught up to me. "Rinse what off? What did . . .

How did this happen?" Then she looked closer, and her eyes got wide. "Miranda, hand me a water bottle. Every water bottle we have. NOW."

Mimi must have grabbed them from Laurel, because faster than I could blink, Mom started pouring water over my head. All along the platform, travelers in their pajamas and robes were staring. Apparently the fact that the train had broken down in the middle of the night was nothing compared to watching a grown woman trying to drown her daughter with bottles of water.

To make things even more horrifying, Travis came running over. "Holy smokes! What's going on *here*? Can I help?" he asked, his voice coming from somewhere behind me.

"Bring any water bottles you have! It's probably too late, but . . ." Mom answered.

Travis ran off, then came back. "Got some, ma'am! Should I pour it right on her? Here we go!" There was another, icier splash of water as Travis added his bottle to the Drown the Idiot game.

I couldn't help it. Tears hit my eyes hard and overflowed. Pushing past Travis and Mom, I ran toward the side of the platform, where at least the lights were dimmer. Seconds later Mom and Mimi came running after me.

"Sara? What the—" Mom stuttered before finally blurting, *"What's going on here?"*

I tried not to sob. "I'm sorry! I didn't . . . I was only trying to dye the ends blue. It was only the bottom few inches. Well . . ." I sniffed. "It was supposed to be, anyway. I had to make it even. But I didn't know this would happen!"

Mom stared at me like I was from Mars. "*Dye the ends blue?* Where did you even get the hair dye? Why did you think this was okay?"

I didn't answer. I couldn't.

"Your hair . . . ," she started, then paused, shaking her head.

I sunk to the ground, not caring that I was sitting in a puddle of gross water.

"It's not my fault! The dye was only supposed to stay on for twenty minutes! How was I supposed to know the train would break down?"

"The train has nothing to do with this! I can't believe you used such poor judgment. But meanwhile . . . your hair is *gone*. You'll need to cut off most of what's left, to even it out. You'll be lucky if it comes down to your chin. And furthermore . . ."

She paused so long, I finally looked up, and the look on her face was NOT good. "*What?*" I asked. "Why are you looking at me like that?"

"Sara," she said, squatting down next to me. "You've also managed to dye your left ear a vivid ultramarine blue. It's not coming off. At all."

My hair. Is gone.

And I'm dyed blue.

I stared at her, thinking that she would fold me into a hug, telling me it wouldn't be so bad.

But Mom wasn't done. "What on earth was going through your head? What made you think this was okay? Honestly, Sara, I'm . . . well, I'm speechless! Did you consider for a minute that you should have asked permission?"

"Carol, why don't we calm—" Mimi tried to say, but Mom shot her a look, and she went quiet.

"Well? Can you answer me?" she asked, still glaring.

"You would have said no!" I shouted.

"You're darn right we would have! What a ridiculous, misguided . . . Why did you even do this in the first place?" she asked.

I put my ruined head between my knees and covered it with my arms. "I was . . . I wanted an outwardly visible way to show I've changed," I mumbled. I closed my eyes. I wanted more than anything in the world to be home, in my bed in Shipton, with this whole thing a bad dream.

Mom kept talking, but I pressed my arms tighter over my head.

Just then Laurel and Root came over. "What's going on over here? We found the bathrooms, if anyone needs them," Laurel said, crouching down next to me. "WHOA! What happened to you, Say-S—I mean, Rae?"

I shook my head. I couldn't even form words.

But Mom could. She glared at Laurel. "Sara took it into her head to dye part of her hair blue, only she managed instead to permanently damage her hair *and* dye her skin."

Root murmured something about toxic chemicals in beauty products, but I didn't even look up.

Laurel put her arm over my shoulder. "Oh, poor So-So," she said. "That's a bummer, for sure. But don't freak out. It's not that bad."

I peeked out. Although her arm was around me, Laurel was looking at Mom. "Jeesh, Mom, this is hardly the end of the world. Hair grows back, and as for her blue ear, well—"

"THAT IS *SO* NOT A HELPFUL ATTITUDE!" Mom bellowed. "And I would think that you'd at least realize now that your example is the last thing your sisters need!"

Laurel stood up so that she and Mom were standing over me. I stayed on the ground, picking off pieces of my hair and letting them fall all around me. It was like being in my own tiny hairy snowstorm.

"*My* example?" Laurel said. "How is this possibly my fault? And tell me exactly, what's so horrible here? That she tried to dye her hair? Let me guess . . . you think that's too dangerous!"

"Well, the chemicals *can* be carcinogens, so that is pretty dangerous," Root said, but they both ignored him.

"You know very well what I mean—" Mom said, but before she could say anything more, Laurel interrupted.

"Sara's trying something, and even if it didn't work out, it's not the end of the world. She's allowed to take risks. *I'm* allowed to take risks! Because not everyone wants to play it safe all the time—"

"There's a difference between taking thoughtful risks and the kind of dangerous or nonsensical choices you're making these days," Mom said. "Focus on your education for once, instead of—"

"UGH! I can't *deal* with you anymore!" Laurel had her hands on her hips. "My education doesn't only happen in the classroom!"

Mom looked like she was going to throw something. Both of them had forgotten about me and my hair. I hadn't seen them fight like this since before Laurel moved to Alaska. I hated it.

Mom glanced around at the silent platform, and lowered her voice to an angry whisper. "That might be true, but the classroom's where you *need* to focus your time. Enough! Enough of your endless distractions!"

"Distractions?! Is that what you call the rest of the world?" Laurel laughed, but it wasn't a funny laugh. "I've had enough of the classrooms! What I *need* is to get out there and actually learn from the world around me! In fact," Laurel yelled, stepping away from Mom, her arms out in front of her, "I'm DONE!"

Mom opened her mouth, and closed it again. She looked at Mimi, who was holding Ladybug and standing next to me. I looked up at all of them from my wet miserable hair-covered spot on the ground. Laurel was bright red, her eyebrows scrunched together and mad, and Mom didn't look any better.

"What do you mean, Laurel?" Mom asked finally, her voice quieter.

Laurel didn't even pause. "I'm not sure I'm going back to Berkeley," she said, and her voice was quieter too, but no less mad. "There are a lot of important things our world needs right now, and I'm not going to sit around and ignore that."

I stared at her. Even my hair didn't seem that important all of a sudden. Drop out of school? Laurel? I glanced at Mom, and found her staring at me.

"Come on, Sara," she said, walking by Laurel as if she weren't there. "Let's go into the bathroom and try to get rid of the dye."

Ladybug peered over Mimi's shoulder. "Oooh, Say-Say, your ear's a really pretty blue. I wish my ear was blue!"

Mimi shushed her.

I got up silently and went with Mom. Laurel just watched us go.

Now we're back on the train, which got fixed, temporarily at least, and will take us to Chicago. I didn't see Travis again after he poured water on my head. . . . Who knows what the heck he thinks about us now? I don't even know if Mom and Laurel are talking to each other, or if

Mom is talking to me. For the rest of the night we were all pretty silent. Once we got on the train, everyone went right back to bed. I'm writing by flashlight, but there's no bullfrog snoring and no ocean waves.

I don't think anyone is getting any sleep tonight.

Sorry this page is so wet. It's stupid to care, with everything going on with Laurel, but I can't help crying. My hair! I've been growing it for four years, and honestly, it was the only cool thing about me. I haven't even looked in the mirror yet. I'm too scared. I guess I got an "outwardly visible sign" all right. . . . Now I'll look as freakish and horrible as I feel.

Chapter 16

Fun Fact!

The Chicago Cubs baseball team had the longest losing streak in baseball history, until they won the World Series in 2016. Before that, they had not won since 1908. (I sympathize. Feels like I'm at the start of a historic losing streak myself.)

August 17–8:30 a.m.

We're all up and packed before the train arrives in Chicago. I'm so tired, I feel like I have sand in my eyes. Mimi and Mom don't look much better than I feel. . . . They're staggering around in silence, clutching their coffees and packing one-handed. We're all pretending things are normal, passing each other stuff and moving out of each other's way. But it's weird. Root stopped in to get the water bottles to refill and said Laurel was "taking the morning to recalibrate her energies" and would see us in Chicago. Mom nodded and handed him the bottles. He stood there like he was going to say something else, but then he left.

Why does he keep leaving these notes? I CANNOT BE-
LIEVE I'M GOING TO HAVE TO FACE HIM WITH
MY TORCHED-HAYSTACK HAIR. UGH. I am com-
pletely mortified.

Dear Rae,

Wow...what a night! Sorry I couldn't stick around,
but Auntie Georgia wasn't feeling great, so we were
trying to keep her comfortable, or as comfortable as
you can be when you're yanked out of bed at 3:00 in
the morning! Still, I guess we should be glad it wasn't
worse...and at least on a train you're not way up in
the sky when something goes wrong!

Anyway, sorry for whatever happened to your head.
(I'm not sure what did happen....Is everything
okay?)

Trav

P.S. I thought you might find this funny....I did a
sketch of Rupert Presley and his favorite snake.

Travis is a pretty good artist. The snake looks good with sideburns. But still . . . on a scale of one to ten, my humiliation is around 463.

Oh, and Mom and Mimi left for the café car, and put these on my suitcase:

☆ A light cotton scarf (Mimi's) to hide my blue ear

☆ A big straw sun hat (Mom's) to hide my machete-chopped hair

☆ Several barrettes and hair clips (Ladybug's)

Also, I missed breakfast, and now we're pulling into Chicago. My stomach is growling so loudly, Ladybug got all excited, thinking someone had a dog. I hate my life.

10:00 a.m.

Laurel, Root, and I are sitting in a café, where I'm FINALLY getting some food. The NTFs were quite concerned about our lack of breakfast and have been twittering and clucking around us and making sure we're fed. Let me correct that: Gavin and Travis have been twittering, practically force-feeding us from their stash of trail mix, beef jerky (seriously, no), and peanut M&M's. You would think that Miss Ruby and Miss Georgia would be the ones wanting to feed us—after all, my nana practically assaults us with baked goods when we go to visit her. But these women couldn't care less. They were too busy arguing over whose turn it was to carry Elvis. Because, yes, they are now carrying around the life-sized Elvis cutout.

Travis on the other hand seemed to honestly fear for our lives. And I'll be honest. I don't like to skip a meal *at all*. (In fact, Laurel once bought me a T-shirt that says, "I'm sorry for what I said when I was hungry.") But even I don't take my meals quite as seriously as the Texans.

Once we got out in the daylight with the NTFs, having to deal with luggage and maps and travel stuff, Mom and Laurel were kind of normal. Or normal-ish. I mean, they ask each other questions and answer them, so there's no obvious Silent Treatment happening, but they're avoiding eye contact, and no one is saying much of anything beyond the bare necessities. Still, for Laurel that's not bad. I hope they make up soon. . . . It's hard enough being miserable about my hair without having to worry about them.

Meanwhile I've got Mimi's scarf flung casually (I hope) around my neck, and the hat pulled down low. Luckily, we're eating outside, so it looks pretty normal. Maybe. I barely had time to look in the mirror before we got off the train, and it's bad. Oh, it's really bad. Mimi said she'll take me to get a haircut today in Chicago, so at least I won't have grayish flakes of once-was-hair falling off anymore. But I don't know what I'm supposed to do about my ear.

Anyway, we're here, and just finished eating some kind of bacon-with-a-side-of-sausage special that had Root looking a little ill but made me and Laurel very happy. Once they made sure we were fed, Gavin and Travis went off with Mom and Mimi, figuring out some tour information, and Miss Ruby and Miss Georgia (and Elvis) left to ask the waiter to take their photo. It seems like everyone's busy, but I'm afraid they're staring at me. I can't tell how much of my hideous hair–blue ear combo is showing, so I keep adjusting the scarf. Laurel just slapped my hand down and told me to leave it alone or she'll grab the scarf and hide it.

I guess I'll just see if there's more bacon.

· · · · ·

TO: EmilyGirl, SaanviTheFab
FROM: SaraJF
SUBJECT: Me in Chicago and some news

Hey, you guys!! I miss you INSANELY much. Or maybe I'm just going insane . . . hahahahahaha. Kidding. Sort of.

Actually, I have to tell you something. Or a couple of things, really.

First: My hair is officially . . . different. I'm not going to say anything more right now, but it is definitely changed. So I guess I can check that one off the Reinvention List.

Second: While the blue dye didn't quite work as planned, it turns out that it's pretty strong stuff. My ear is actually blue. We're not sure if it will wash off. I mean, OF COURSE IT WILL WASH OFF! Eventually. It just hasn't yet.

Third: Laurel and my mom had a huge fight and Laurel says she might want to drop out of college! Mom is Freaking. Out. Not sure how they're going to manage the rest of this trip.

So . . . yeah, that's the big news. Other than that, I guess the trip is going fine. I mean, we've seen some really cool stuff. We're in Chicago now. Check out the photo—that's Ladybug in a clear glass box on the Skydeck. I'm telling you, Google the Chicago Skydeck. Is that nuts or what?? You're literally suspended over the street off the 103RD FLOOR!!! AS IN YOU ARE OVER 1000 FEET UP IN THE AIR STANDING ON A PIECE OF GLASS!!!

I was too chicken to do it. Big surprise there.

Okay, enough of that! Tell me the gossip from home? How's surf camp?? Vi, how's the design stuff? Do you miss me?? TELL ME YOU MISS ME!! It feels like I've been gone a million years.

XOXOXOXOXO Rae

P.S. I'll send you a picture of my hair, but . . . not yet. I just can't deal.

P.P.S. That dude in the photo with Ladybug is Travis, one of the other National Rail winners. Some facts about him:

1) I told you I wasn't lying about the cowboy hat.
2) He's so friendly, it freaks me out. First I thought it was all some sarcastic game, but I think he really might be that friendly. Weird, right?
3) His two great-aunts are on the trip with him, and honestly, they're kind of awesome. When we're ninety, we should take a train trip, if trains are even still a thing. Maybe we'll have flying cars by then.

XO Rae

• • • • •

TO: SaraJF, SaanviTheFab
FROM: EmilyGirl
SUBJECT: re: Me in Chicago and some news
    Oh. My. God. SARA!!!!!! I mean, RAE!!!!!! What is going on with your hair? Send photos!! I'm sure it's amazing! But:

First: I've been wimping out of doing my pink stripe, but maybe I'll do it tonight. I'll send you photos!

Second: Your ear is blue? Does that mean you *did* dye your hair? Anyway, that dye has to wash off your ear, right?? I mean, people don't generally walk around blue, and tons of people dye their hair. So yeah. I'm sure it'll be gone soon.

Third: WOW, your mom must be freaking! That's crazy—does Laurel really want to drop out? What would she do? What's Root think of all this? (Also, ROOT! How's he been as a travel companion? Do tell!)

Fourth: That Travis boy is kind of cute! Maybe he could loan you his hat, if you don't like your new hair. KIDDING. Kidding. Sort of.

Home is fine and boring. It's only been a few weeks, and you know Shipton, nothing ever really changes here. Chicago sounds amazing. Even with all the hair and Laurel craziness, I'm still jealous! Of course we miss you. . . . The three musketeers aren't the same when one of our musketeers is gallivanting around the country! :(

XOX Em

How best to catch up on our journey? Well, last night there were . . . ructions. Lots of drama, lots of excitement, lots of surprises and revelations. All the things, in fact, that make a great story! However, out of respect for the players here, I will hold off on the details, as there are a number of hurt feelings, bruised egos, and worried parents in the mix. I'll just say that lemon juice does seem to help fade hair dye stains on skin, in case any reader needs that tip someday. I'll also say that bacon, when applied liberally, can help mend fences between angry and frustrated multi-generational family members.

So while there are some frayed tempers and Vesuvius-like volcanos waiting to erupt, we are still trying to keep the Love Train moving here! We are living in the moment, even if the moment involves a surly Scribe and an overly sugared-up Animal Planet who might have eaten some wheat product, because holy cow, she has gas that could make strong men fall to their knees. Cowboy Senior had the misfortune to be downwind as we walked to the Art Institute. He let out a low whistle and said he knew of industrial pig farms that were less powerful. Our poor little Animal Planet.

However! She is feeling better, and we will keep LIVING IN THE MOMENT, because that's why we're here. We've seen Wrigley Field, home of the Chicago Cubs, and the vertigo-inducing skyscraper the Skydeck, as well as the gorgeous art at the Art Institute. But the highlight by far has been the splash fountain. Everyone—the Activist, Tree, Animal Planet, Cowboys Jr. and Sr., and Grammy One and Two (as I've started calling the older aunties traveling with the Cowboys)—ran right in. Even Superwoman took off her shoes and splashed around with Animal Planet.

Poor Scribe ... well, it's not easy being twelve. She was wearing white shorts, and Animal Planet might have splashed a bit more than expected. The Scribe's underwear has red and orange polka dots. That we could all see quite clearly. Tree generously offered his poncho as a cover-up, but somehow Scribe did not seem any happier.

> MIMI: Going forward I should probably make it clear to Ladybug that not ALL public fountains are for swimming in, since we learned that the hard way.

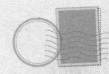

HI FROG!! THIS IS CHICAGO AND THIS STATUE LOOKS EXACTLY LIKE A BEAN BUT IT'S NOT CALLED THE BEAN IT'S CALLED CLOUD GATE. I DON'T THINK IT LOOKS LIKE A GATE. I THINK IT LOOKS LIKE A BEAN. I ALSO JUMPED IN TWO FOUNTAINS TODAY! ONE I WAS ALLOWED TO AND ONE I WAS NOT ALLOWED TO BUT I DIDN'T KNOW THAT. THE AUNTIES WE MET ON THE TRAIN JUMPED IN TOO. THEN GUARDS CAME AND WE HAD TO LEAVE. LOVE, LADYBUG!

8:00 p.m.

Back in the hotel. Ladybug, Laurel, Root, and Travis are all playing cards in Travis's room. And Mom and Mimi are downstairs in the restaurant, having a Parents-Only Conversation about Laurel. So I'm alone for the first time since we left Shipton. But for some stupid reason, instead of being relieved to *finally* have some peace and quiet, I feel like I'm missing out. Which is idiotic. I don't even like card games.

Maybe I'm just exhausted. Mimi and I went off and found a hair salon to deal with my hair, and they had to cut off practically all of it. Not Laurel-buzz-cut short, but definitely too-short-for-a-ponytail short. Mimi says it looks amazing and chic and reminds her of a young Audrey Hepburn, whoever that is, but I feel naked. Which, given that my ear is still a kind of faint blue after the lemon juice, isn't my favorite thing. I guess I got my "outwardly visible signal," though.

Chicago was pretty cool, I admit. The Art Institute was my favorite—incredible paintings and sculptures, and also air-conditioning. Of course when I got all excited about these amazing Hindu paintings, Mimi got even MORE excited and wanted "In your own words, sweetie!!" for me to tell her my impressions of the art. I don't want to be horrible, but she's the one getting paid—she can say it in *her* own words. My words are my own, and this stupid million-page journal is the only place they're going.

Ugh. Maybe I'll go see what's happening in the card game. At least then I'll have something to do. But then they'll think I want to hang out with them.

Never mind. I guess I'll just get ready for bed.

9:00 p.m.

Another note under the door. He's SO weird. But in a nice way. I guess.

Hey, Rae!

Wish you'd wanted to come down and play cards. Did you know your little sister cheats like crazy? Jeesh, you could warn a guy. She also passed wind and we had to leave the room and play in the hallway until it aired out. WOW. I didn't know someone that little could make such a big, big smell. (Okay, I mean "farted." Sorry if that's rude, but I never heard "passed wind" until now when I asked my dad for a polite word for "fart." "Passed wind" just sounds ridiculous.) Anyway, I didn't have a chance to tell you at dinner, but your hair looks real nice. Auntie Ruby said you were "hiding an old-time movie-star face under that mop" and that it was a huge improvement. (Also, don't mind Aunt Ruby... she meant it as a compliment.)

Well, I know you're busy writing, but if you ever want to—you know—stop writing, let me know.

Trav

It's pretty cool Miss Ruby thinks I look like a movie star, even if she did say I had a mop before. I sure don't have a mop now. More like a Swiffer.

Ugh. Mom came in to have a conversation with me about "poor choices" and "impulsivity" and "choosing good role models."

All I did was try to dye the ends of my hair, for crying out loud! You would think I'd tried to run away and join the circus. I said that, which I think was a mistake.

Mom exploded, in a quiet, don't-wake-Ladybug kind of way. "You may think this is funny—" she started, but I interrupted.

"I definitely *don't* think it's funny. Believe me, burning my hair right off my head is the last thing I'd find hilarious," I said.

But she kept going. "—but I assure you, Mimi and I are *not* laughing. Not at all. Your sister has been modeling some very . . . misguided behavior, and I don't want you to think—"

Just then Laurel and Root came in. Root took a look at me and Mom and scuttled into the bathroom, but Laurel kind of squared her shoulders like she was heading into battle. Which I guess she was. Because she turned to Mom and said, "You know, freaking out at Sara—sorry, *Rae,* because of her hair seems pretty superficial, don't you think? It's hair. It's going to grow back. It's not permanent. And you know something else? If I take some time off from college, that's not permanent either. You get that, right? I can always go back. But you're such a perfectionist, you can't bear the thought that we might do something that you didn't plan out for us."

Well.

Consider that a shot fired in World War Mom and Laurel. Mom pretty much blew up. She immediately started protesting that she lets us make mistakes, plenty of them, but her job as a parent is to guide us, and help us avoid the most costly and dangerous mistakes. Then Laurel started in on how at twenty she could use her own judgment on these things, and didn't Mom have any faith in how they'd raised her, and Mom got kind of teary and shiny-eyed and said she hoped so, but that wasn't enough to keep her girls safe.

By now they both were crying and whisper-shouting, trying not to wake Ladybug or bother Mimi, who had holed up in the bedroom to write. I was stuck wondering what to do. . . . At least Mom wasn't freaking out over my hair anymore, but it seemed kind of cowardly to bail on Laurel when she had jumped into the fight to save me. So I stood there, swiveling back and forth between them like I was watching a tennis match.

Finally Laurel put up both hands, like she was stopping traffic. "We're not going to agree on this, at least not tonight. And I don't want to ruin our trip. So let's just . . . let it lie for now. Okay?"

Mom paused, mid-blast. "Let it lie?" she repeated.

"Like letting a field go fallow," Root said, emerging from the bathroom. "Helps the soil replenish the nutrients that have been used up. Great metaphor, you know?"

Mom and Laurel both stared at him. Mom finally kind of exhaled in a big sigh, and her shoulders dropped a little. "Sure. We'll . . . let it lie."

She walked over and hugged Laurel, who hugged her back, hard. Then Mom hugged me. "And as for your hair, there's not much we can do about it at this point. I think you've pretty much been punished already. We'll just . . . let that lie too."

When she walked out of the room toward the bedroom, I looked over at Laurel. She seemed lost, standing in the middle of the living room. Root was busy setting up the sofa bed, and I felt like I should say something, or try to talk to her. But before I could figure out what to say, she walked into the bathroom and shut the door.

Midnight

I was actually asleep for once, when I woke up and realized it was quiet . . . like no-bullfrog quiet. Sure enough, Mimi and Mom were awake, whispering. Then I realized Mom *wasn't* awake; Mimi's whispering to herself, trying to figure out her book, I guess. She sounds pretty freaked out, actually. I don't think it's going very well.

Chapter 17

Fun Fact!

In the 1830s, Princeton, Illinois, was settled by families from the New England and Mid-Atlantic states. Its name was, according to legend, drawn from a hat. Its former nickname, the City of Elms, is no longer used due to an epidemic that struck the elm trees and killed off almost every single one of them. (Dead trees. . . . Again I ask, who's in charge of these "fun" facts??)

Fun Fact!

"Kewanee" is a Native American word for "prairie chicken." Kewanee, Illinois, is also the acknowledged Hog Capital of the World, holding an annual Hog Days Festival every Labor Day weekend, complete with parade, flea market, and carnival.

(Okay. Now, that is a for-real fun fact!! I now know a Native American word for "prairie chicken," though it doesn't tell me what tribe or language or anything. Still . . . I can definitely use it in trivia contests. Also . . . Hog Capital of the World. I can't believe we're missing the festival, because I'm pretty sure the whole thing would be wrapped in bacon.)

New Train alert! Goodbye, *City of New Orleans*. Hello, *Southwest Chief.* This one goes all the way from Chicago to Los Angeles. It's kind of wild, really. . . . If I look at a map, we're still way closer to Massachusetts than to California, but we're halfway through our trip. Two more weeks. Two more trains. So much more country to travel.

Everything is so spread out here. . . . It seems like it'll take forever to get to California. This time we're on the train for almost twenty-four hours straight, and part of me is actually relieved. If we're on the train, I can curl up away from Mom, who still looks at me like I tried to tattoo my entire body, instead of just dye a few inches of my hair. And away from Mimi, who has purple shadows under her eyes and a kind of frantic fake smile. And even away from Laurel, since I don't really know what to say to her. I mean, dropping out of school? The last thing I want to do is sound like Mom, but I can't help being a little freaked out. Also, I feel like such a loser. . . . How would she ever care about my stupid hair or my Reinvention

Project when she's got all this stuff on her mind? Anyway, there's something safe and peaceful about having a whole day to find my own corner and be left alone.

I decided to do another check-in on the Reinvention Project list:

☆ Learn Latin (Started strong, but wow, there are a lot of verbs. Must recommit.) *(Hmmm. The recommitting didn't really work. Better try again. I have managed some spectacular insults, though. For instance, the next time Vi's little brother bugs us, I can just say, "Quis est haec simia?")*

☆ Learn to surf, at least the basics (Obviously this is going nowhere.) *(Still no change. Obvs.)*

☆ Practice yoga every morning to develop Inner Peace and Mindfulness (Hmmm. Not bad, considering. I hit my nose and got a nosebleed when I tried turtle pose, but otherwise I'm getting there.) *(This is really coming along! Almost mastered camel without crashing over.)*

☆ Change hair (*Note: this is Vi's idea. I've been growing mine for four years, and I'm definitely not cutting it, but dying the ends . . . that I can do.*) (Nothing yet.) *(Well . . . I guess I nailed this one.)*

☆ Start wearing dark gray or navy-blue nail polish (*and try not to pick it off in ten minutes*) (Note: this is Vi's idea too. We'll see.) *(I colored my nails in with*

188

Mom's Sharpie. Does that count?) (The Sharpie has faded and now I look like my nails are rotting. Ugh.)

☆ Read at least five nonfiction books (Two down . . . *Loving I Am Malala!) (Finished Malala and on to Chasing Lincoln's Killer! Who knew nonfiction was so exciting?)*

☆ Pick a signature social cause to care about (*Note: This one's Em's idea. I have lots of causes I care about, but apparently we each need a "signature cause."*) *(Maybe the environment? Laurel's got me pretty worried.) (Ugh. Nothing. How am I supposed to choose??)*

☆ Eschew with a firm hand all old camp, soccer team, and dumb club shirts and sweatshirts, even if they are soft and cozy (*Since I didn't pack any, I am totally nailing my new style! Still, I miss my old Hidden Valley Camp T-shirt.) (Since I've added Mimi's scarf to cover my blue ear, I guess my style is coming along. Ish.)*

☆ Consider jeggings (*Not sure this one's going to stick.)*

☆ Drink coffee (*Nope.) (Still haven't been brave enough to try again.)*

☆ Rebrand myself as Rae, not Sara (*Hmmm . . . So far Travis is the only one who remembers every time, and how useless is that?) (Since no one in my family is talking much, it's hard to say.)*

☆ Work on a novel, or at least figure out a good
story (Nothing. Haven't written a word. Phooey.)

Ladybug has officially been adopted by the NTFs. She
and Travis play endless rounds of Frog Juice and Spit, or
she curls up with Miss Ruby, who is teaching her—and
Laurel and Root!!—to knit. I have visions of Root knitting himself an organic hemp poncho and trying to convince us all to take shelter under there in the cold. But I
shouldn't be mean. . . . After all, he's already way better
at it than Laurel. So far she's only managed to tear a hole
in her T-shirt with a knitting needle and send a ball of
yarn all the way down the aisle under the seat of three
sleeping German tourists. Of course they woke up as
Root was crawling under their seat, with only his (hairy)
feet and legs sticking out. *That* was a fun conversation.
Luckily, Mom speaks German.

We're all in the café car, spread out in different seats.
I'm alone in a corner booth with this journal, but I can't
help listening in to everyone else. Mimi and Gavin are at
a booth behind me, talking writing. It's actually pretty
interesting how Gavin outlines his novels. . . . He has a
whole notecard system. Even though Mimi's book is totally different, she seems pretty fascinated. In fact, she
sounds excited about writing for the first time in a while.
Gavin's offering to do "word wars" with her, where they
set a timer and write until it goes off, and whoever wrote

the most words wins. Then the loser has to buy lunch for the winner. Knowing Mimi's weird competitive streak (seriously, play Scrabble with her someday), I'm betting this will help her get the words flowing.

On the other side of the car, Travis seems to have a bizarrely large appetite for playing really dumb kid games. He keeps giggling . . . and yes, he has his fairly hilarious TEEHEEHEEHEEHEEHEE giggle thing going on, which makes Ladybug crack up too. Right now they're laughing over who would win in a battle, Giant Elvis or Tiny Bruce.

LADYBUG:

Traaaaaavis! You're being silly! Bruce is a ROMAN CENTURION! Don't you know what they are? They're fighters who fought big battles and stuff!

TRAVIS:

TEEHEEHEEHEEHEE! That li'l bitty thing? Giant Elvis could crush him like a little gnat. Wouldn't even notice he was doing it. You ever seen Elvis perform? I mean before he was dead and all? Man could *move,* I'm telling you. That Brent—

LADYBUG:

BRUCE!!!

TRAVIS:

(under his breath) Teeheeheehee. (louder) Oh, right. Bryce—

LADYBUG:

(standing on the seat) BRUUUUUUUCE!!

TRAVIS:

(trying not to burst out laughing) Sorry 'bout that, Ladybug, old gal. But still, Elvis would kick that poor Bobby—

LADYBUG:

(now laughing) TRAVIS!!!! HIS NAME IS BRUCE!!! AND HE IS A ROMAN CENTURION!!!

MISS RUBY:

(glancing up from her knitting) Lord, child, they heard you in Missouri. Simmer down. Now, Laurel, how you doing on that corner stitch? Oh, honey. No, that's okay. I've got another pair in my bag. They break all the time.

Apparently Laurel managed to spear Miss Ruby's glasses with her knitting needle and fling them across the train. I didn't even know someone could do that if she tried.

Miss Ruby seems kind of crusty and rude, but she's

actually awfully nice. She didn't even blink when Laurel, all pierced tongue and shaved head, asked if she could learn to knit. Miss Ruby pulled out an extra set of needles and found some yarn and started in on the basics. And when Root said he wanted to learn too, she sent Travis off to get Miss Georgia's knitting bag and added him to the class. Miss Georgia's resting, apparently. While Miss Ruby seems strong enough to keep up with anyone, Miss Georgia's more . . . well, more like a typical old person. She's kind of shaky when she walks, and sometimes falls asleep in the middle of things. But when she *is* awake, watch out. She and Miss Ruby are probably worse than me and Em and Saanvi for giggling and arguing and goofing off. Can't imagine if they'd been in middle school together. . . . I'm betting that they wouldn't be allowed to have the same lunch period, that's all I'm saying.

LIFE IN THE GREEN LANE

Well, fearless readers, we're in the middle of the country now! I'm currently on a train traveling from Chicago toward the Southwest. And do you know what's outside our windows as we whiz by at speeds topping 100 miles per hour? Corn. Yep, corn, corn, and more corn. My little sister Li saw it and was all excited (even though she has some grain allergies and can't always eat corn) because we'd seen some homeless people in Chicago and she figured here was TONS of food for them to eat.

And I get it. You'd think you could feed an army on all this food, and in fact, it looks wonderfully fertile, the breadbasket of America, waiting to feed the hungry. Except that most of this corn isn't really going to nourish anyone, because it either gets ground up and used as cattle feed, or it's turned into high-fructose corn syrup and poured into soda and junk food, or it becomes ethanol and is added to gasoline.

Here's a fun idea . . . YOU try explaining that to the six-year-old who wants to feed the hungry. It went over about as well as you'd expect. She kept saying, "But it's food, right? Isn't it food? And people are hungry, so why can't they eat it?"

I'll tell you, it's enough to make a girl mad.

You know why bad things happen, why people can go hungry or be mistreated? I'll tell you, it's not up to the bad guys. When good people do nothing, well . . . that's the first step. And I don't want to be one of the people who does nothing.

Is that wrong?

Peace, Laurel

Ah, as the famous Dickens said, "It was the best of times, it was the worst of times." Of course, he was writing about the French Revolution, and I am writing about a family train trip, but really, in some ways they're both violent, exhilarating events. (Even if most of our violence is acted out between a tiny plastic Roman soldier and a life-sized cutout of Elvis Presley.) Anyway, we are back on the train, and for once I'm finding a way forward with the writing, thanks to the talented and inspiring Cowboy Senior. Having a fellow writer aboard helps with some of the challenges of writing a book about a family train trip while actually being *on* a family train trip.

We are together, the whole family, thousands of miles from home, and yet each of us has our own journey as well. Spread out around the train as we travel through America's heartland, we are each experiencing the world our own way. In the sightseeing car we have windows all around us, affording views of the fields and farms and high-summer sunlight. But inside we have made new friends, ranging in ages from teens to grandparents, we have talked of our lives and listened in on others, and we have been willing to share our stories and our interests. This is the beautiful contradiction of train travel . . . we are moving fast and sitting still; we are all together and yet able to find our independence. What a gift.

Well, that was weird. I stayed in the sightseeing car after everyone else left, and was perfectly happy, staring out the window. There was a little sliver of orange-and-rust sunset in the sky, and we'd crossed the Missouri River and are going to be in Kansas soon. I was thinking about going back to our room, but the car had emptied out and I liked staring out at the endless flatness and the last bit of daylight.

Then in walked Miss Ruby and Travis. They didn't see me, since I was all curled up at the end of the car. I didn't mean to listen in or anything, but now I feel like . . . I don't know. Like I learned something maybe I wasn't supposed to know.

Travis started by asking Miss Ruby if Miss Georgia was doing "okay, given the circumstances."

Miss Ruby sighed. "She's stubborn and mean and useless, so yes, I suppose she's fine," she said, sounding totally exasperated.

Travis gave a snort. "Oh, like stubborn don't come around here!"

Miss Ruby hit him with her backpack, which, I happen to know, has tons of knitting stuff and boxes of some kind of peanut brittle and around four books.

"Ouch! I take it back," Travis said, rubbing his arm.

He looked like it might have actually hurt, and honestly I wouldn't be surprised. Miss Ruby doesn't mess around.

"You'd better take it back. I'm not near as stubborn as that woman on my worst day. She's riddled up with the cancer, and likely in all kinds of pain, not that she'd tell *me*, course not. And here we are chasing our fool tails around the country. Hmmm-mmm-mmm." She shook her head and sounded annoyed.

I turned my head so I could hear better. Cancer? Miss Georgia?

But Travis nodded. "I hear you. But she's going to be feeling the same, whether at home in her bed or on the train. So long as she wants to do this—"

"Oh, she wants." Miss Ruby sighed, huge and loud. "And I want to be here too. Of course I want to be with her. The Grand Canyon! Seeing that with Georgie will be a memory for a lifetime!" She laughed a little. "Even if that lifetime only lasts a little longer."

I shook my head, not even realizing I was doing it. Was Miss Ruby sick too??

But Travis gave another snort and shoved Miss Ruby's arm (although way more gently than Miss Ruby had shoved him). "Don't you start with that. You've got years left to go, right? After all, you want me to grow up without you telling me how to be? What will Daddy do if you're not there to tell him what's what?"

They both laughed a little, softly at first, but then Travis started his TEEHEEHEEHEE laugh.

"Remember when you and Auntie G went away for a week? And he put dishwashing soap in the washing machine? Said he figured soap was soap and it didn't much matter what kind, it would get our clothes clean?"

"Lord, I will remember till I leave this earth! Those photos you sent! Looked like a snowstorm in that bathroom! Bubbles up to your knees, and you laughing like the village idiot." She shook her head, still laughing. "That man. Amazing that he manages to get himself out of bed in the morning."

"You say that, but that's not what we heard at that award ceremony last month. Remember? It was all 'Gavin Alexander is changing the face of rocket propulsion!' And you were so proud!"

"Man's a fool," Miss Ruby said, waving her hand at Travis to shush him. "He may be a genius, but he's also a darn fool." She groaned and stood up. "Better go to Georgie. Walk me back?"

Travis got up too, taking the bag. "Course I will. I was raised right." He put out his arm for her, and she took it, and held on as the train swung and wobbled around.

"Darn straight you were," Miss Ruby said, clutching tight. "Thanks to me."

Huh. I admit I haven't wanted to spend much time with the NTFs, but that doesn't mean I . . . I mean, obviously

I wouldn't want anything bad to happen to them. Poor Miss Georgia. And poor Miss Ruby, if her best friend's so sick. I can't imagine how horrible it would be to try to stay fun and friendly and silly if Em or Saanvi . . .

And then there's Travis. He obviously loves Miss Georgia like crazy. And he's always doing things for her and helping her and laughing at her jokes. He must feel *awful* inside.

Well, anyway.

The moon's up now, and I should probably head back to the room. But I'm not quite ready for bed.

I feel kind of bad that I've been such a jerk to Travis. He's a pretty good guy, taking care of his aunt, and dealing with Ladybug. I should have been nicer. I guess I still can be, right? Okay. Starting tomorrow I'm going to be friendly. Er. How hard can it be?

Chapter 18

DEAR FROG, WE ARE IN COLORADO!!! AND WE CAN SEE THE ROCKY MOUNTAINS!!!!!!!!!!!!! SEE THIS POSTCARD? IT'S FROM THE TRAIN STATION WHERE WE GET TO STRETCH OUR LEGS. THE SIGN HERE SAYS WE'RE CLOSE TO THE MIDDLE BETWEEN THE ATLANTIC OCEAN AND PACIFIC OCEAN. MOM SAYS ASK YOUR DADS TO SHOW YOU ON A MAP. MOM SAYS I CAN'T DRAW A MAP HERE BECAUSE THERE IS NO ROOM. MOM SAYS—

Carol here! Ladybug is in time-out, sorry. It's been a long day on the train, but we want to get this in the mail. Jason and Tom, if you get a chance, look up La Junta, Colorado, on the map with Frog—it's close to the midpoint between the two coasts! Best, Carol

August 19—10:00 a.m.

Well, that was a pretty cool stop. We're in Colorado, and the landscape has changed all over again. Now it's prairie grass and, way far in the distance, enormous snowcapped mountains. Miss Georgia was so excited, she punched Miss Ruby. Like, actually hauled off and punched her on the arm. Miss Ruby punched her back (of course), saying, "Why would you think the right way to celebrate God's beautiful earth is to hit somebody? What's *wrong* with you? I suspect your mama dropped you on your head when you were little. Mmmmm-mmmmm."

And of course Miss Georgia wasn't about to take *that,* so she says, "If my mama dropped me, it was an accident, and probably broke her heart. Your mama? She likely dropped *you* on purpose. Coupla times. Hoping it would shake some sense into you!"

Then Miss Ruby said God gave cows more brains and a better-looking face than He gave Miss Georgia, and Miss Georgia said that God had been looking at a joke book when He came up with Miss Ruby's hair, and then they both burst out laughing, hitting their armrests and hooting.

The entertainment value is high with those two, I have to admit.

Now I'm going to beard the lion in his den, as Mom always says when she has to do something she's dreading. Specifically, I'm going to try to be . . . argh . . . *friendly* to Travis. Not that I wasn't friendly! I was. Ish. It's not a crime to want to be alone, even if Mimi keeps giving me awful looks like I kicked her dog or something. (Which, obviously I'd never do, because I love dogs. And I love people! Well, some people. But I wouldn't go around *kicking* anyone, for goodness' sakes! Anyway, the dog has nothing to do with the whole lion in its den thing. WHAT WAS I EVEN SAYING??????)

Right. I'm going to try to chat with Travis. In a normal,

casual-type way. Nothing weird or overly friendly. I don't want him to think I *like like* him! Ewwww. Or that it's all about *cancer*. Because that would be awkward, obviously. No, just normal-level friendly. That shouldn't be so hard, right?

10:15 a.m.

Okay, it's totally hard. I wasn't rude before, but I made it pretty clear I wanted to be left alone, and he was Chatty Chad, talking and talking, even when I barely answered. Today he's off with the aunts and Laurel, minding his own business. What a time to take a hint—right when I decide to be nice! So . . . do I wander over and tell him I've changed my mind and he doesn't need to leave me alone? Or ask him if he's read anything good lately? Or what??

10:25 a.m.

IS THIS SO HARD FOR EVERYONE ELSE??? I mean, being normally nice to someone? I have a terrible feeling that there is something seriously wrong with me.

11:00 a.m.

This is ridiculous. I kind of sidled over to where Travis is playing cards with his aunts and Laurel, then got totally self-conscious, because who wants to be interrupted in the middle of a game?? (I mean, assuming they like playing games. Which I don't. But clearly Travis does.) Now I'm back in my seat on the other side of the sightseeing car while gorgeous scenery whips past the windows and they laugh and jabber over there like they're having the time of their lives.

I'm going to get up and go over. This is pathetic.

Great. Now Ladybug's here, asking what I'm doing.

"I was going to see if maybe Travis and Laurel wanted—"

"COME ON, THEN!! LET'S GO SEE IF MISS RUBY WANTS TO DO MORE KNITTING!"

I guess I'll stop writing for now. Ladybug's trying to drag me to their table while making noises like a hooting owl. Apparently this is their "knitting signal." I have no idea why. . . . Maybe she was knitting an owl cozy??

I cannot believe this is my life.

3:00 p.m.

Huh. That was a lot easier than I expected. Travis looked up like he was expecting me when Ladybug dragged me over. (And she did drag me—it was like those tugboats we saw hauling the huge barges in New York. Or like trying to get Amos into the cat carrier for the vet . . . all claws and creepy low growls. Not that I was growling. STOP, BRAIN, STOP!)

Anyway, Travis looked up, put his cards down, and said, "Aunties, you know I'm only going to keep taking your money. Ready to quit?" And he stood up and gave his seat to Ladybug, even lifting her up and swinging her onto the seat with that big ridiculous smile. THEN he put his arm out like he was going to *escort* me somewhere, and said, "Want to go get a Coke?"

"High-fructose corn syrup!" I answered, which is officially and undeniably the stupidest thing I have ever said in my life. New book title: *Stupid on a Train: A Memoir*.

He looked at me politely, his head cocked to one side, as though to say, "Pardon me? Did you blurt out random ingredient lists, or have I misunderstood?"

But he didn't say anything, and I just faked a cough like maybe there was a tickle in my throat or something. RIGHT.

Anyway, finally I managed to say I don't like Coke but maybe we could go get a snack in the café car, and we headed off. I admit I was cringing a little, in case his aunts or his father were the type to do the embarrassing OOOHHHH LOOK-AT-ICKLE-TRAVIS-WALKING-WITH-A-GIRL sort of thing. But no one gave us a glance, except for Miss Georgia, who called out to bring her a Snickers and a beer.

Travis didn't answer, which I think was wise.

Once we started walking, it was actually pretty normal. That's partly because, as I've mentioned, Travis talks A LOT. He's not a loudmouth, but it's kind of like a running faucet. . . . He keeps chattering and chattering unless you turn it off. So I stayed pretty quiet and let him do his thing. I was also still holding on to his arm, since I had literally *no idea what on earth* I was supposed to do. Drop it? Just let my arm go kind of limp and see if it slipped out? WOULD SOMEONE WRITE A MANUAL ON THIS STUFF, PLEASE? It was actually fairly helpful, embarrassing as it sounds, because the train was going around these crazy twists and turns, and I nearly went flying into the wall a few times.

The other thing about Travis talking . . . it's not a monologue. He actually pauses and waits for a response, even if it's only a nod or "uh-huh" or whatever. So it's not ridiculously hard to break in and say something. When we got our drinks (Coke for him, lemonade for me) and our snacks (smoked almonds for him and Cheez Doodles for me—Do not judge! I can't resist their orangy cheesy goodness), we sat and stared out at the landscape. He talked about being so excited to see his mom, and all the things they were going to do in LA.

I wanted to ask Travis when his mom moved to Los Angeles, or if he used to live there and then moved to Texas with his dad, and if they got divorced or what. But as someone with two moms, I know all too well how annoying family questions can be. If I had a dollar for every time someone said "So, which one is your *real* mom?"

I'd be rich by now. So instead I asked, "Do you like LA? Would you ever want to live there?"

Travis gave a sort of thoughtful nod. "That's a real good question. I ask myself that sometimes. I miss my mama, of course, but we talk every night, and she usually flies back every month or two. She works for an airline, so she's up in the air a whole lot anyway, which makes living with her sort of inconvenient. Plus I'm an only, and Dad and the aunts would miss me something awful. And I've got good friends, and we have the goats—"

"You have goats?" I asked, interrupting. "Do you live on a farm?"

He snorted a little, laughing. "Naw. We're barely even in the suburbs. But Auntie G decided a few years back that Aunt Ruby needed goats. Fainting goats, to be exact."

"Fainting goats," I repeated, a little confused. I couldn't help wondering if this was a real thing. Maybe he *was* making fun of me. "Are you making this up?"

He shook his head and put a hand over his heart. "Scout's honor. Here." He typed something into his phone and held it up.

I read the screen. It was Wikipedia. "Hmmm," I said. "*A myotonic goat, otherwise known as the fainting goat, is a domestic goat whose muscles freeze for roughly 3 seconds when the goat feels panic. Though painless, this generally results in the animal collapsing on its side.*" I looked up. "Seriously?"

Travis grinned. "Yep. And they're pretty much what you'd expect. They're goats . . . who faint when they get, well, provoked: nervous or stressed or really anything. They're not the smartest things. They're in danger from a predator? They fall down. Not the best survival instincts." He started typing again on his phone. "I've got photos, and trust me, they're cute enough to make up for the dumb. Darn cute. That's why we still have them. I think Aunt G figured we'd laugh about them and then find them a new home, but . . . well, see for yourself."

He held out the phone again and—OMG. I now officially want a fainting goat! They are insanely cute.

"Right?" he said, when I made a kind of cooing noise. "That one's Blue. And here's Gansey. He's the most stubborn but probably the best-looking. Doesn't it always go that way?"

"Fascinating," I said, and I wasn't even being sarcastic. "What do you do when you're not hanging around with goats?"

"Computers," he answered, so fast that I blinked. Travis usually talks kind of slow and mellow, but the way he said that seemed like it was pretty important.

"Like, video games?" I asked. I tried to keep my voice neutral, but I have to say I'm with Mimi and Mom on this one . . . most games are so boring, and it seems like every boy in my class is obsessed with some game or another— they don't even play basketball at recess anymore, they're so busy huddling in a corner to talk about who got what score.

"Kinda. I code, so I've written some games, and some apps. Also some programs that help manage hospital pharmaceutical protocols."

I stared. Travis stared back.

"What?" he asked, but his voice sounded like he was trying not to laugh.

"Nothing!" I said, but I said it too fast.

He laughed, his ridiculous TEEEHEEHEE laugh. "You're thinking I am shoveling pure-grade Texas bull manure, right? Because how does a kid like me start doing all this?"

"NO!" I protested, but then I got a little mad. "Well, kind of! I mean, how does *any* kid start doing this?"

He stretched his feet out and leaned way back in his seat. "Well, that's a good long story." He glanced at his phone, then out the window, where endless nothingness was flying by. "But luckily, it seems like we have plenty of time."

It *was* a good thing we had a lot of time, because Travis tells a very thorough story. I heard about his parents meeting each other when his dad was at a conference in Los Angeles, how they got divorced when Travis was seven, and he and his dad moved back to Texas. It sounded like his mom and dad are still good friends, which is cool. My friend Sheena's parents divorced, and *her* dad moved to

Florida and she hasn't seen him in three years, which is pretty awful. Anyway, Gavin and Travis moved next door to Miss Georgia and Miss Ruby, who basically became his other parents. And Gavin does some hotshot computer technology with NASA—yes, *that* NASA—which is how Travis started learning to write computer code when I was learning how to send an email.

But that's the seriously shortened version. . . . I left out around five hundred details about where they live, and a whole bunch of Travis's thoughts about life—moving, Texas, computers, his mom (who he calls Mama), and more. Mimi should write about *him* for her project. He'd be a dream come true.

Chapter 19

Fun Fact!

Raton Pass is the highest point on the *Southwest Chief*'s route, at 1,881 feet. The ascent is also the steepest part of the route, and when you enter the half-mile-long tunnel along it, you pass from Colorado into New Mexico.

Fun Fact!

A butte known as Wagon Mound, seen out the window after Raton and before Lamy, is in the shape of a wagon and horses, and was used as a landmark on the Santa Fe Trail.

Not-So-Fun Fact!

According to Laurel, while most history books talk about "savage Indian attacks on traders and settlers" who were traveling the Santa Fe Trail, the reality was that tens of thousands of Pawnees, Comanches, Cheyennes, Kiowas, Arapahos, and other indigenous people were kicked off their land, robbed, or treated badly by the incoming settlers.

On the *Southwest Chief* the landscape changes dramatically hour by hour. Open plains give way to the foothills of the Rockies. Then the desert of the American Southwest comes into view. Out the window endless crops, mostly beets and corn, wave in the hot summer wind, and in the distance the snow on the mountains gleams so clearly, you almost want to touch it. Occasionally, a ruined Spanish mission or old fort reminds us of the settlers who traveled this way before us.

But as enticing as the scenery is outside the train, and as delightful as it is to sit in the totally glass-enclosed sightseeing car and stare out, it is even more wonderful to gaze on the scene within. In one area, Animal Planet is learning to knit. Yes, Grammy One and Two have found a well of patience that neither Superwoman nor I have ever found, and—go figure—Animal Planet's a natural. She says she's knitting little cat sweaters for Amos and Boris. . . . How lucky for our cats!

Meanwhile, in another part of the train, a miracle has occurred. The Scribe, it appears, has laid down her quill and is actually speaking words to Cowboy Junior. She has also stopped wearing the fifteen clips and barrettes and is letting her new hairstyle fly free, and I'll be honest, she looks so grown-up and lovely, I can't quite take my eyes off her. I have no idea why she started talking to Cowboy Junior. I have no idea what they are talking about. I have no idea of anything, which is pretty typical in my life with the Scribe. However, I am finally wise enough to avoid asking questions and simply enjoy that it's happening.

Rock on, Scribe. Enjoy the journey.

We're going through the most outrageous landscapes. There are rocky canyons barely wider than the train— seriously, it looks like I could reach my hand out the window and touch the side of the rock face—and also gorgeous mesas and buttes, these enormous rocks that stick straight up toward the sky in all kinds of wild shapes. And we've been zigzagging around sharp turns—dry riverbeds and scrubby trees and red rocks as far as the eye can see.

And there are ruins . . . like old hotels or settlements from the 1800s that seem like they must be part of a movie set. It's weird, where I live near Boston there are obviously tons of old historic buildings and sights. I mean, Plymouth Rock, where the Pilgrims landed, is only a few hours from our house! (Also, most boring field trip EVER. It is literally a rock. In a kind of underwater cage. That we all just stared at. Then Harry Blackman, who's a total doofus anyway, dropped his camera inside the grate thing and we all had to try to fish it out. Second of all, don't EVEN get Laurel started on the whole Pilgrims and Indians thing. . . . I realize the story has to be simplified for little kids, but really? That discovered-America-and-made-friends-and-shared-turkey-dinner story? Totally wrong. Though I think I was a little traumatized by Laurel's revised version when all I wanted to do was make a handprint turkey for a centerpiece.) Anyway, what was I saying?

Oh right. Old stuff. Well, even though lots of the old forts and monuments here are actually more recent than stuff at home, they *seem* older. Or at least realer. (Is that a word? This isn't supposed to be graded on grammar, is it?)

Anyway. I've been talking with Travis pretty much nonstop, except that we keep interrupting each other to point out the window and gasp. So our conversations go something like this:

SARA:

```
Yeah, I was supposed to learn to surf
this summer but—
```

TRAVIS:

```
BUTTE!
```

SARA:

```
No, I said "but"— Oh, wow! Yeah, butte!
That's amazing!
```

TRAVIS:

```
Anyway, yeah, I've surfed a few times
with my mom. It's pretty cool. I mean,
your arms get tired and your eyes get
all stingy from the salt, and you keep
getting knocked down and it all seems
stupid. Then you get one little, puny
wave that none of the good surfers even
want, and—
```

SARA:

OMG! Antelope! Did you see that? There
were totally antelope out there!

TRAVIS:

We can't elope! I hardly know you!

SARA:

Shut up.

You get the idea.

But basically, Travis is some kind of boy-genius. Or
at least a veryveryvery smart guy. According to him he's
just normal with a little extra help from his dad (because
of the whole rocket-science-y computer stuff), but I don't
buy it. Plenty of my friends have parents with cool jobs,
but we're not exactly prodigies. Travis is a prodigy. When
I said that, he got kind of mad, though.

"Why? What's wrong with being a prodigy?" I asked,
because he was clearly not liking that word, even though
he's too polite to actually say anything.

"Well, think about it," he said. "A prodigy is only special because he does something early. So it's a kid who
read all of Shakespeare by six. Or wrote a symphony at
twelve. But then what? What about when they're twenty?
Or fifty? Are they still doing cool stuff? Or did they peak
early and wind up doing nothing special for the rest of
their lives? I don't want to be some game show question:

'What thirteen-year-old boy created a hospital program, then went on to do absolutely nothing?' Jeesh."

I stared a little, barely noticing the landscape. Travis plays at being so easygoing, but . . . wow. I wasn't worrying about how to make my mark when I grow up. Even Em and Saanvi, who I think of as pretty motivated, are more interested in finding out our middle school schedules than our futures. I thought back to my conversation with Laurel at the Greensboro civil rights museum.

"Do you . . . ," I started, but then I stopped.

Travis poked me. "What?" he asked.

I shrugged. "I don't know. It's just . . . you're already doing pretty cool stuff. And Laurel, well, did you know she told our moms she wants to drop out of college? She wants to . . . I don't know . . . volunteer full-time with some protesters, I guess. To her, being in school is a waste of time, compared to trying to make the world a better place. And you're all worried about your *legacy*—"

"Well, that makes me sound like an idiot," Travis interrupted. "It's not a legacy! I just don't want my best moments to happen before I'm even old enough to drive a car!"

"Sure, but I was trying to dye my hair blue because I want to start middle school with a new look!" I said, waving a hand in the general direction of my head. "I mean, how lame is that? You and Laurel are at least concerned with real things! My whole list is dumb stuff."

"What list?" Travis asked.

I groaned. Just because we were actually talking and he was actually decent didn't mean I was about to tell him everything. "Just a list me and my friends made of stuff we wanted to do this summer. You know, before middle school. And now I can't help wondering what the point is, you know?"

"What do you mean? It sounds fun," Travis said.

"It was fun, but what's . . . the real point? How is that going to change the world?" I sighed and groaned again. "I wanted to learn to drink coffee! And maybe be able to say things in Latin, to confuse people!"

Travis laughed, his TEEHEEHEEHEE laugh. "Well, you can always call someone a *spurcifer*! That'll confuse them." He shook his head. "Rae, girl, relax. Sometimes fun is as good as it gets. So you might as well enjoy it." He gave his big grin, relaxing his shoulders and shaking out his arms like he was loosening up before a run.

"Says the guy who's worried about his next high-impact computer coding project."

He nodded like I'd made a good point. "Fair enough. Maybe I need to chill out too."

"Well, do you think Laurel should chill out? I mean, it's pretty intense to leave school, but maybe she should. She wants to make a difference in the world."

He shrugged. "How should I know? Pretty sure if you took a data set of people who changed the world, you'd find some went to college, some didn't, some dropped out, some went late. . . . I mean, what I'm trying to say is that there's no *causality* between changing the world and college. You know what I mean? Not saying college doesn't matter, just saying you couldn't make an equation saying one leads to the other."

I know what "causality" means (mostly), but before I could tell him, Ladybug came up to show us her cat sweater, and we wound up playing Go Fish. You know what? It's not actually *that* bad a game.

The train attendant's coming through, telling us we're going to be at the Lamy station soon. We have to get all our bags and books and knitting and drawings of mesas (Ladybug) and legal files (Mom) and so on. . . . It looks like we've been here for weeks. Mom and Laurel managed to be sort of normal. As far as I know, they've been "letting it lie" and not mentioning college. So we were able to all sit at lunch and talk about the scenery and people's favorite movies and fainting goats, without anyone fighting.

It's amazing that we've been on the train a full twenty-four hours already. I guess having someone new to talk to really does change things. Mimi's been madly clacking away on her computer, which is good. Ish. I mean, I don't want her miserable and freaking out, though I do wonder what she's writing. Every once in a while she'd glance over at Travis and me and look way too pleased. Ugh.

We're almost at Lamy, New Mexico, where we'll get off and take a shuttle to Santa Fe. Travis and I kept talking, but not about serious stuff, just about school and our friends and families. His most recent idea: he wants to write a postcard to my friends at home. I must be really bored, because I said yes. I wonder what Em and Vi will think!

Dear Emily and Saanvi,

Greetings from New Mexico! You're probably wondering who's writing this, and I'd like to introduce myself as Travis Alexander, third-generation Texan and friend of Rae. We've been chatting on our train journey, and I figured, after hearing about what good friends y'all are, you might want to know who she's been hanging out with. So here we go, two truths and a lie:

1) I have fainting goats, and the smallest one likes to be held like a baby, on its back with its little hooves up in the air.

2) My daddy works for NASA and met the president once.

3) Rae's feet are bigger than mine.

Good luck guessing! Anyway, hope you're having a great time in Shipton. It sounds like a mighty nice place to visit.

> And if you're ever in Texas, feel free
> to stop in and see your new pal,
> Travis

Chapter 20

Fun Fact!

Santa Fe is the Southwest's oldest city, founded in 1610, and the country's highest state capital, at 7,000 feet.

Fun Fact!

Santa Fe was formerly the royal city of the Spanish conquistadores, and was known as Villa Real de la Santa Fe de San Francisco de Asis. (Note: probably good that they shortened it. Imagine writing your home address with that!)

• • • • •

LIFE IN THE GREEN LANE

Ah, Santa Fe, crossroads of natural beauty, tribal history, and Spanish influence! It's hard to imagine a cooler place than this funktastic artist haven, and I think Root is half tempted to get off the train here and call it home, if he could. It's *that* gorgeous. But let me tell you, when your sister asks what's up with all the Spanish names, it gets you thinking. And I'm not throwing anyone under the bus here, but I will say that when a twelve-year-old doesn't really know that the Spanish conquistadores who came to this area were . . . not nice people, to put it mildly . . . well, you wonder what they teach in school these days. (Also, when the Spanish words inspire your youngest sister to sing " 'Mariposa' Means 'Butterfly' " five hundred times in a row, you might find yourself angry at the *entire* teaching staff of Shipton, Massachusetts.)

So I took on the unenviable job of trying to explain, in PG-13 language, why those conquistadores were bad news. And I get it . . . every story has two sides. For Hispanic Americans some Spanish explorers are heroes! They set off bravely to unknown worlds, willing to face wild dangers (such as falling off the earth—remember people weren't totally sure the earth was actually round). But for a whole bunch of the Native American tribes—including Pueblo, Apache, Navajo, and more—these "explorers" were rated-m-for-mature-video-game levels of brutal in their treatment of the people who had long lived in the lands they were "discovering."

So here we are in beautiful Santa Fe, where there are conquistador-themed statues, hotels, and more, and I'm thinking . . . how does it feel for today's Native American men and women to see this celebration of such a dark chapter of history?

I guess what I kept telling my sisters, and I need to remember myself, is one thing: the winning team writes the history books. So remember to question everything.

Peace, Laurel

It feels so good to be off the train, breathing fresh mountain air and walking around Santa Fe. In some ways I can't believe we're still in America—it's so foreign. The buildings are Spanish-looking and exotic compared to the plain wood and brick buildings at home, the people are mostly Hispanic or Native American, and almost everyone—men and women—wears tons of awesome silver and turquoise jewelry. All around, the landscape's striped red and orange with a deep blue sky. And even the air smells different: spicy and piney and clear-smelling, somehow. So *not* like the thick salt and seaweed smells at home. We're staying at a small inn, and for once I'm not feeling like Goldilocks, with everything (and everyone) either too old or too young for me. Laurel, Root, Travis, and I did a self-guided tour of the chocolate shops of the city—yes, you read that right!—while his aunts rested and Gavin and the moms and Ladybug went off to a bug museum. (Something, I might add, that I was perfectly happy to miss.)

It was kind of cool having it be the four of us. . . . Root and Travis talked a lot about computer technology and sustainable agriculture (okay, in fairness, Travis talked a lot, and Root said "right on, man!" and "radical!" a whole bunch). And Laurel and I got to talk. It's been weird, since the Hair Disaster night we've been together a ton, obviously—we're all together every single day—but we've barely talked. Not about school or her fight with Mom and Mimi or any of it. Finally, though, while Root and Travis were in front of us babbling about transparent solar panels, I asked her.

"Hey, Lo-Lo? Are you . . . Did you . . . Is it definite? You know, not going back to school?" We were walking by some giant church, and Root had stopped to read the plaque.

Laurel shrugged a big, heavy shrug, and rolled her neck a few times, like she was exhausted. "I don't know. No, I haven't decided anything for sure. But I wasn't just saying it! I mean, I've been thinking about it for a while, you know?"

I didn't really know what to say, so I nodded.

"I guess . . . a lot of people talk big, about joining protests or getting arrested or whatever, but I don't want to be one of those people! I don't want to just *talk* about the change I want in the world. Sometimes I worry that people look at me and see just another white college kid who thinks she can carry a protest sign and make a difference." She looked at me. "So I wanted to do something serious, to show that I'm not just going through the motions, but that I'm really committed. Does that make any sense?"

I looked back at her. And let me tell you, Laurel looks amazing. She's got headbands that keep her spiky hair tamed flat, and around four different choker necklaces with different braids or pendants, and even with her sort of scary nose ring and tongue piercing, she looks *good—*

friendly and fun, with crinkly smiley eyes and freckles and a giant toothy grin. She's pretty too, though that's not really what you notice first. Mostly she looks real.

But she still feels like other people see her and think she's a fake.

I couldn't help it. I started laughing.

"What? What's your deal, wacko?" Laurel asked, but she started giggling. "Why are you laughing?"

So I told her all about the Reinvention Project and my list and that I'd been too embarrassed to tell her about it before because it felt so stupid compared to her wanting to change the world.

"Let me see the list," she said, stopping and holding out her hand.

"No way! It's too embarrassing," I said.

"Say-Say! Don't be such a chicken. I won't laugh," she said. Then she tilted her head. "Okay, I might laugh. But in a nice way."

I stuck out my tongue. "I don't even have it with me. Maybe later. Anyway, it doesn't really matter. About school . . ."

But she waved her hands like she was brushing off a fly. "I don't feel like talking about it. I'm letting it lie. Okay? I need to think on it awhile. Tell me something else. What's the news from home? How are Em and Vi?"

Hanging out with Laurel always leaves me thinking about something new. . . . We're surrounded by history and big ideas and LIFE, and I care about all of it, but at the same time I'm wondering if Em kind of likes this guy from the school play last year, and if the Moms will let me get a phone next year. Laurel pays as much attention when I'm blathering about this stuff as when we're talking about conquistadores and Hispanic culture and the status of native tribes. I love that about her.

Anyway, we're about to have dinner, which is apparently going to be a big Southwestern feast, and we're celebrating Gavin's birthday. The aunts have some sort of birthday surprise planned. Travis threw out a couple of ideas, but I sincerely hope he was joking. A gorilla jumping out of a cake? Ew. That sounds like a recipe for hair in the frosting, and there's no call for ruining a cake like that.

7:10 p.m.

Ah. Apparently they tried to do the gorilla jumping out of the cake two years ago. Miss Georgia wore the gorilla costume, and Miss Ruby wheeled in this ENORMOUS cake. But the corner of the cake table caught on the doorway and knocked the cake sideways, so Miss Georgia fell out, instead of popping out of the top. According to Travis she came out swearing like a sailor. He said he learned a bunch of new words that day.

Now I'm really nervous about dinner. Though Travis isn't too sure if it's going to be so wild this year. As we were walking back to the hotel, he started to look a little . . . not sad, but not his usual super-happy self. When I asked him what was up, he said, "Just fussing a little about Auntie G."

I didn't know what to say, because we hadn't ever talked about what I overheard on the train that night. Finally I said, "Is she . . . okay?"

And Travis grinned a sad echo of his usual giant smile. "She's dying. But we knew that. And this trip was planned so that she could have her last hurrah, and so far I think she's been having it. But now she seems a little . . . less. Less alert, less silly, less interested in doing much other than sleeping."

"Do you think—" I started to say, but Travis kept talking.

"She says she's saving her energy for the Grand Canyon. And of course tonight she and Auntie Ruby have some shenanigans and tomfoolery pulled together for Dad. Not sure what it'll be, but apparently the hotel's providing a karaoke machine."

I looked at him, and he looked back, and we both started laughing, kind of quiet at first, but then Travis did his TEEHEEHEEHEEHEE thing, and we were both hysterical.

Finally he wiped his eyes and started walking again. "Let's get to it, Rae, old girl. Karaoke waits for no one!"

I didn't get a chance to tell him how sorry I was that Miss Georgia's sick. But hopefully he knows.

Well, that was something! Who would have thought that Miss Ruby and Miss Georgia would know all the words to Beyoncé's "Single Ladies," let alone the choreographed dance moves.

Let me back up. I suppose without explaining, that probably sounds weird. Well, it *was* weird, but still. The birthday dinner was amazing, though Root spent a fair bit of time poking at the black beans and tomatillos and empanadas, saying things like, "Do you suppose there's bacon in this?" and "Does anyone else smell lard?"

But the rest of us had a serious feast. It makes me feel a little bad for the Mexican restaurant in Shipton. Apparently small oceanside towns near Boston aren't really the last word in Mexican or Southwestern food. As Laurel said, the difference between what we were eating and the restaurant at home is like the difference between a New England clambake on the beach and a McDonald's Filet-O-Fish. Anyway, when we were all stuffed and happy, and when Gavin was drinking one of several fancy drinks with fruit and umbrellas in them while making sappy toasts to his family and to all of us, Miss Georgia and Miss Ruby disappeared. Then they came back with a massive dish that was on fire—apparently some kind of flaming fried ice cream specialty—*and* the karaoke machine and the giant Elvis.

GAVIN:

I am so blessed. So blessed to be surrounded by the youth of today, who will
make the world better tomorrow, and my
dear aunts, who have already— WHAT THE
HEY???

MISS GEORGIA:

Hold 'er steady, Rube! That nearly took
off my eyebrow!

MISS RUBY:

Someone hit play! We're approaching melt-
down! It's about to be Chernobyl around
here!

What followed was an Elvis version of "Happy Birthday," sung into the karaoke machine as a duet, with lots
of elbows and hissed whispers about sharing the mic.
Then Gavin blew out the burning ice cream and we all ate
(well, all except for Ladybug, who had a special dish of
mango sorbet instead). *Then* "Single Ladies" happened.
Apparently it was intended as a kind of surprise birthday encore, and it was pretty fabulous, though at the end
one of the fringed sleeves of Miss Ruby's outfit landed in
Root's leftover ice cream. Still, I was impressed. We all
cheered and whooped and hollered. Then Laurel got up
and sang Janis Joplin's "Me and Bobby McGee," and Tra-

vis sang some kind of country-western-rap thing that was pretty impressive. They tried to get me up there to sing, but there was no way. I'm not up for that Olympic level of embarrassment. Now Ladybug's in bed, and Travis and I are going outside to try to see some meteor shower that always happens this time of year. We'll see.

For the record, if that sounds kind of romantic and ooooooh-maybe-it's-a-date, NO. No it is not. I really like Travis, and he's pretty much the first boy who's a friend. But there's no butterfly-ish feeling in my stomach, no nervous sweaty hands, no nothing. So now I know . . . this is what it feels like *not* to have a crush on a boy. Good to realize.

1:00 a.m.

I don't . . . I'm not sure where to start. Miss Georgia's been taken to the hospital.

Gavin and Miss Ruby went with her. Gavin tried to get Miss Ruby to stay behind with Travis, and Miss Ruby nearly stomped right over him and climbed into the ambulance. Then the driver tried to tell her to follow in the police car, and she told him to shut his mouth because he'd have to knock her out or handcuff her to get her gone. Really, in those words.

And the worst part is that we nearly weren't back for it. The meteor shower was amazing, not that it matters now, but we must have seen twenty shooting stars, and we kept sitting out there, talking and talking (yes, mostly Travis but me too), about everything . . . about our parents and our friends and what we want to do when we grow up and space and the planet and . . . seriously, everything. And it was after midnight when we finally realized we were freezing and so tired, and started walking back to the hotel. There were tons of lights and sirens, and we were still half a block away when we started to run. My first thought was that my moms had called the cops when I hadn't come home, but I realized that was stupid, they would have come looking for us first, and we were in the park around the corner. My next thought was Ladybug and allergies, which is when I really started to run.

It sounds horrible . . . it IS horrible . . . but I actually had a moment of such relief when I saw Ladybug in Mom's arms and the stretcher with Miss Georgia. I think I am not a good person.

While I was staring at Ladybug, Travis gave a kind of croak and ran over to Miss Georgia.

She took his hand and held tight. "Travis-man, don't you start. This might be a fire drill, right? And we've practiced for these fire drills. You know what to do."

Travis nodded, and he wasn't crying or anything, but it's the only time I've seen his face without even the tiniest bit of a smile.

"You sure? You don't look like you know your own name. And that's not going to work, right?" Miss Georgia said, not letting go, even while they were wheeling her toward the ambulance and trying to get an oxygen mask on her. She batted it away with her other hand, looking annoyed. "For Lord's sake, let me talk to my boy. I'm not dying this minute."

"I'm sure. You don't have to worry," Travis said. He kept walking alongside her, and finally managed a half smile. "My name is Travis Walker Alexander. I'm not going to forget it, and I'm not going to forget our plan. But how about you get yourself fixed up and come right on back, and we can save that plan for later, all right?"

Miss Georgia let go of his hand as they loaded her in. "I'll see what I can do. But, Trav?"

He ran up to the ambulance and stuck his head in. I couldn't hear what she said, but his half smile fell right off. But he nodded. "Yes, ma'am. I know." Then he paused. "I love you, Auntie G. Love you so much."

Then they slammed the doors and took off, sirens blaring.

Now Travis is alone in the room he shares with his dad, and Mom and Mimi are trying to get Ladybug back to sleep. I wish I knew what was happening. Or maybe I don't. Maybe if I don't know, I can pretend for a few more minutes that everything is still as awesome as it was under the shooting stars.

Chapter 21

If I were the superstitious sort, I would say that we tempted the gods with our laughter and joy yesterday. But of course I'm not, and I don't really think any gods worth their pedestals would smite people for snort-laughing over bad karaoke. But it is a fundamental truth of this world that trouble can come at any time, that the wolf is always outside the door, whether we are worried and vigilant, or relaxed and joyful. And when disaster strikes while traveling, it can be doubly challenging if you are not well prepared. Last night Grammy One went to the hospital. She may not come out. Apparently she has been battling cancer, and this trip took place with the knowledge that she was not going to be getting better.

Watching Grammy Two standing with her friend as the ambulance came, watching Cowboy Jr. try to keep his gorgeous smiling face cheerful for his family . . . well, it is enough to break my heart. All we can do for these lovely new friends, for these used-to-be-strangers, is to offer a hug, a listening ear, a shoulder to cry on.

Having said all this, one gift that traveling offers is a chance to see the kindness of strangers unfold in front of your eyes. People who were unknown to us mere days ago become friends, willing to do what they can to help in times of crisis. From innkeepers to fellow travelers, people offer their time, their money, and even just their sympathetic shoulders. It is moments like these that make us realize that, in spite of it all, we are blessed.

Mom and I just left the hospital, where Travis and Gavin and Miss Ruby are taking turns clustering around Miss Georgia's bed, and we stood around the waiting room, awkward and fidgeting and useless. It sounds like I'm complaining, but I'm not, not really. I wanted to go to the hospital, actually, and made Mom take me while Mimi took Ladybug off to some playground. But once we got there, I realized there is literally not one single thing I can do to help. Still, Travis and I went down to the cafeteria for a bit, and at least I got to see him. He seemed . . . okay. Ish. I mean, he seemed worried, sure, but still himself. Luckily, he can still talk as much as ever. I wasn't sure what the heck to say, or if I should ask questions, or what, but he chatted on, like usual.

"So what's going on?" I asked finally. "Do the doctors . . . I mean, is there any . . . news?"

Travis shook his head. "She's failing. That's what the doctors are saying."

We both sat there, staring at the ugly plastic cafeteria table.

"I hate that!" he said suddenly.

"What?" I looked around.

"That word. 'Failing.' Like, you know, she's flunking kidneys or liver or something, and if she'd only tried *harder*, she could get a passing grade. Like, gee, is there some extra-credit work a ninety-year-old can do? Can she retake a midterm or go back to her twenties and drink more milk?"

I was kind of confused, but I tried to keep up. "I'm sure they don't mean it's her fault," I said. "It's just the word they use."

"I know," Travis said, his voice quiet again. "But I don't like it. Sounds like she should work harder, when one thing about Auntie G is that she always—ALWAYS—worked as hard as she could. That's probably half the problem. She's like a car with a hundred-and-fifty-thousand-mile warranty that's already gone to two hundred thousand."

I nodded. It was a little hard to follow what with him going from failed midterms to car warranties, but I figured it was better to agree with him. Then he leaned back and changed the subject.

"So that meteor shower was pretty awesome, didn't you think?" he asked after a minute. "I mean, the Texas sky can get pretty, but that was something else. You seen anything like that before?"

I shook my head. "Not even close! I've only seen three

shooting stars in my entire life, and I've spent, like, *hours* staring up at the sky. My friend Em has shooting star luck. She always sees them. She's made around a hundred wishes."

Travis did his TEEHEE laugh, but it was kind of tired-sounding. "Girl, you know they're not stars, right? We're talking about astral debris, up there. You know . . . sky garbage! You're wishing on sky garbage."

"Shut up, dream killer," I said, and pretended to look mad, shoving him a little, to make him laugh some more. "I don't need that kind of negativity."

He TEEHEEHEEed a little louder, which made me laugh too. Then he crumpled up a napkin and arced it toward the nearby garbage can. "Make a wish!" he said. "Go on! Magic garbage flying by!"

"You'd need to light it on fire for it to work," I said.

Then his laughter ended kind of fast, and he gave a big sigh. "You know, Rae, I'll tell you a secret. I know there's nothing magic about those meteors. And all that super-stition about wishing on a shooting star is a load of ma-nure. But when we got back to the hotel, and all those red lights were flashing . . . well."

He stopped then, but I nodded. I knew what he meant. Because for that second when I had thought it was Lady-bug, I'd had an immediate feeling that if I had just paid more attention, wished on every star and eyelash and birthday candle, I might have been able to stop it.

"I'll look for another one tonight and make a wish, just in case. Can't hurt, right?" I said.

He shrugged, looking lost. "I suppose. Can't hurt."

Now my family's all back at the hotel, resting, since no one got any sleep last night. I'm going to try to nap, so that tonight I can go out on the hotel porch and look for more shooting stars. If I see one, I know what I'll wish for.

9:00 p.m.

Another night in Santa Fe, even though we were supposed to get back on the train today to head toward the Grand Canyon. Gavin and Mom were on the phone for a while, and Mom kept saying "I *know* we can leave if we want to. We don't want to. Not yet anyway. Let's see what tomorrow brings."

Finally Gavin said thank you and that since we were staying, he'd be bringing Travis back to the inn for the night. He and Miss Ruby were going to stay close. In case.

I can't quite put a name on what I feel right now. Dread is part of it. Dread of the "in case," which I know is in case Miss Georgia dies. But I also feel . . . I don't know. Weightless? Like I don't really have roots or an anchor? I feel like those tumbleweed plants that roll for miles and miles across the desert because there's nothing to hold them in place. And weirdly, I also feel guilty, not like it's

my fault that Miss Georgia's in the hospital, but like . . .
our family is still together, still healthy, still heading off
to the Grand Canyon and on to California, and Travis's
whole world is turned upside down. It's not fair. (And I
know, I know . . . life's not fair! I don't even need Laurel
to tell me that!)

For now we're hanging around Santa Fe. Tomorrow
Ladybug wants to go back to the bug museum, and Mimi
said she'd bring her. Maybe I'll go along. Take a few photos of Bruce and the bugs. Ladybug would love that. And
honestly? I don't know what else to do.

Chapter 22

We're back on the train, heading to Williams, Arizona, where we'll spend the night before heading out in the morning for the Grand Canyon. We stayed two extra days in Santa Fe, but nothing changed with Miss Georgia, and finally Mom and Mimi decided we had to keep going. Saying goodbye to Gavin and Travis and Miss Ruby was one of the hardest things I've ever done. I mean, we might see them in a few days, but . . . we might not.

We might never see them again.

Gavin promised to call when things change, which, if I'm being honest, means when Miss Georgia dies. Because she's dying. Right now. The doctors say there's nothing more to be done, and that since she refused "extraordinary measures" to keep her alive, like feeding tubes and stuff, it's just a matter of time.

She's alive now, but soon she won't be. And with all the science and computer stuff, with all the shooting stars and giant Elvis cutouts, with all the fierce love that Travis and Miss Ruby are throwing at her . . . even with all of that, nothing's going to make a difference.

It's almost sunset, and the sky over the desert is crazy beautiful—all ultra-bright orange and hot pink and even purple in wiggles and zigzags across the sky. It's ridiculously gorgeous . . . the kind of thing you'd see on a poster or something. And it's right outside the window, flying by us as we whip along the mesas and canyons. We just had dinner in the dining car, and it's fancy here, with flowers on the table and cloth napkins. And I never would have thought I'd write this, but with only the six of us it seemed . . . *quiet*. I'm sure people were still staring. . . . Laurel got a tortilla stuck under her tongue stud and had to remove it, and Mimi decided it was a good night to sing "Johnny Appleseed," a kind of grace-type prayer before the meal that has lots of clapping, because she thought we needed cheering up.

But without Miss Georgia and Miss Ruby fighting over the bread basket, and Travis TEEHEEHEEHEEing at everything, and Gavin and Mom talking some kind of random legal patent stuff . . . well, yeah. It feels too quiet. Funny how fast things can change, then change again.

10:00 p.m.

We're at the hotel in Williams, and there was a message waiting for us. I guess Mom and Mimi's phones didn't get a signal on the train. Miss Georgia never woke up. She died this afternoon, just a few hours after we left. She's gone.

239

Root, we're not angry. Not at all. In fact, it's rather... heartwarming...to know you would take such pains to keep Ladybug safe. But since the "villain" in this instance was an actor who's hired by the train to perform a pretend train robbery, you understand how surprised and upset he was to be incapacitated—without injury! You did an excellent job!—by you and your jujitsu hold. It was a pretty impressive hold, by the way. I had no idea you were capable of such things.

In any event, we've talked to the head of rail security and the station master, and there will not be charges pressed. In fact, there was even a brief discussion of getting you a costume and having you disarm the "villain" on the train, maybe even rescuing the "helpless maiden" who he'd take captive. However, Carol made it clear that will NOT be happening.

All this to say, thank you for looking out for Ladybug, but maybe in the future, talk to the police before taking action. After all, there were three security guards very nearby, as we quickly found out.

Love,
Mimi

Chapter 23

LIFE IN THE GREEN LANE

THE GRAND CANYON: Land of literal and cultural vertigo! Look one way, and there are hundreds and hundreds of tourists, each holding up a camera, a phone, or both, some sporting sweatshirts with questionable political values, some clearly from other nations. Some of them step off their tour buses into the oven-like heat (think hair dryer set on high blowing straight at you), take a photo, and then climb right back into the air-conditioning. Look the other way and . . . gods and goddesses, heroes and mortals all fall on their knees in amazement! Blazing red rock, endless ripples and rows of cliffs extending into the distance, a drop thousands of feet to green-blue river water below. . . . It is beauty so wild and enormous, it slaps you across the face.

It's easy to trash the Grand Canyon as a cliché: mobbed with tourists and souvenir stands. But that's too easy. Because the glory of this spot can't be ignored, and this is our country, in all its outrageous beauty.

Nothing's quite as simple and obvious as it seems. Are these horrible tourist buses despoiling the earth? What if these tourists go home, touched by what they've seen, and pledge to make the natural world a little safer, keep it a little cleaner?

There's a special Grand Canyon train that brings people here, with an old-fashioned steam engine and people dressed in costumes talking about the history of the land. As our train approached the Grand Canyon, a fiddler and guitar player (both hired by the train to provide "authentic Western music") played in the observation car. And again, it would have been easy to roll my eyes and sigh that once again crass commercialism was taking over. But then they played the old folk song "This Land Is Your Land."

You know the one:

This land is your land
This land is my land
From California to the New York island
From the redwood forests to the Gulf Stream waters
This land was made for you and me

And as they played, people joined in. Americans of course who know this song from their summer camps or Boy Scout jamborees, but also Japanese, French, and Argentinian tourists who, somehow, knew the words. As we sang, I looked over at Root, and tears were streaming down his face. Out the window the landscape flew by, more intense by the minute. Inside, human beings from all around this crazy planet shared their amazement at the sight, and sang.

Peace, Laurel

• • • • •

Fun Fact!

The Grand Canyon is 277 miles long, 18 miles wide at the widest point, and 6,000 feet deep at the deepest point.

Fun Fact!

The Grand Canyon is over six million years old, though newer controversial studies suggest that this estimate may be off by more than sixty million years, and that the canyon may have formed over 70 million years ago. (Okay, that is a heck of a miss. I mean . . . sure, it's old and all, and I could see being off by a few thousand years. But 70 million? I feel better about my last math test.)

Not-So-Fun Fact!

Of the 4.5 million people who visit the Grand Canyon each year, around twelve people die here. Deaths are from natural causes, medical issues, suicide, drowning, and traffic crashes. Usually two or three deaths per year are from falls into the canyon.

August 24–9:00 p.m.

Well, we're finally here, and without the NTFs. The Grand Canyon was the place Miss Georgia was most excited to see. On the train she kept saying she'd wanted to see it her whole life, and now she was on her way, thanks to her best friend, the most wonderful person in the world. And Miss Ruby would always say it would be a darn shame if someone knocked Miss Georgia right into the canyon for being such a fool, and Miss Georgia would say that she'd grab hold and drag Miss Ruby down with her, and they'd laugh and laugh.

Funny how a few weeks ago I would have been so relieved to get rid of them. And now all I can think about is how Miss Georgia and Miss Ruby would have loved posing Elvis on the Skywalk, and how Travis would have been all fired up to see the view. It's still amazing, of course. I mean, how could it not be? As Laurel said, after we got off the train and stared for a few minutes, barely able to talk, "Well, now I get what all the fuss is about."

And I know what she means. Of course I've heard about the Grand Canyon, and seen photos. But I had no idea.

How can I describe it?

Well, if I were doing a writing exercise and needed to put in as many details as possible, I guess I'd describe the swoops and spikes of the rock walls, the way they're all striped in these even horizontal designs of red and brown and orange that almost look painted on. There are so many layers of cliffs and rocks that they go on and on and on to this incredibly faraway horizon, like some kind of exercise in depth perception. And the farther away these cliffs are, the more the colors change, from orange and red and brown to pink and purple and gray. And the sky is a deep dark blue—somehow way more *blue* than an everyday blue sky at home.

But I'm not sure how well this really describes it.

Mostly I want to stare. I can barely make myself blink. We're spending two nights in a lodge right by the rim of the canyon. Even when we're inside, the view is there, demanding that we keep looking. Ladybug just said, "Mom, close the curtains. The Grand Canyon is staring at me."

And she's right. I can barely read my book—it's too hard to concentrate.

I can't help wondering how Travis and Miss Ruby and Gavin are doing. Or where they are. Last Mimi heard from them, they were trying to make decisions about "the remains" and figuring what to do next . . . whether to return home to Texas or keep going to California.

Ugh. Miss Georgia should not be "remains"—I hate that.

• • • • •

TO: EmilyGirl
FROM: SaraJF
SUBJECT: Re: Hellooo?

Hey, Em—

Sorry it's taken so long to write back. I did get your email when we were in Santa Fe, but things got a little hectic. Remember the two old women who were part of our train travel group? Well, one of them was really sick and had to go to the hospital a few days ago, while we were still in Santa Fe. And we just found out she died. It feels so awful, Em, and I didn't even know her that well. I can't help thinking about Travis, who must be heartbroken. Anyway, would you believe I miss them? Wouldn't have thought so, but I do.

I'm attaching the photos we took of the Grand Canyon at sunset. I know it looks like some picture off a calendar in the science room, but IT ACTU-ALLY LOOKS LIKE THAT. No, seriously, this place is amazing. It doesn't even seem real. It's so gorgeous, it's hard to do anything but stare, swiveling my head around. (Not all the way around like an owl. Not that owls can actually spin their heads *all* the way. It only looks that way. ANYWAY.)

Thanks for sending pics of your hair. . . . It looks So. Good! Never knew pink could look so fierce! Is Vi still being a wimp? I totally wouldn't have thought she'd be the scaredy-cat. And you and Vi are insane, by the way. I do NOT look like a model with my short hair and scarf. I look like someone who's trying to hide the fact that her ear is *still* pale blue! Honestly, at this point I'm hoping it'll be gone by school.

But in answer to your question, I haven't really looked at my Reinvention Project list in a while. I've read a bunch of nonfiction, and have been doing yoga most mornings . . . though I'm not sure I've developed much calm or mindfulness. But I can touch my toes, so that's something.

Anyway, I miss you so, so much. It seems like a million years since we were hanging out together. I can't wait to see you guys. But in a weird way I don't want the trip to end. Strange, I know.

XOXOX Sara

P.S. I'm giving up on "Rae." The only person who remembered to call me that was Travis, and honestly, it felt stupid. If I ever see him again, I'll tell him to call me Sara.

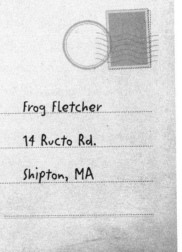

DEAR FROG! THE GRAND CANYON IS REALLY BIG! AND REALLY HOT! AND REALLY PRETTY! THERE ARE LOTS OF PEOPLE HERE AND GUESS WHAT? I TOOK PICTURES OF BRUCE WITH SOMEONE FROM THE HOPI, NAVAJO, AND HAVA-SUPAI TRIBES! ALSO BRUCE AND I RODE A BABY HORSE BUT I GOT ALLERGIC. BUT I LOVE IT HERE!!!!!!!!!!!!!!!!!!!!!!!!!!!!!!
LOVE, LADYBUG

Frog Fletcher

14 Ructo Rd.

Shipton, MA

When I was a kid in Toronto, I wanted a few very specific things. I wanted a hoopskirt (blame my love of Louisa May Alcott books), I wanted to swim with dolphins (checked that one off at a somewhat sketchy resort in Florida a few years ago), and . . . I wanted to see the Grand Canyon.

I can't explain why the Grand Canyon was such an obsession. I had seen a photo of it in a book on the Wonders of the World, and for some reason, I was hooked. More than the Pyramids, more than Niagara Falls, I was dazzled by the image of red rock and blazing cliffs. And unlike the Pyramids, or far-off exotic vistas on South Pacific islands, the Grand Canyon is relatively easy for a North American to visit. But I never quite got there.

Now, after almost a month of cross-country train travel, I am standing here with my beloved family. And honestly, it is beautiful, majestic, and truly awe-inspiring. I no longer want a hoopskirt, and I am happy to admire dolphins from afar, but I am deeply satisfied to be able to see the Grand Canyon.

At the risk of having my dream stomped on by a bunch of six-, twelve-, and twenty-year-old feet, I thought it would be worth it to ask each of my traveling companions to offer a sentence or two of their perspective.

Superwoman: I visited the Grand Canyon as a very young child, and have always kept a vision of it in my mind. Coming back forty years later, I was ready to be disappointed, and to find it smaller, diminished. Instead it is more awe-inspiring and mind-blowing than ever. I am grateful—so few childhood memories live up to present day, but this one did.

The Activist: What can I say? It's radical. I expected the crowds and the commercialism, but I didn't expect this level of amazing gorgeousness. Everything else kind of falls away when you stare out at it.

Tree: It's a beautiful world, man. Let's hope we can keep it alive. Because it would be a real shame to lose it.

Animal Planet: I LOVE THE GRAND CANYON!!! IT IS MY FAVORITE PART AND I GOT TO RIDE A BABY HORSE BUT I THREW UP BUT I STILL LOVE IT! (Note: it was a mule. And that was very unfortunate. But the mule driver was a really good sport.)

The Scribe: I don't really know how to describe the Grand Canyon. . . . It seems like most words are kind of weak in comparison with the real thing. But one thing I know is that I'm glad I've seen it. Standing next to the ocean at home, I think I'll always have a bigger appreciation for this country now that I've seen this side of it too.

> MIMI: Sara commented! Insightfully! And without sarcasm! Do I thank her? Pretend I didn't notice?? Hard to know how to play this one. . . .

Mimi got an email from Gavin saying they're coming to the Grand Canyon tomorrow. Apparently Miss Georgia had made it her dying wish that they continue the trip . . . with Elvis.

I'm really glad. It's been weird being here without them. And I totally wished Travis had been there today. I saw someone who—for real—could have been Rupert Presley, Elvis's long-lost herpetologist brother. Velour jumpsuit, snake tattoo, and big sunglasses. Oh, and sideburns. I tried to get a picture, but let's just say Ladybug's explosive reaction to the mule distracted me.

Chapter 24

Hey, Rae,

I guess I got in the habit of writing from being around you, so I figured I'd write, even if I'll hand it to you tomorrow. Crazy, I know.

Anyway, we're back on the road. We rented a car and drove from Santa Fe yesterday, heading toward the Grand Canyon. It feels weird to be in a car, and weird to be without Auntie G. (Well, we have her ashes with us, so I guess in a sense she's still here, but that's hardly the same. Actually it's downright creepy if I think about it.)

Aunt Ruby mostly slept in the backseat—she stayed at the hospital the whole time with Auntie G, and she looked dog tired. She got into that seat, put Elvis in her lap, used her purse as a pillow, and was snoring like an industrial fan before we hit the interstate. So it was just me and Dad. Which was good. We talked a lot, about the aunties, and about dying, but not in an awful way. We talked about what made a good death, and we agreed that for Auntie G, being with all of us, having this train adventure almost across the whole country, holding Aunt Ruby's hand, and going quick in the end...well, that's a good one. Wish she could have seen the Grand Canyon, though. Sure do.

We're going to be there soon, though it'll be late and I don't think we'll see y'all tonight. But I'll see you tomorrow, and it's weird, how good it'll be to see you all, and hear what you've been up to, and sort of get back to normal. Funny that normal is hanging out with someone I just met, but there you have it. Normal's a little different these days.

Love,

Trav

GOOD MORNING! You may not believe it, but we all slept EIGHT HOURS. Do you know what this means? It means we have all learned to sleep through Mimi's bullfrog imitation! This trip has been a true success based on that alone! In other news, Gavin and the rest of them arrived quite late last night and are planning to meet us at breakfast. Mimi and I have gone out for a walk and will see you there. Can someone please remind Ladybug that she should AVOID ALL MULES if you guys go outside before breakfast? Let's not have another "incident," shall we?

Love, Mom

August 25–3:00 p.m.

Whew . . . it gets seriously hot here. We're inside now, taking our siesta, which really just means getting the heck out of that blazing sun for a little while. Poor Root . . . he dropped his huge hat and it blew away, and now he's kind of a blotchy pink-and-red. Laurel's trying to convince him that her organic sunscreen isn't going to hurt him, but he's not buying it.

Meanwhile I spent the whole day with Travis. I saw

him as soon as I got up—we were actually the only two at the breakfast table. By the time I got down there, everyone else had headed out. At first I was a little embarrassed. . . . I wasn't sure if Travis would be different. What if he was crying? I mean, Saanvi cried a *ton* when her dog got hit by a car. (It was AWFUL. . . . I cried too, but nothing like Vi. She had to stay home for two days.) Anyway, I would hug her and pat her back and sit with her, but with a boy it's different.

But Travis was the same as before, with his way-too-big smile and way-too-big cowboy hat, and before long he was laughing at my stories about Root trying to apprehend the guy dressed up like a train robber. But his laugh is more teeheeheeheehee, not TEEHEEHEEHEEHEE.

After breakfast we went out hiking, and he told me what had happened with Miss Georgia. It was easier to talk about while we were moving somehow—the trail was narrow, and we had to walk in a line, taking turns in front.

I asked him if it had been awful, and he paused, then shook his head.

"It wasn't awful, not really." He started walking again. "I mean, it was in some ways. It was awful at first, when the doctors were all up in a frenzy, trying this and that to help her, and Aunt Ruby was losing her darn mind, swearing at everyone and ordering them around. That was pretty bad."

I nodded, and wished he was a friend like Vi, because I would have hugged him. Because honestly, it sounded more than "pretty bad" to me.

"But once they realized they weren't going to save her, it actually got a little better. I mean, everything calmed down, you know? Does that sound weird?"

I shook my head, slowing a little to check out a particularly funky-shaped cactus. "Not really. It's like . . . maybe this is a stupid comparison, but you know when you need to get a shot? And you get really freaked out and panicked and you have a hard time taking a deep breath and stuff, even an hour before you're going to the appointment? And then, when you finally get the shot, sure, it hurts, but it's *nowhere* near as bad as the freakout before. Is it like that?"

"Exactly!" he said, stopping so fast, I bumped into him. "That's exactly it. I was dreading and dreading hearing that this was it, that she was going. Heck, I've been dreading it for months now. And once they said there was nothing more to do but make her comfortable and make sure she had what she wanted . . . well, it was bad, but kind of better too." He nodded a few times, looking a little relieved. "Glad you got that. I felt sort of awful for feeling that way, but I think I was just glad the dread part was getting to be gone."

"Yeah, I totally get it," I said, and it felt really good to see his giant smile appear again.

He also told me something that is part really cool and part really freaky: they had Miss Georgia cremated, and brought her ashes here. Their plan is to release them over the canyon at sunrise tomorrow.

"Are you allowed to do that?" I asked. "I mean, can you just fling someone's ashes anywhere, or do you need . . . I don't know, a permit or something?"

Travis shrugged. "No idea. Don't plan to ask. Aunt Georgia always used to say it's better to ask forgiveness than to ask permission. I figure this is one of those times."

We walked in silence for a minute while I thought about this. It was an interesting motto. I bet Laurel would approve, though the moms probably not so much.

As though he were reading my mind, Travis asked, "So what's going on with Laurel and your moms? Any more fireworks, or what?"

I thought for a minute. The fact was, they hadn't fought since Santa Fe, since Gavin's birthday and Miss Georgia and everything. And last night in our room, while Root and Ladybug played their five trillionth game of cards, Laurel curled up with her feet in Mom's lap, the way she used to. (Also . . . Root. I mean, seriously, he is a really good guy. How many people would be willing to play that many games of cards with a cheating six-year-old?)

"They're okay, I guess," I said finally. "Laurel and I talked some in Santa Fe, and she's still not sure what she wants to do. I mean . . . she's actually not sure she even *wants* to leave school. But I don't think she's told them that. Basically everyone's been pretty quiet for a few days, which is good. Laurel said she needs space to get her 'head together.'"

Travis stopped to get a rock out of his shoe, and we both stood to the side, letting a group of very fit-looking Canadian hikers blow past us. He looked at me. "What does she really want, do you think?" he asked.

I stared out at the view, which looked like it could be on the cover of *National Geographic,* then down to the rest area ahead, which was mobbed with people, then to the trail under our feet, where someone's crumpled candy wrapper lay on the path.

Bending down, I picked up the wrapper and shoved it into my back pocket. "I think she really just wants to do something that matters, you know?"

Travis nodded. "I get that," he said. "But after this past week, when Dad had to make calls and let everyone know about Auntie Georgia, I wonder what that even means. Back home, when they heard about Auntie, literally more than a hundred people called us, asking when we'd be having a service, sending us memories and pictures and stuff. So what really matters? I mean, Auntie G never did anything most people would consider important. She was a receptionist for a car dealership for ages, but nobody says that would change the world. But . . . it did. She helped grow that business and she was friends with everyone there and she helped people buy their first cars, and in some cases she helped them keep their cars when they were short on cash. She knew everything about everyone who walked in there, and if anyone needed anything, she knew about it before they walked out." He stopped talking for a minute, and we walked in silence.

"Anyway, I can't picture a world where Laurel wouldn't make some kind of difference," he said, and I nodded.

He was right. Miss Georgia and Laurel were alike in that way—no matter what they did, they'd make the world better.

By the time the others met up with us, we had stopped talking about Miss Georgia, Laurel, or saving the world, and instead were laughing (though not rudely . . . we were quiet. Ish.) at the different tourists who were coming down on mules. Anyway, we stopped when I was about to point at someone who wound up being Root, and eventually we all climbed onto the mules they had arranged and went back to the top. All except for Ladybug, who hiked back with Mom on an easier path due to the whole mule allergy issue. I will say, the swears Miss Ruby fired off while riding that mule are really going to stay with me. I had no idea there even *were* so many words for that particular body part. Wow.

DEAR FROG! I HIKED INTO THE CANYON
TODAY AND IT WAS VERY VERY VERY
HOT. I GOT TOO HOT TO WALK AND
MOM CARRIED ME AND SHE WAS
REALLY MAD. BUT I BROUGHT BRUCE
AND TOOK LOTS OF PICTURES!!!!!!!!!!!
LOVE, LADYBUG!!
    I didn't get mad, I was just
tired...never mind. —Carol

Frog Fletcher

14 Ructo Rd.

Shipton, MA

Wow. That was amazing. And horrible. And beautiful. And . . . wow.

We just came back from the "memorial" for Miss Georgia, though it wasn't like any funeral I could imagine. For one thing, Elvis Presley was there, at least for part of it.

But I'm getting ahead of myself.

Mimi woke us at 5:00 a.m.—apparently the fact that it's summer means that the sun rises over the Grand Canyon REALLY FREAKING EARLY. Anyway, I got up right away. . . . Honestly, I'd been awake half the night, it felt like, thinking about life back home and about how easy it is to hang out with Travis and about Miss Georgia.

Three weeks ago I had never met her; five days ago we were laughing while she and Miss Ruby sang karaoke . . . and now she's gone.

When we got outside, the sky was still mostly blue-black, and there were stars . . . wild numbers of stars. But in the east the light was starting, and there was the deepest purple not-black color creeping up the canyon. Laurel and Root came out, yawning (Root was still wearing his Cat in the Hat pajama bottoms . . . honestly, I have no words), and we headed over to the canyon's edge to meet up with Travis and his family. By the time we got there, it was already a little bit brighter.

They were all clustered as far east as it's possible to be, near an edge that, if I look right over it, makes my head spin. It dropped straight down the cliff face, into blackness that I knew would turn to shades of red and gold as the sun got higher.

Miss Ruby had the cutout Elvis with her, which made me do a double take—at first I thought it might be a park ranger or something. But no, it was only Elvis.

Once we were all there, Gavin started to speak. He didn't say a lot, not like a big preaching thing. He talked about how Miss Georgia had helped raise him, how she and Miss Ruby had been a part of his life for so long, he wasn't quite sure he'd be able to stop talking to her, but that he had every confidence that she would still be listening, wherever she was.

Then Travis said a few things, mostly about how much he was going to miss her. Then—and this will probably sound dumb, but it was really beautiful—Miss Ruby sang. She didn't sing a church song or anything; she sang Elvis Presley's "Love Me Tender," and she sang it really slow and sweet. When she was done, we wiped our eyes (we were all crying at this point). Then Gavin took the lid off this jar he was holding, and spread his arm out in a giant arc, spreading ashes as far over the edge as he could.

The sun had been rising, and by now it was more light than dark, with crazy, touched-by-God rays of sunlight starting to break over the canyon in pink and gold stripes. The ashes caught the light as they fell, and honestly it looked like magic.

That was when Miss Ruby said, "I think she'll want company. It's time." And took a step closer to the edge.

Gavin roared, "NOOOO!" and rushed toward her, Travis right behind him.

But before I could even figure out what was happening, she took Elvis and flung him right over the side, right after Miss Georgia's ashes. He went pinwheeling, feet over head over feet, out of sight.

Gavin and Travis froze on either side of her, and Miss Ruby laughed. "Did you think I'd do that to you boys? What kind of a devil do you think I am, anyway?"

Gavin snorted, then started to laugh, then did a full-on belly laugh, with Travis TEEHEEHEEHEEHEEHEEing along with him. At first I was too shell-shocked to laugh, but it was contagious, and before long we were all cracking up, literally slapping our knees and laughing our heads off. Laurel had to sit down, she was laughing so hard.

Then Ladybug moved forward, I guess to take yet another picture of Bruce, and there was a horrible scream.

"NOOOOOOOOOOOOOOOOOOOOOOOOOOO!" she shrieked, so loud that I thought my heart would stop.

I thought she'd fallen.

I honestly thought, for one horrible, terrible moment, that she was gone.

But she was right there.

She was fine.

Bruce wasn't, though.

Ladybug had dropped Bruce, and the camera with *all* the photos, right over the edge.

Chapter 25

DEAR FROG BRUCE IS GONE. I WANTED TO TAKE ONE LAST PICTURE WITH HIM AND MISS GEORGIA, EVEN THOUGH MISS GEORGIA IS NOW ASHES. BUT I DROPPED HIM AND MY CAMERA AND HE IS GONE FOREVER. MY HEART IS BROKEN. LOVE, LADYBUG

Frog Fletcher

14 Ructo Rd.

Shipton, MA

10:00 a.m.

I don't even know what to say. I mean, I feel horrible for Ladybug, who is absolutely devastated. But at the same time . . . we were all still wiping our eyes after Miss Ruby sang, and then cracking up after Elvis went over, then the totally disgustingly scary horror of thinking Ladybug *had fallen* . . . and then BRUCE?! As Gavin muttered under his breath, "Oh, Georgie would have loved all this."

Ladybug was inconsolable. She sobbed in Mimi's arms,

totally desolate. I had mostly stopped crying after Miss Ruby's song, but I started up again, hearing Ladybug so upset. She kept wailing over and over, "But I love Bruce! I love him! He can't be gone! I love him and he's gone!"

And of course I—and probably everyone else—was thinking about Miss Georgia, and how she was gone too, even though people loved her so.

After we got back to the hotel, Root went to take a walk, and Mom and Mimi went off to talk to the rangers. Ladybug curled up in my lap, sniffling into my neck.

"Why do things leave, Say? Why do they go away when we love them?" She burrowed in and her tears tickled my shoulder.

And it's so bad—I can't help but cry when I'm with someone who's crying, so of course my eyes kept spilling over too. But all I could do was pat her back and smooth her hair and hold her tight until she fell asleep, sniffling and snorting. My shirt was wet—Ladybug always sweats hard when she cries, so between the sweat and tears, I was pretty gross. Plus there was probably some drool or snot mixed in. . . . Who are we kidding? When you cry as hard as Ladybug, it's a full-body experience.

Laurel came in and sat next to me, but we didn't even talk. She just leaned against me so that Ladybug was half on me and half on her. We sat there for a while, with Laurel drawing pictures on my arm with her finger for me to guess, while Ladybug snored quietly.

When Mom and Mimi came back, they were pretty relieved to see her sleeping. Mom gave a big sigh and plopped down next to me on the couch.

Mimi went and got a glass of water, then flung herself down next to Laurel. "Oh, girls, thank you," she said, leaning over to peer at Ladybug. "You're a godsend. She's so upset, the poor little duck. Sleep's probably the best thing for her."

I nodded, trying not to move my shoulder. "No problem. She's pretty wrecked."

"Of course she is," Mom said. "She had to say goodbye to Miss Georgia, who, even though we just met her, became close to us and was pretty special. And while Bruce is 'just a toy,' it's another goodbye. No wonder she's so bereft."

As though in answer, Ladybug whimpered a little and curled up tighter. Mom leaned closer to me and opened her arms.

"Here, hand her over to me. You must be starving. Travis is downstairs in the restaurant, if you want to join him." She looked over at Laurel, and her voice changed a little, sounding more formal. "Lo-Lo, if you're willing to hold off, we'd love to catch up and talk, if that's okay?"

I glanced at Laurel, wondering if she'd go into explosive mode. But she nodded. Her eyes had dark smudges under them, and her usually spiked hair was flat and sort of tired-looking. "Yeah, that works. I wanted to talk to you too," she said. She smiled a little. "I think I've 'let it lie' long enough."

I was *starving,* actually, since we hadn't had breakfast before heading out. But for some reason I wasn't super-eager to jump up. Part of me was exhausted—exhausted by the early morning, by the emotion of saying goodbye to Miss Georgia, by Ladybug's seemingly bottomless pool of tears. It was a relief to sit, holding tight to my hot, sweaty little sister, surrounded by my family. I clutched her tighter, once, then loosened my arms. She was fine. Bruce was gone, but really . . . we would survive that. We were all still here.

I slowly leaned toward Mom until she could get her arms around Ladybug. For a minute Mom's arms were around both of us, and she held on tight, and I pushed into her, glad to have her there. Mimi put her arms around Laurel, then reached over to squeeze us closer. Laurel squeaked a little, then laughed, and for a second we were all together, smushed and cozy and damp and smelly and *family.*

Ladybug's words echoed in my head: *I love him and he's gone.* My eyes felt scratchy again, and I pictured everyone's faces in that early-morning blaze of light. Finally Mom let go and pulled Ladybug onto her lap.

I slid myself away from them and stood up. Mom looked at me over Ladybug's head. "You know, your hair really does look lovely," she said. And she smiled. "I love you, Say-Say. So much."

Of course I knew this. But it felt good to hear it anyway.

Downstairs Travis was somehow managing to look somber even while eating a double stack (FIVE!) of huge pancakes with a side of bacon and sausage. He looked glad to see me, but his smile was much lower than its usual blinding level.

"How's your sister doing?" he asked, pushing the platter of bacon toward me.

I grabbed a piece and jammed it into my mouth, too ravenous to be polite. "Sleeping," I mumbled through the bacon. "So that's good."

He nodded. "Poor thing. She looked plumb worn out. That was a hard morning for her. Well, it was a hard one all around."

I looked up, hoping to see the waitress, and Travis moved his plate closer. "Here, you can share. This is my second plate," he said, pulling a silverware roll over from the other side of the table.

I looked at him, then at the plate.

"What? I don't have cooties," he said, his grin starting to amp up. I felt like I should get sunglasses, it was so blinding after the past few hours.

"No, I just don't want to starve you. After all, you've only had six or seven pancakes. Don't want you to waste away," I said. But sarcasm is seriously wasted on that boy. He only smiled brighter (sunglasses! Now!) and politely said that he could always order more. So I dug in.

"Do you think Miss Ruby will be okay?" I asked, after a brief silent moment of shoving pancake into my mouth as fast as possible. I was *starving*. Apparently high drama and tears make a person hungry. Or maybe they were just really good pancakes.

Travis cut a bite and ate it, looking thoughtful. "I reckon she'll be fine," he said finally, after swallowing. "But I don't know that she's going to be the same. I can't really explain it, but she and Auntie G . . . they were like bread and butter. They went together. I reckon she's going to be a little different from now on."

I thought about the two of them arguing and giggling and finishing each other's sentences. And even though I hadn't known them long, I agreed. It was hard to imagine how Miss Ruby would *be* without Miss Georgia. I wondered, not for the first time, if they'd been a couple. I wasn't sure how to ask Travis, or if he'd freak out at the question. After all, it's not like we'd discussed my moms, and asking someone if his great-aunt is a lesbian (sorry, Saanvi!) is a little weird.

I asked a different question instead. "Were either of them ever . . . you know . . . married, or anything?"

He nodded. "Yup. They weren't *together* together, if that's what you're wondering. Auntie Ruby married young, married a guy from their high school who Aunt G *hated*. Apparently she was right, because he turned out to be a real jerk. Aunt Ruby left him two years later and got a restraining order. Auntie G, now, her husband was a great guy. I don't remember him much, because he died when I was pretty little. Lung cancer. He smoked like it was his second job. They used to live right next door to Auntie Ruby, and a year after he died, Aunt Georgia told Ruby to pack up and move on in, because it was too much work to keep two kitchens clean."

I laughed a little. I could picture that conversation.

Travis laughed too. "They had been best friends since kindergarten, and when Aunt Ruby left her husband, she moved next door to Aunt Georgia and Uncle Jessie. And the three of them used to do so much together that folks in town called them the three amigos, or the three stooges, depending. But when Aunt Ruby and Aunt Georgia moved in together, they turned right back into schoolgirls, my dad always said. Said it was slumber parties and gossip all the time."

Travis gave me a sideways look. I had finished his pancakes and was trying, unsuccessfully, to clean myself up. "Here," he said, dipping his napkin into an unused water glass. "Try this." He handed me the wet napkin, and I mopped up my sticky hands and—ugh—hair. Apparently I had done full-contact pancake eating.

"People gossiped about them," he went on, once

I was no longer a toxic syrup zone. "Making guesses. But Auntie Georgia used to say she hated when folks asked her, nosy-like, if she and Ruby were 'only friends.' 'There's nothing "only" about friends,' she used to answer. 'Friends is as good as it gets. Jess was "only" my husband, if you're going to talk that way.' Used to confuse a lot of folks."

"That's kind of a good point," I said. "After all, who gets to decide that our boyfriend or girlfriend is the really important relationship, and our best friends are an afterthought?" I thought about Em and Vi and wondered if we would be together in fifty years, traveling the country and punching each other and playing cards. It was fun to imagine.

Now I'm back in the room getting the last of our stuff packed up before we check out. We'll go back to Williams and take the *Southwest Chief* to Los Angeles . . . our last overnight train. Mom and Mimi and Ladybug are off at the park ranger station, to lodge an official lost-item report, not that anyone thinks that Bruce or the camera will ever surface. We looked over the canyon—I made myself go to the edge and peer down, and holy cow. Not to be awful, but that Roman centurion is GONE. There's no trace of Bruce, the camera, or even the life-sized Elvis, which tells you how far down everything fell. So there's no recovery mission happening, but I guess the thought was that at least Ladybug would know we did EVERY-

THING POSSIBLE to get Bruce back. She'll know we tried, anyway.

It is inevitable, when traveling, that some things get left behind. Maybe it's a pair of socks or a computer cord, or maybe it is something more precious. Sometimes lost items can make their way back to us; the miracle of mobile phones, Google, and the US Postal Service all working together to return our lost keys, sunglasses, books. But other times, those items left behind are truly gone forever. Please, my fellow travelers, take good care of your journals, your cameras, your beloved baby blankets or stuffed animals. Don't create any more goodbyes than you absolutely must.

Chapter 26

Fun Fact!

The Cajon Pass, at an elevation of 4,190 feet, lies between the San Bernardino Mountains and the San Gabriel Mountains and was created by the movements of the infamous San Andreas Fault. (Note: I asked Laurel why the San Andreas Fault was infamous, and apparently, to sum it up, EARTHQUAKES. Tons of them. Awesome.)

Fun Fact!

In 1873, Eliza Tibbets received two Brazilian navel orange trees sent to her by a friend in the US State Department in Washington, DC. The trees thrived in the Southern California climate and soon led to a different kind of California Gold Rush: the establishment of the citrus industry. Now more than one billion dollars' worth of citrus fruits are grown here every year.

Not-So-Fun Fact!

Apparently California's drought is breaking historical records and the state's running out of water.

Other Not-So-Fun Fact!
Ladybug has barely stopped crying since we left the Grand Canyon. If only we could create an irrigation system with her tears.

9:00 p.m.

Back on the train, heading west, away from the Grand Canyon, and by extension, away from Bruce (and Elvis, for that matter). Even getting on the train was brutal. The nice sleeping cabin attendant (Russell, this time) asked if Ladybug was the little girl with the bitty soldier and did she want to take a picture. Apparently word had spread about Ladybug and Bruce. Needless to say that automatically led to a new flood of tears. Russell felt horrible—he brought Ladybug an ice cream (which she couldn't eat), then folded her towel into a swan and put his attendant's hat on its head, but still she wouldn't stop. Then we tried to get Ladybug excited about seeing the sunset out the window from the observation car—it's a gorgeous red and orange and purple kaleidoscope out there—but she sobbed harder and said she didn't want to see it without Bruce. Finally Mimi carried her off to bed.

Miss Ruby was sitting with me and Travis, watching the sky get crazier and crazier. She shook her head. "That poor little girl. She's going to cry herself sick. Does she always get so riled up?"

I shrugged. "Not really. I've never seen her like this." I glanced down at my shirt, which was still damp from where I'd tried to cuddle her before giving up and sending her off with Mimi. "I wish I could help."

Miss Ruby gave a sigh. "Sometimes the heart just has to grieve. Nothing to be done but give her time, I suppose."

Travis leaned over and gave her a squeeze. "Wise words, Auntie. But I'm worried about you too. You doing all right?"

She snorted and slapped at him a little, but I noticed she squeezed him back before letting go. "I'll be fine. Your auntie and I knew this was coming. Like that little girl, I just need time to get used to things." But she looked straight ahead while she said it.

"If only Ladybug hadn't dropped the camera too!" I said. Travis groaned. It was not the first time I'd said this.

But I kept going. "No, seriously. I think she'd be okay if we had the photos of Bruce, at least. She was so proud. . . . She wanted pictures of him all over the country. And jeesh . . . she probably took a thousand. Honestly, it would have been a pretty fun album." I sighed. "So many other people took photos too. I wish we had some way to get them."

Travis looked at me. "Well, now . . . ," he started; then he trailed off.

"What?"

"It's probably nothing," he said finally. His mega-smile, which had started to light up, dimmed again.

"*What?*" I asked again.

"Well, I was thinking about the *other* photos out there. The ones other people took. We might be able to find 'em. But even if we did, what's the point? I mean, we can't print them out or give them to her. I guess you could once you get home, but who knows if she'll even care by then. Maybe it'd just make her sad all over again."

"Well, if we had the photos, we could make a photo book online, and pick it up in San Francisco. That's pretty easy to do, actually." I looked at him. "What? Haven't you ever done that? I've made tons of them. We made one for Laurel when she went to college, and another for Vi when her dog died. It's pretty simple." I waved a hand at him. "But what's the point? We don't have any photos! That's the whole problem."

The mega-smile came back. "Oh, I don't know if that's a problem," Travis said, sounding excited.

I stared. "How are you going to find them? I mean, I know Mimi has a few emails for people she was going to contact for her book, but other than that . . . ?"

Travis jumped up. "Auntie, keep Rae . . . Sara here company for a minute! I'll be right back!" He took off down the car, running so light and fast between the seats that he looked like he was dancing.

I stared after him.

Miss Ruby snorted, then coughed a little. "Fool is going to crash into the wall, running like that while we're moving." But her voice sounded like she was complimenting him.

"Do you know what he's doing?" I asked. I couldn't imagine she did, but what the heck did I know? Maybe he had a cape and magic wand hidden in his roomette.

She waved a hand impatiently. "No idea, but I'll bet you a jar of nickels that it's got to do with a computer. That boy thinks he can get to the moon and back just by pressing a few buttons. And the darnedest thing is that he usually can. Sits in his fuzzy slippers at the kitchen table and chats away with Russia, Egypt, Australia . . . you name it."

Sure enough, before she'd even finished, Travis was rushing back, his computer under his arm.

"The other photos!" he burst out once he sat down. He opened the laptop and started typing like mad, fingers flying faster than I could follow. "There are a couple of different ways we can search for them . . . reverse image lookup, travel blogs, hashtags, rail travel chat rooms . . ." His voice trailed off as he focused on whatever he was doing.

I shot Miss Ruby a look. She was gathering her bag and mug, starting to stand up. "I'm too old and this is too boring. You young people tap all night on that thing. I'm going to bed." Her hand rested on Travis's head for a second.

Travis looked up immediately. "I'll walk you back. Train's going around all kinds of curves, and—"

She slapped his head. "Don't you dare. I don't need help walking down a train hallway, for crying out loud. I'm not dead yet, Travis Alexander."

He nodded, full-bright grin turned on. "Yes, ma'am; duly noted," he said, and leaned up to kiss her. "Sleep tight. Tell Dad I may be a while."

Miss Ruby gave me a look. " 'Be a while' is his code for 'up all night.' You may want to get a cup of coffee."

Once she left, we were the only ones in the observation car. It was fully dark out now, and for a few minutes I just watched Travis's hands typing madly.

"Check it!" he said finally, pulling the computer back so that I could see the screen. On it were tons of—literally a hundred or more—photos of Bruce!

"What?? How?? Where??" I was apparently stuck in the land of one-word questions. "How did you find these?" I finally sputtered.

"The Internet is *not* a private place. Believe me, if you put something out there, even just to a few friends or on a social media site, it's pretty easy to find it." He raised one eyebrow, which, by the way, is something I've been trying to do since I was five. "Keep that in mind when you're partying with your friends and thinking about posting those photos."

I blushed a little, which was stupid, because it's not like I'm doing anything that would be embarrassing to post, but still. "Whatever. So you . . . what? Hacked into people's Instagram and Facebook accounts? Nice work."

"No hacking needed. I just searched for an image match. These are all set to public viewing! That's my point . . . there's no privacy! But for our purposes now, that's a good thing, right?"

I looked over his shoulder. There were photos of Bruce in Atlanta, with the dogs at the inn in Eutaw, even on the High Line in New York almost a month ago! There were a bunch of him on the train with different passengers—including Darrell, our first sleeping cabin attendant, who had apparently posted the photo on the National Rail travel blog.

I smacked Travis on the shoulder. Miss Ruby was rubbing off on me. "Are you kidding me! Who wants privacy? We can totally make a book from these! Here . . . open another window and I'll start designing the book."

Travis was still clicking around. "Didn't you say your mama has the emails of some of the folks you met? Why don't you go get them? Maybe we can get a few more pictures. I'm going to download these into an album, so it'll take a bit." He glanced at the time on the corner of the screen. "Yeah. It's going to take quite a bit. How about we play cards until it finishes?" He jumped up, doing his arm-shaking-neck-cracking thing. "It's going to be a late night."

11:00 p.m.

Travis crept off to the café car to see if there's any candy around. We've only gotten halfway through the photos, and people keep emailing us new ones. On the plus side, the book is starting to look awesome.

2:15 a.m.

If I put enough sugar and milk in it, I can drink coffee. So that's good, I guess.

4:40 a.m.

We uploaded the Bruce the Magnificent photo book. It should be done by the time we get to San Francisco tomorrow night. Or tonight. I'm losing track of time. Even Travis's megawatt mega-energy burned out around an hour ago. But he kept at it, helping me pull photos from emails and the web until I was able to mostly re-create our journey. There aren't a ton of photos of Ladybug and the rest of our family. (Though there is the one that the nice German woman took back in Atlanta. . . . Apparently she has a well-regarded travel blog called *Gute Fahrt*. I am not even making this up. . . . It means "Have a good drive" or something. How do the Germans not fall down laughing, I wonder?)

Anyway, there are more pictures of random strangers, and we've managed to include fun facts, memories, and even—this was Travis's idea—some quotes that Bruce himself might have said while sightseeing. The best one? Someone at the hotel in Santa Fe had posted a photo of Bruce, Elvis, Ladybug, Miss Ruby, and Miss Georgia. Miss Georgia is laughing so hard, her face is kind of blurred. But she's there. She's laughing and she's there.

My eyes are so tired that I can't stop rubbing them, and my mouth tastes like something died in it around five hours ago. But I'm too excited to sleep. And Ladybug's worth it. Seeing her smiling again will make it all worth it.

It's our last night on the *Southwest Chief,* and of sleeping on a train—tomorrow we'll take the *Coast Starlight* to San Francisco, and that'll be it. It'll be over, or almost. A few days seeing friends of Mom's from law school, and then we fly home. I NEVER would have thought it at the beginning, but I'm actually going to miss the train, with its rumbling and chugging and constant movement. There's something about us all being together, so cozy and snug, knowing that Mom and Mimi are right there, that Laurel's only a few feet away, that we're all in one place, safe. It reminds me of camping trips, the way it felt when we all went to sleep in the tent. But even cozier, in a way, because the train rattles and swings, and outside in the corridor there are occasional footsteps or the quiet voice of the car attendant. (Of course, it also feels cozier than camping because we never—and I mean *never*—managed a camping trip where it didn't rain. It was like a jinx.) Anyway, I'm not sure I can give Mimi the satisfaction and tell her, but truth is, I love it.

Who am I kidding? I'm not a total monster. . . . Of course I'll tell Mimi how amazing this was. I haven't heard her say anything about her writing in a while. She was writing a lot with Gavin before the whole Miss Georgia thing, and since then she's been typing away, but she hasn't talked about it in ages.

It's weird. At the beginning of the trip the two most important things were making it through my Reinvention Project and keeping Mimi from writing anything embarrassing about me. But now neither of them seems like that big a deal. I wonder if I should tell Mimi I don't really care that much anymore. Who knows . . . maybe it would be fun to be in a book. Even if it *is* embarrassing, it's kind of cool. It's a way for this trip to be around forever.

I'm not sure I'm going to sleep. I think I'll wait to watch the sun rise. Funny to think we've gone all the way across the country. No sunrise over the ocean here. . . . It's West Coast all the way.

Chapter 27

Sara!

Imagine! You managed to stay asleep while we all got up, darted in and out of that tiny bathroom, and got dressed. It was SO impressive that Mimi wanted to check that you were breathing! Well done—you've learned to sleep like a teenager! WE ARE VERY PROUD! I do believe you may have pulled what the kids call an "all-nighter"—is this true? If so, CONGRATULATIONS AGAIN! That's a very teenage thing to do. You're clearly ahead of the game. Meanwhile we're all eating breakfast. Join us when you wake up!

Love, Mom

Fun Fact!

Founded in 1781, Los Angeles was originally known as El Pueblo Sobre el Rio de Nuestra Señora la Reina de los Angeles del Río de Porciúncula. (Again, imagine writing that as your return address. Short and simple, people. Short and simple is the way to go.)

Fun Fact!
Los Angeles is home to people from more than 180 countries speaking over 140 languages.

Not-So-Fun Fact!
Apparently homelessness has risen sharply in Los Angeles, and on any given night some 82,000 people are homeless. It seems like most of them live at the train station.

August 27–8:00 a.m.

We're in Los Angeles, City of Angels, the place where we say goodbye to Travis and Miss Ruby and Gavin and get on our last train north to San Francisco. Outside it's all palm trees and strip malls and highways and cars as far as I can see.

Meanwhile I feel like someone smacked me over the head with a frying pan. Seriously, there should be little stars and tweety birds around my skull, like in the old cartoons. I guess not sleeping gives you a headache? I wish I had known that yesterday. Still, I'm pretty excited. If all goes well, there will be a most amazing photo book waiting for us when we get to San Francisco this afternoon. I only wish Travis could be there to see it too.

Okay. Ten minutes of yoga (three sun salutations, some warrior one and two, and cobra and child pose to round it out), then . . . breakfast. With coffee! If nothing else I can claim that this trip's a success on that front.

· · · · ·

LIFE IN THE GREEN LANE

The American Road Trip is a tradition so famous, it's almost a cliché: from Mark Twain to Jack Kerouac, it's a story that's been told dozens of different ways. But there's a lot of cool discovery still to be found on this road trip, or rail trip, really, since we're crisscrossing the country not in the lonely solo vibe of a car, but in the community of a train full of strangers. Things that surprised me:

• How friendly people are, how willing they are to talk and tell their stories, and ask me mine.

• How easy it was for me to judge people based on where they live and what they wear, and to be proven wrong again and again.

• How hard it is to say goodbye to people we've just met and landscapes I've only just seen but that have started to feel like home.

We're close to the end of our journey, and man, I'm struggling with the end of this particular road. Confession time, Reader-Friends. I was sure of a whole lot of things when we started out. Sure of what's right and what's wrong, and where I belong, and how the rest of the world should fall in line. And now, less than a month later, I've learned I don't know nearly as much as I thought I did. I had a plan, and the plan, man, was a good one. I was going to BE THE CHANGE. I was going to MAKE LOVE NOT WAR. I was going to DO THE WORK.

And these are all good plans.

But you know what? There are a ton of ways to fight for what matters. And if I'm going to fight, I need to arm myself—not with weapons—but with knowledge. Another thing I realized I don't know? I don't know nearly enough about successful and low-cost environmental alternatives to help our planet. So before I rip up my hands tearing down the old world, I think I'll spend some time learning how to build a new one.

But here's one thing I *am* sure of: my family is the most amazing, wacky, beautiful group of people in the world. And the hardest goodbye of all will be saying goodbye to them, my sisters and my moms, because a month of togetherness . . . well, that's a gift that might not come around again real soon.

Perspectives.

This trip has offered some good ones, not only on the country we live in, but on those people I thought I knew best.

Happy trails, readers. Here's to you all discovering a road trip of your own. Who knows where it might lead you.

Peace, Laurel

Dear Em,

Here we are in sunny LA! Can you imagine me surrounded by movie stars? Yeah, me neither. I'm actually surrounded by huge crowds of people taking the train up the coast for work or vacation or whatever it is that has five million Californians trying to jostle around the train platform. Still, there are palm trees, and somewhere on the side of the station there are big cameras and stuff, because apparently they're shooting a TV show. Welcome to the big time!

I'm mailing this as soon as I finish writing, but I'll probably beat it home. Three days! It's going to be weird, I think, being back. But SO GOOD to see you. I know it's only been a month, but trust me, a lot has changed. And not just my hair.

XOXOXOX Sara

Noon

UGH. We had to say goodbye to Travis and his family. His mom, who seriously looks like she *could* be a movie star, was waiting on the platform when we pulled up. We were all together, mushed in near the doors with all our bags and stuff, Ladybug in Root's arms because he was the only one willing to hold her after she spilled a big cup of pineapple-orange juice all over herself. Root's honestly kinder than anyone else I've ever met. I don't even mind his poncho anymore.

Anyway, Travis was peering out the window as we pulled in, and there were a ton of people all crowded around and I couldn't see anything, but as soon as the door opened, he half jumped, half fell out and bellowed "HEY THERE, MAMA!!" at the top of his lungs. And this gorgeous woman with big sunglasses and a fancy-but-casual wraparound dress came charging toward us like a linebacker, pushing people out of her way. When she got to Travis, she hugged him so hard, his arms were pinned to his sides, and he stood there and took it. Then Gavin and Miss Ruby got off and hugged her too, and she hugged them back until Miss Ruby shoved everyone, saying, "We're making a spectacle, and blocking the door, to boot. Now get a hold of yourselves." But she was wiping her eyes.

Finally we all got ourselves off (Root's sandal strap caught in the gap by the door, and he nearly went flying into three very old Japanese men, who looked seriously startled and bowed as they scampered out of his way). By then, Travis and his family had moved over to by the station and were waiting for us. I felt a little shy, suddenly. I'm still wearing the now pretty nasty T-shirt I wore for our all-night photo project, and my hair . . . well, it's so short that there's really no taming it after an all-nighter and minimal sleep. Compared to Travis's glamorous mom, we all looked pretty bad. But she swooped in and hugged me like she had hugged him, so tight, I couldn't move.

"You people!" she said when she'd finished hugging us all. "You people must be some kind of special. I've heard from Gavin and Travis all through this trip, and mostly what I heard was about these lovely folks who made everything so much more fun. How they celebrated Auntie G, how they took Travis in as one of their own, how they were just . . . salt of the earth." She wiped her eyes and swooped over to look at Ladybug. "And this one! I talked to my Georgie one day before she passed, and you know what she told me? She said, 'I'm sure glad I met that little girl. She knows how to find joy in everything, so she brings joy to everybody. She has a gift.' That's what she said. What do you think about that?" She looked at Ladybug.

Ladybug stared back for a second, then buried her face in Root's shoulder. "But Bruce is gone. I loved him, and he's gone. And all my pictures are gone too!" Her voice was muffled, but I could hear her start to cry.

Travis's mom shook her head slowly. "I know, baby. I know. And you miss him. Of course you do. But you had this trip with him, right? You had this magical, marvelous trip, and—photos or no photos—you're not going to forget that anytime soon, are you?"

Ladybug sniffled.

"Well? Are you?" she asked again, and this time we all stared at Ladybug, who took her head out of Root's shoulder and stared back.

"No," she whispered, finally. Then: "NO!" she said, much louder. "I will NOT forget. I will never forget him!"

Travis's mom nodded emphatically. "That's right! NO you won't! Now," she said, turning to the rest of us. "I want to buy you people some lunch. It's time to celebrate new friends!"

"And to say goodbye," Mom added. "Our train leaves in a few hours."

"And to say goodbye," Travis's mom agreed. "But first we celebrate!"

And we did. Even though Miss Georgia wasn't there, even though we didn't have Elvis or Bruce, it reminded me of our dinners together at the beginning, when everyone around us would stare. But instead of being embarrassed, I was kind of proud. We looked like we were having way more fun than anyone else, and I bet everyone who saw us secretly wished they were sitting with us . . . wished they were in on the story.

Saying goodbye to Travis and the rest of them—that part wasn't so good. Ladybug cried (of course—she's constantly damp these days, like a little mini-swamp). And I admit I was kind of teary myself. It wasn't just saying goodbye to them, it was also the end of the trip, and knowing that I may never see any of them again.

Travis held out his hand, all formal-like, but I grabbed him and hugged him instead. Who cares if he's a boy and I probably smelled like the salsa Ladybug spilled on me at lunch? He hugged me back, hard. He's still shorter than me of course, but he gives good hugs.

"You take care of yourself, you hear?" he said. "I haven't known you long, but girl, you're downright dangerous—burning your hair right off your head, dying yourself blue, writing who-knows-what in that darn secret book of yours."

I let go and punched him (though not as hard as Miss Georgia would have). "Shut it, you. You're the one hacking into everyone's private photos and taking on secret coding projects for the government!"

He laughed. "We made a good team," he said. "Mama promised me we're going to hit the East Coast next summer. She wants me to try lobster, Lord knows why. Last thing I want to do is eat a giant sea bug, but—"

"You'll see! It's delicious! Better than that mud-feeding catfish you told me about," I interrupted him, pretending to frown, but he just pulled his full-watt get-the-nuclear-shield smile.

"Take good care, Rae or Sara or whatever you want to be called," he said. "And write me a letter sometime. You got enough words in that darn book. Write a guy a letter instead. And not an email!" he added. "Anyone can read those, you know?"

"It's Sara. Just Sara Johnston-Fischer. And believe me, I may never write another email or post another photo again," I said. "This creepy guy I met told me stuff that scared me off the Internet forever."

Everyone else was already on the train, and I had to go. But I'm not going to lie . . . it was hard.

"Well . . . ," I said, finally stepping onto the train.

"Safe travels, Sara Johnston-Fischer," he called, one last time. "See you on the flip side!"

I watched him until the train pulled around the curve. He was there waving, his mom and dad and Miss Ruby by his side, until they were completely out of sight.

Chapter 28

Fun Fact!

A little-known piece of history exists beyond the grasshopper-like oil pumps of Ellwood Oil Field. On February 23, 1942, Captain Kozo Nishino surfaced his Japanese submarine in the Santa Barbara Channel and fired sixteen rounds from his 140 mm deck gun toward the oil field. He inflicted little damage, but it was the first attack on continental United States soil since the War of 1812.

Not-So-Fun Fact!

This train is totally pathetic. There are a ton of business travelers, and nobody talks to anybody. Hardly a real train at all.

I'm sitting in the sightseeing car staring out at the Pacific Ocean. . . . We're winding and flying around curves, the water always there, and even though it's not my home ocean, even though we're thousands of miles away, there's something very comforting about that line of deep blue water meeting robin's-egg-blue sky. (Though it seems really freaking weird to see the sun get lower over the horizon. . . . Sunsets aren't supposed to be there!) But still, it's almost like my eyes were thirsty—I can't seem to look away.

4:00 p.m.

Ladybug's napping with Mom and Mimi . . . all three of them sacked out in the regular lounge chairs. We don't have a sleeping cabin or anything, so we're spread out all over the seats. Root's off reading, and Laurel's been sitting with me. With everything else that's been going on, I hadn't really thought about the fact that she'll be staying here in California. She and the moms came up with a plan: she's only taking three classes this semester so she can do more volunteer work. That was her compromise. She'll continue working toward her degree, but will also get an internship and "be more present in the Movement"—which Mom wasn't totally thrilled about, but I thought sounded impressive.

Anyway, when we fly home in a few days, she won't be with us. Thinking about saying goodbye to her makes me want to cry.

We sat in silence for a while, staring out at the winding coastline. Then she bumped my shoulder. "Whatcha thinking?" she asked.

"I'm thinking . . ." I hesitated. I cried when she left in the fall, and I know it made her feel awful. But telling the truth felt more important. "I'm thinking how much I'm going to miss you," I said. "And I'm not saying that to make you feel bad. But I . . ." I trailed off.

She put an arm around me. "I know you're not saying it to make me feel bad, Say-Say. Jeez, I would never think that. I hate leaving you too, you know. I didn't tell you, but I was pretty homesick last year at the beginning of school."

I stared at her. "You were?" My fearless sister Laurel, who chained herself to a fence near the White House, who sat in a kayak in front of some giant oil tanker, was homesick?

"Oh yeah. And again after winter break. I got back to California in January and *hated* it. I hated the sunshine, and all the people chirping around in T-shirts and sandals. I wanted cold and winter and cozy sweaters—and you guys! I wanted to go sledding with you and Ladybug, and talk to people who know that maple syrup is from maple trees and not from a plastic bottle in the supermarket."

I smiled a little. When we were little, Laurel had wanted to start a petition that companies couldn't call their syrup "maple" syrup if it wasn't the real stuff. Mom convinced her it was likely to be more work that it was worth, but Laurel never really got over it.

"Yup, I was full-on homesick," Laurel went on. "And I'll tell you the truth—I'll probably cry like a baby when you guys leave."

"Then why don't you come back?" I said. "Why don't you switch to a college near us?"

Laurel laughed a little and hugged me. "Little girl, haven't I taught you anything? Just because it's easy doesn't mean it's right, you know? I'm learning a ton at Berkeley and meeting cool people, and figuring stuff out. It's not supposed to be easy all the time."

I nodded. "I'm really glad we had this trip," I said, snuggling against her. "I'm sorry I was kind of obnoxious about it at first. I can't believe I was so obsessed with my Reinvention Project and so freaked out about Mimi's book. It seems kind of dumb now."

"Will you finally let me see that list?" Laurel said, reaching for my journal. "Come on, let's see how you did."

I was a little embarrassed, but I pulled it out. Together we looked at it.

☆ Learn Latin (Started strong, but wow, there are a lot of verbs. Must recommit.) (Hmmm. The recommitting didn't really work. Better try again. I have managed some spectacular insults, though. For instance, the next time Vi's little brother bugs us, I can just say, "Quis est haec simia?")

☆ Learn to surf, at least the basics (Obviously this is going nowhere.) *(Still no change. Obvs.)*

☆ Practice yoga every morning to develop Inner Peace and Mindfulness (Hmmm. Not bad, considering. I hit my nose and got a nosebleed when I tried turtle pose, but otherwise I'm getting there.) *(This is really coming along! Almost mastered camel without crashing over.)*

☆ Change hair (*Note: this is Vi's idea. I've been growing mine for four years, and I'm definitely not cutting it, but dying the ends . . . that I can do.*) (Nothing yet.) *(Well . . . I guess I nailed this one.)*

☆ Start wearing dark gray or navy-blue nail polish (*and try not to pick it off in ten minutes*) (*Note: this is Vi's idea too. We'll see.*) (I colored my nails in with Mom's Sharpie. Does that count?) *(The Sharpie has faded and now I look like my nails are rotting. Ugh.)*

☆ Read at least five nonfiction books (Two down . . . Loving *I Am Malala*!) *(Finished Malala and on to Chasing Lincoln's Killer! Who knew nonfiction was so exciting?)*

☆ Pick a signature social cause to care about (*Note: This one's Em's idea. I have lots of causes I care about, but apparently we each need a "signature cause."*) (Maybe the environment? Laurel's got me pretty worried.) *(Ugh. Nothing. How am I supposed to choose??)*

☆ Eschew with a firm hand all old camp, soccer team, and dumb club shirts and sweatshirts, even if they are soft and cozy (Since I didn't pack any, I am totally nailing my new style! Still, I miss my old Hidden Valley Camp T-shirt.) *(Since I've added Mimi's scarf to cover my blue ear, I guess my style is coming along. Ish.)*

☆ Consider jeggings (Not sure this one's going to stick.)

☆ Drink coffee (Nope.) *(Still haven't been brave enough to try again.)*

☆ Rebrand myself as Rae, not Sara (Hmmm . . . So far Travis is the only one who remembers every time, and how useless is that?) *(Since no one in my family is talking much, it's hard to say.)*

☆ Work on a novel, or at least figure out a good story (Nothing. Haven't written a word. Phooey.)

"I don't think this is dumb," Laurel said finally. "Think about it. You've been practicing yoga almost every day, you've got a fabulous new haircut, you're officially drinking coffee. . . ."

I shrugged. She was right, although I still wasn't

willing to call my haircut anything but a barely saved disaster.

"Maybe you should make a new list," Laurel said. "And for the record, I don't think there's anything wrong with trying nail polish. Or jeggings. So you want to change up your look! Why not! Being told *not* to care about what you look like is as bad as being told you *have* to care. It's all about freedom, man."

I nodded, but my mind was already on to something else.

"Hey, Lo-Lo," I asked. "Was Mimi . . . did she ever send part of her book to that New York publisher?"

Laurel turned and looked at me. "Why don't you ask her?"

I shrugged. "I don't know. Because I was kind of a jerk about her writing, and I feel bad. Like, if she didn't write anything good, it's partly my fault."

Laurel laughed and hugged me. "You're sure putting a lot on your shoulders. Were you responsible for writing her book? If it's a big hit, do you get the credit? No? Well, then I don't think you can take the blame either."

I rolled my eyes. "Obviously that's not what I meant. But—"

Laurel interrupted me. "Sara. Listen. You're only the boss of you. Not the boss of Mimi or her editor or her book. Mimi's the boss of her own self."

"Of course I am," Mimi said, coming up behind us. "What are you girls talking about? And scoot over and make room for your weary mother, will you?" she continued, scootching us until we were squeezed into the seats. "Mom and Ladybug are still sleeping, but some fool on his cell phone was talking so loudly about V-chip futures and second-round financing that I wanted to bean him with my purse." She yawned loudly. "So anyway, what's this about me being the boss of me?"

I rolled my eyes at Laurel. I wasn't really sure what I wanted to say to Mimi. As amazing as the trip had been, I was still kind of mad. She never asked my opinion, never checked with me to see if I wanted my every move splattered in her book. Still, she's wanted to write a book for so long, and when it really came down to it, I had done everything possible to sabotage it. It would have been nice to be asked, but really, the only answer I ever should have given was *of course*. How bad could it be? She's my *mom*. Mimi turned toward me a little. "Say-Say, honey, before you say anything, I need to tell *you* something. I'm sorry. Not for taking you on this amazing trip, which, frankly, we're all pretty lucky to be on. But for not taking you seriously and respecting your voice. There was no way we were going to skip this opportunity, but that doesn't mean I should have ignored your feelings about it. And I'm sorry."

Laurel elbowed me, hard, in the ribs. I cleared my throat. "I . . . um, thanks, Mimi. This has been amazing. Obviously. And I'm sorry too. I shouldn't have given you such a hard time. It was pretty Veruca Salt of me. And honestly . . ." I paused here, because I knew once I said it, I couldn't really un-say it. "Honestly, I'm fine with whatever you wrote. Really. I'll even try to add more of my, you know, thoughts and words, or whatever you want."

Mimi squirmed until she could get her arms around me in a kind of awkward sideways hug. "Oh, sweetie! You're no Veruca! You're such a good kid. And you should know, Mom and I had a long talk, and I told that editor I wasn't interested at this point. It's not fair to the rest of you."

I stared at her. "What do you mean, you told her no? Did Mom think that was a good idea?"

"It was my decision, but we both agreed that our family deserves its privacy, and that this was the right choice."

I felt dizzy. She had turned down the fancy New York publisher? "You should call her back! You can still do that, right?"

Mimi looked at me. "I don't know. Probably. But the point is that—"

"The point is that someone wants to publish your book! I'm fine with it! Totally fine!" I paused. "Maybe . . . you know, try not to make me look too ridiculous."

Mimi sighed and laughed. "You know? I'm not sure if I want to call her back. I'll tell you, with Gavin's help,

I started again, writing up some of our adventures as a novel, instead of nonfiction. It's still a very rough draft, but I *think* I'm writing a children's book. We'll have to see how it turns out, but I had this idea about this hilarious family traveling cross-country. Not *our* family, but one that shares some of our stories."

At this I sat up. "You're writing a novel? For kids? Like, my age? Who are the main characters? Are they sisters? When can I read it?"

Mimi laughed and pulled me back. "Yes, for kids your age. But in my book they're all boys. I've already thought of a title: *The Roling Family Rides the Rails.* And yes," she said, squeezing me. "Of course you can read it. I'll count on you to be my first editor."

I squeezed her back, but my mind was still racing. "Are you sure?" I asked. "Are you sure you don't want to call that Krista person and tell her you changed your mind?"

"Nope," Mimi said. "I decided to be brave and try to write a novel. If you and Laurel can be brave, I can too! I'm so lucky." She squeezed me tighter, then reached around and grabbed Laurel. "So lucky," she repeated. "Seriously. This is the good stuff, right here."

A few minutes later, Mom, Ladybug, and Root came over and sat across from us. We talked about Mimi's new book, and about the funny things that could happen to her (fictional!) characters. Then we talked about Laurel's internships, because Mom went all Judge Johnston and called everyone she knew. Now Laurel has these cool legal aid and Environmental Justice Coalition interviews lined up. Then Ladybug said she was bored and could we play cards, so we did. She still cheats like crazy, but I played anyway. After all, as we say in Latin, *Nisi eos tibi valde adiungere potes, eos vince.*

August 28

> Laurel, Root, and Sara,
>
> I know you're off on your SPECIAL MYSTERIOUS ERRAND, but I'm not sure we can keep Ladybug awake much longer. So far she has eaten seven dumplings and chased three different cats around our guesthouse. If we're not in the room when you arrive back here, please come down to the courtyard IMMEDIATELY, as it means I have pulled out all the stops and am trying to launch the paper kite we bought in Chinatown. You may recall from your own youths that I do not particularly ENJOY kites, as they bob and weave and suddenly DROP with no provocation. I hope your surprise is worth it.
>
> Love, MOM

DEAR FROG, GUESS WHAT? SARA AND OUR FRIEND TRAVIS DID A MAGIC TRICK AND FOUND A MILLION PHOTOS OF BRUCE EVEN THOUGH THE CAMERA IS AT THE BOTTOM OF THE GRAND CANYON!!!!! THEY MADE ME A BOOK WITH SO MANY BRUCE PHOTOS AND NOW I HAVE THEM ALL!!!!!!!!!!!!!!!!! ALSO DID YOU KNOW THAT SAN FRANCISCO HAS A FAMOUS LUNAR NEW YEAR'S PARADE WITH DRAGONS? I AM GOING TO TRY AND FIND A DRAGON. WE WILL TAKE A PHOTO OF OUR NEW DRAGON ON THE GOLDEN GATE BRIDGE!!! I WILL SEE YOU SOON AND BRING YOU A DRAGON!!!!!!!!!!!!!!!!!!!!!!!!! LOVE, LADYBUG!!!!!!!!!!!

TO: Travis Writes Code

FROM: SaraJF

SUBJECT: I know I said I wouldn't email but . . .

Hey, Trav,

I know I'm not supposed to email, but I thought you'd like this photo of all of us on the Golden Gate Bridge. Take a look at Ladybug: notice anything new? That's Josephine, the fire dragon she bought in Chinatown. Ladybug is planning to take photos of her all through San Francisco and on our plane home tomorrow. I think I'll tell Mom to text you all the photos as she takes them . . . just in case.

Also, Root and Laurel had the idea for the second photo I've attached here. We asked our guesthouse to print out a picture of Elvis, and I guess in San Francisco that kind of request isn't considered too weird, because they asked us if we wanted full body or just his face, and whether he should be wearing a jumpsuit or not. Anyway, here he is, hanging out with us on the bridge. We thought Miss Ruby might like that one. Tell her we say hi.

Ladybug loves her book so much. Thanks, Travis. Seriously. Thank you. I can honestly say that nothing about this trip would have been as good without you.

Love, Sara

Chapter 29

We're at the airport, waiting for our flight back to Boston. Laurel and Root just hugged and kissed us goodbye and we all cried . . . even Mom. Even Root. There was something about this trip together that I can't really explain. The best way I can describe it is that it's like when you plant something and water it and wait and watch it grow. It's plain dirt at first, and you wonder why you care, but then it's really really really exciting when the first green sprouts come up. Way more exciting than if you just go to the store and buy flowers or carrots or whatever. And this month's train trip . . . it was like we planted something all together, we watered it and watched it and celebrated it together. We grew it together.

All in all, I guess I do feel pretty reinvented. I mean, I definitely don't feel like the same person who got on the train almost a month ago. And thanks to my hair and scarf (and the really cool new silver bangles I got in Santa Fe), I don't look like her, either. And I learned a lot (not even including all the "Fun Facts!" which, as mentioned, were often seriously un-fun).

I learned that it's possible to become good friends—maybe even best friends (after Em and Vi, because nobody's *ever* replacing them, no matter how awesome)—with someone I just met, and who's totally different from me. And I learned to appreciate Root, and how he really truly believes he can try to change the world. And I learned that just because people might notice us (and let's be honest, it's hard not to, with my family), it doesn't mean they won't like us. And that Laurel gets homesick, and misses me just as much as I miss her. And that she's not always brave, and that I can be, sometimes.

I took Laurel's advice this morning, when I couldn't sleep, and tried writing a new Reinvention Project list. There are actually a bunch of the originals on there, plus others that I never EVER would have imagined. Let's be honest, Saanvi was the only one who wanted me to wear gray nail polish, and I'm pretty sure she'll be so impressed with my new scarf look that she won't even care.

So here it is: the final new and improved Reinvention Project list for the new and improved Sara Johnston-Fischer:

☆ Learned several key Latin phrases and insults that I can use to confuse/impress people

☆ Started morning yoga routine. Not sure about calm and mindfulness, but I'm definitely more flexible!

☆ Changed hair: not exactly as planned, but still, it's definitely different! Also Mimi said that maybe, no guarantees, I can get a blue streak.

☆ Read six nonfiction books. They were actually seriously interesting. I now know way more about Temple Grandin, Malala Yousafzai, owls, voting rights, President Lincoln, and hip-hop.

☆ Officially love coffee (as long as it's mostly milk and sugar)

☆ Figured out how to be friends with a boy

☆ Learned about Internet privacy (and am never EVER posting things online!)

☆ Created signature scarf look (I kind of like Mimi's scarves . . . I might wear them to school, especially if those jeggings work out)

☆ Realized that even Laurel thinks about what she looks like and who she wants to be

Things that are no longer on the list:

☆ Wear nail polish . . . honestly, Sharpie is faster and more fun

☆ Pick a signature social cause. Sorry, Em, but that's way too much pressure. And I like caring about a bunch of things.

☆ Rebrand myself as Rae. You know, this was one I was really excited about. But honestly, even if people had remembered, it kind of seems pointless.

Things that will be on the next list:

☆ Learn to surf. Hopefully I can do this next summer . . . maybe even when Travis visits.

And finally . . .

☆ Work on a novel, or at least figure out a good story. I don't know if I'll ever figure out the mermaids or selkies, but I have to admit . . . this trip would make a pretty good story someday.

Anyway, like I said at the beginning, I'm sorry this journal got to be so long. Nothing about this summer went as planned. But maybe that's okay. Maybe the best stories always turn out that way.

Latin Glossary

caudex: blockhead

malus nequamque: no-good jerk

Mihi molestus ne sis: don't bother me

Nisi eos tibi valde adiungere potes, eos vince: If you can't beat 'em, join 'em.

nugatory ac nebulo: trashy pipsqueak

Quis est haec simia?: Who is this monkey?

semper audax: always brave

spurcifer: scumbucket

stultissimi: total idiots

Author's Note

I made up a lot of stuff in this book, which is half the fun of writing fiction. I'm an author, so making stuff up is part of my official *job*, after all. But I didn't make up *everything*. (Obviously. I didn't make up the English language, or the idea of trains. Or sisters.)

But I digress. My point is that in a book like this, there is a lot of made-up stuff, but there are a bunch of facts as well.

To make sure I got the real parts right, I did a lot of research on railroads, learning about travel routes, jobs, and dining cars, among other random subjects. The *Crescent,* the *City of New Orleans,* the *Southwest Chief,* and the *Coast Starlight,* are all real Amtrak trains. The names alone sound so amazing to me; they take me back to the long-ago time when rail travel was exotic and sophisticated, and really the only way to see the country.

I read a lot of books, such as John Pitt's *USA by Rail* and Jim Loomis's *All Aboard: The Complete North American Train Travel Guide.* These books offer invaluable information about the specific trains mentioned above. They explore everything from the history of the trains themselves to the landscape beyond the tracks. and I am indebted to their authors. Also useful were Amtrak's route guides. These guides are free on Amtrak's website and offer a station-by-station guide to each train's route and what travelers might see out their windows if they pay attention. Here's an example of the *Crescent* line route guide: amtrak.com/ccurl/680/728/Amtrak-Crescent-Train-Route -Guide.pdf. You can look up the others if you're interested.

All the "Fun Facts" in the book came from the abovementioned books or the route guides. I've done my best to ensure they're correct, but you should double-check anything you read here before pinkie-swearing that it's true. Also, if you happen to take one of these train rides and learn something new, please write to me and tell me!

Finally, a word on the Latin. I admit, I don't actually know Latin insults all that well. But the Internet is a wonderful place to find things, and lo, I found a University of Oklahoma student group that had put together a list of just what I wanted. I then asked my marvelous brother-in-law Paul Ringel, who happens to be a professor of history, if he by chance knows any Latin scholars. Of course he *does* (because historians are awesome like that), and Professor Jacqueline Arthur-Montagne took a look and ensured me that they were accurate. All that being said, if I messed something up, I'm the *malus nequamque*, not her!

Happy trails, readers. Hope your next journey is a good one.

Acknowledgments

(As written by Sara Johnston-Fischer)

OMG, no one told me that when you finish writing a book there's still approximately a million more pages of writing (okay maybe five, but still), not to mention revising it, and then revising it again, then fixing all the dumb little things that only my English teacher and my moms actually care about. Still, it's kind of cool when all these awesome people —who have WAY more important things to do than fix my kind of pathetic ramblings—actually take the time to help me. And no one even laughed at me. I mean, not to my face, at least.

Honestly, I can promise you all that this whole thing would still just be a big pile of poo (that's a metaphor . . . it was never actually poo. That would be totally disgusting) if not for my writing besties. Seriously, without Jen "I want Root to come to my house for Christmas" Malone, Rachael "First of all: it doesn't suck" Allen, and Kate "Okay, here's what I think you mean" Boorman, I would totally give up on life, let alone this book. They write such awesome books, and it's kind of humiliating that they had to read all about my sisters and Bruce and of course the Reinvention Project (which, now that

I'm older, is literally the most embarrassing thing in the world and I cannot BELIEVE people are actually going to read about it. GAH.). But Jen, Rach, and Kate did read it. In some cases *cough cough KATE BOORMAN cough* they read it like five different times, which is the kind of thing that might be used for torture in less enlightened countries. (I should ask Laurel about that. Now that she's working with Amnesty International, she knows these things).

Anyway, I'm not quite sure how these acknowledgments are supposed to go, but I DO know that I'm TOTALLY lucky to have Krista Vitola, Beverly Horowitz, and everyone at Delacorte Press/Penguin Random House working on this book. I mean, not every editor or publisher would think a book about my totally lame family was a good idea. (Honestly, it's possible it wasn't a good idea, but they are seriously smart and publish awesome books, so I'm just going with it).

And OBVIOUSLY Marietta "What about Sara Choo Choo?" Zacker and the team at Gallt & Zacker Literary Agency are total superstars. I mean, with title suggestions like Sara Choo Choo, I don't think anyone needs more convincing that we're talking genius-level business savvy. I'm so seriously lucky . . . you guys don't even know.

Okay, I think that's it. Is that it? Am I supposed to write something else? This whole writing thing was WAY harder than I thought it would be. . . .

Further Acknowledgments

(as written by Dana Alison Levy)

I think Sara pretty much nailed it.

But I have to add in big love to the usual suspects, both online and "in real live life." as my daughter used to say.

First, a HUGE thank you to all readers of the Family Fletcher books! Parents, teachers, librarians, and most of all—kids! Your emails and letters and comments at school visits make my writing days so much brighter. I hope you enjoy Sara's story. I wrote it especially for all the readers who asked why I don't write more girls. This one's for you.

Second, a shout-out to my writer-peeps on Twitter, FB, LBs, and the various secret writing lairs where I can be found skulking. The online community is rich in camaraderie and smart, savvy folks who make me a better writer and a better person. I so appreciate it, especially those of you who work tirelessly to diversify children's literature. You are my heroes.

Third, as Sara said, the Delacorte and Gallt & Zacker folks are pretty much the best in the business, and I'm grateful I wound up in such capable hands. Thank you for keeping Sara's train trip on track. (SORRY! I couldn't resist).

And finally, to my family, Patrick, Noah, and Isabel, who are every bit as weird and wacky as the Johnston-Fischers. From Paris with narwhals to Ireland with Dermot the fisherman and Delaney the cow, I wouldn't want to be on this journey with anyone else.

About the Author

Dana Alison Levy was raised by pirates but escaped at a young age and went on to earn a degree in aeronautics and puppetry. Actually, that's not true—she just likes to make things up. That's why she has always wanted to write books. Her previous books about the Family Fletcher have garnered starred reviews, been named to multiple Best Of lists, and are Junior Library Guild selections. Also, her kids like them.

Dana was last seen romping with her family in Massachusetts. If you need to report her for excessive romping or if you want to know more, head to her website, danaalisonlevy.com.